"What's your name?" she asked softly.

He frowned and opened his eyes a crack. "Cut it out, Katherine. The joke's stale."

"Please tell me," she asked, and when he only scowled at her, she persisted with logic. "Look. First, you've been hurt. Second, you yourself admitted to being lost, then you couldn't remember where...home...was. So tell me, what is your name?"

"Okay, okay. I'll play, Doctor," he slurred. "I'm Sam McDonald. And you're Katherine. And we've been married for ten years, and I've loved you every single day of that time. Satisfied?"

No, she wasn't satisfied. She was stupefied. It was almost as if he had created her fictitious husband himself. That or, somehow or other, she had actually made a fictional character come to life.

Dear Reader,

As usual, this month's Silhouette Intimate Moments lineup is a strong one, but there are two books that deserve special mention. First off, Nora Roberts completes her exciting "Calhoun Women" series with *Suzanna's Surrender,* the story of the fourth Calhoun sister and her successful search for love. You won't want to miss this book; Nora Roberts fans all around the world are eagerly collecting this new series from an author whose name is synonymous with the best reading in romance fiction today.

Another author of note is Judith Duncan. Her name may already be familiar to some of you, in which case you know that *A Risk Worth Taking,* her debut for Intimate Moments, promises reading pleasure well beyond the ordinary. For those of you who aren't familiar with her previous work, let me say only that the power of her writing and the depth of the emotions she captures on paper will astound you. This is a book that will haunt your memory long after you've turned the last page.

But I can't let these two special events keep me from drawing your attention to the other two books we're offering this month. Paula Detmer Riggs is an award-winner and a veteran of the bestseller lists, and *Silent Impact* is a perfect example of the deeply emotional style that is her hallmark. And let Marilyn Tracy introduce you to two characters who truly are *Too Good to Forget*. Memory—or the lack of it—can play strange tricks; in this case, those tricks lead to marriage!

In coming months, look for more of your favorite authors—Emilie Richards, Marilyn Pappano, Kathleen Eagle and Heather Graham Pozzessere, to name only a few—writing more of your favorite books.

Enjoy!

Leslie Wainger
Senior Editor and Editorial Coordinator

MARILYN TRACY

Too Good To Forget

SILHOUETTE·INTIMATE·MOMENTS®
Published by Silhouette Books New York
America's Publisher of Contemporary Romance

SILHOUETTE BOOKS
300 East 42nd St., New York, N.Y. 10017

TOO GOOD TO FORGET

ISBN: 0-373-07399-2

First Silhouette Books printing September 1991

Printed in the U.S.A.

Books by Marilyn Tracy

Silhouette Intimate Moments

Magic in the Air #311
Blue Ice #362
Echoes of the Garden #387
Too Good To Forget #399

MARILYN TRACY

writes romances during the day, and in the evenings she rewrites them into songs on the piano or guitar. She feels that country-western music lends itself most readily to a real romantic story line. Each story she's written has its own soundtrack.

Marilyn didn't always have a quiet place to write romances and music. After several years of working in television news broadcasting and for the State Department in Tel Aviv and Moscow, she jumped from the fast lane and into what she calls a life of paradise in her home state, New Mexico, where she lives with her son. From traveler to homebody, from rover to writer of her own romance novels, Marilyn's sure her life is a dream come true!

Chapter 1

"Think he'll show?" George asked, his words muffled as he chewed on his candy bar. The wrapper had long since disappeared into his bulging jacket pocket.

Sam shrugged, looking not at George, but at the dark expanse of the lonely pier. Nothing ever looked as forsaken as a deserted pier, he thought. It looked haunted by the trips not taken, the dreams already spent. Here, scarcely moving, scraping against the dock with a beggar's scratch, the boats were bound, drained of life, surrounded and encircled by dark wood and darker water.

With any luck, this pier wouldn't be empty for long.

Sam shifted, his hand automatically rubbing against his shoulder. He felt naked without the holster, and more than naked without his gun. However, this was an unofficial surveillance, a mere follow-up on a long-shot tip. And so no weapons, because even if the tip should pay off, he and George weren't after this particular fish—he was small-fry. They didn't need a gun to toss this guy back to the sea. They were after his boss, or his boss's boss. All they wanted was a glimpse of a face, the sound of a voice, any scrap of a clue they could use to connect that mysterious boss with a gun-running ring operating the full stretch of the southeast coastline, and from there to South America.

Sam rubbed his shoulder ruefully. Besides, he thought, they weren't just in Virginia Beach to keep tabs on some gunrunner. Guns didn't fit with linen suits. His hand dropped to his jacket pocket and a soft chuckle escaped him.

"What's so funny?" George asked, his voice barely above a whisper.

Sam shook his head. The humor would translate only to his detriment. His hand curled around the worn pages of the book in his pocket. Here he was, a top Treasury department agent, Mister Action, armed with a spy novel and dressed in a dark-colored suit. Oh, yeah, he thought, he was as ready for potential danger as a baby in a pram.

"Daydreaming about what you're going to say when you meet the beautiful Katherine?" George asked.

Sam glanced at his partner. Sometimes, at times like this, friends of fourteen years' standing knew a little too much. Sam leaned against the wooden pier support, one hand still in his jacket pocket, a finger riffling the oft-read pages of an early Sam McDonald novel. He pulled the battered copy from his pocket, though the darkness made it impossible to see much more than the dim outline of the seductive cover.

"Are you really going to carry that ratty thing into a bookstore and have that classy lady sign it?" George asked. "Why did you bother with the new suit, then? Why didn't you just grab something off a bag man?"

Sam grinned, but said nothing.

"And why are we hanging around here? You know as well as I do this is just an excuse to go to that book signing. You're losing it, pal. You just want it signed so you can shock the poor woman." Though he still half whispered, George pitched his voice a notch higher. "Who do you want it made out to?'' His voice dropped back down. "Sam McDonald. From Sam McDonald's loving wife, Katherine.''

"They're a hell of a writing team," Sam said. He and George had had bits of this conversation too many times in the past few days.

"Yeah. I read 'em. Who doesn't? But you're hooked because he has the same name.''

"Wouldn't you be?''

"I somehow can't picture anybody writing under the name of George Shindowski.''

"Nothing anyone would admit to reading, anyway.''

"That water's pretty deep here, pal. Just keep on talking," George said, but with no malice. "Well, let's hope this little show gets started pretty soon, or you're going to miss your date with your author's better half.''

"It's not until tomorrow afternoon, and hopefully I'll get a chance to meet both of them.''

"Right," George said, but his voice implied otherwise. "That's why you bought a new suit and why you wouldn't even ruin the 'line' of it by wearing a gun tonight.''

Sam grinned again, acknowledging the sure hit.

"Didn't anyone ever tell you that's why all the TV cops wear shoulder pads? Hides the holster, pal. Hides the holster.''

Sam snorted his opinion of shoulder pads for men.

Water nudging the line of boats against the dock was the only sound to be heard for several minutes. George said, "I saw her on one of those late-night talk shows the other day. You know, the kind where they sit around in a fakey on-stage garden room and talk about what they eat for breakfast and what kind of dog food they feed good old Max? I can see why you're hooked.''

Sam had seen that interview. And quite a few others over the past five years of Sam and Katherine McDonald's rise to fame and fortune. To date, though he'd seen Katherine

McDonald some thirty or forty times now, he'd never caught so much as a glimpse of the famous coauthor, Sam. According to the interviews he'd seen with Katherine, the male half of the writing team had been a covert operative for a number of years and still preferred his anonymity.

Contrary to what he'd just told George, not seeing her husband was all right with Sam; the author's wife was something special to look at, and even better to listen to. Her voice was low and soft, it hinted at things deeper, things left unsaid, and her full lips moved in an almost deliberate sensuality, as if she were tasting the words she spoke. Her hair was neither brown nor blond, but a honeyed, rich combination of both, with curls that he liked to think had been untouched by human hands. She was, by her own admission, passionately in love with Sam McDonald. Every time he heard her say it, Sam felt a curious wrench deep inside him. And each time, with her eyes seemingly meeting his through the television screen, he had the odd feeling that she really meant him. Not her husband.

"I think this is it," George breathed.

Sam didn't move from his leaned stance against the dock support, but his entire body tensed. Thoughts of Katherine McDonald reluctantly slid from his mind. From their position at the water end of the pier, they could see whoever might walk the length of wooden darkness. Here was their mark.

Like a typical thug, he walked softly, his head swiveled around, more interested in what might be following him than what might be waiting for him up ahead. He clearly had no idea that the two Treasury agents lingered in the shadows at the end of the pier, the last stop between Virginia Beach and the Atlantic Ocean.

Their mark sported the latest in gunrunning togs, Sam thought with some humor. He whispered as much to George, whose brief broad grin flashed brightly in the night.

George carried the thought further, in a scarcely voiced falsetto. "And here we have your basic commando sweater, dock pants, and deck shoes with socks. This ensemble is a must for any self-respecting gunrunner."

The guy stopped in front of a low-slung sweetheart of a boat. Even in the dark, its sleek rich, power was evident. No beggarly scraping would dare come from this beauty, Sam thought, and then wondered which had come first for this guy, the gunrunning or the boat. Was this one of the young hotshots who ran arms for kicks, or had the money angle lured him in?

"Bingo," George whispered.

Sam's eyes jerked from the mark to the end of the pier. Shadowed by the pier's end, and staying well away from the center of the wooden runway, was a second man. All Sam could really make out was the silvery-white hair and the long coat. Sam frowned. As gunrunning was largely a young man's game, the white hair meant only one thing: this was a head honcho.

"I don't think he's planning to go for a ride," George whispered, confirming Sam's supposition.

The second man stepped from the shadows then and up to the mark. The mark, popping the leather tarp from the boat's shallow cabin, hadn't yet seen the white-haired fellow. When the second man tapped him on the shoulder, he jumped and whirled around, arms akimbo, eyes white and wide with a trapped fear.

Shadows still hid the second man's face from Sam and George, and Sam willed him to turn in their direction.

George apparently traveled the same wavelength, for he whispered, "This way, pal."

Though the older man couldn't possible have heard George over the water lapping against the boats, he turned nonetheless. Smarter than the thug, he wasn't concerned with what could possibly be lurking behind him; he was interested in what obstacles lay ahead. For a single, seem-

ingly endless moment in time, his face was lit by the distant
street lamps of the gravel parking lot feeding into the pier.
His high brow gleamed in the soft glow, his dark eyes
seemed able to pierce the shadows hiding Sam and George.
White eyebrows arched above the dark eyes as if asking who
had commanded his attention at the far end of the pier. His
hard mouth was drawn into a straight, even harder line. A
hard line that Sam knew all too well.

"What the—?" George burst out, involuntarily. His voice
seemed to carry on the moist air, ringing in Sam's ears like
the sound of a glass shattering in a midnight-darkened
kitchen. Sam instinctively jabbed George to cut the rest of
the unguarded betrayal of their presence. He was too late.

The older man started forward. He walked slowly toward them, unhurried, unafraid. In his hand, his ever-
present .38 police special seemed more like an extra ap-
pendage than a foreign, deadly object.

A thousand different images slammed into Sam's mind,
warning him that he was about ready to meet his maker.
Foremost were conflicting images of the man approaching
them...Pete Sorenson, their boss. Their *chief*. The head of
the operations branch at Treasury. In a split second, his
memory opened to show, with no timeworn cast of sepia,
the boss's hard mouth relaxed into a welcoming smile, advising Sam about the ropes at Treasury, introducing Sam to
George, his new partner. Fourteen years of images flickered and took flame. He saw the day the chief had given
George and him a special commendation for a shoot-out
and roundup off the coast of Florida. His mind jumped to
the time the chief had fired that pompous young Paul
something-or-other for a breach of security. And finally, as
if in slow motion, he saw clearly the last time he'd seen the
chief and heard the recorded memory of the last time they'd
spoken.

"Not Virginia Beach," the chief had said. "We've
combed every inch of it. Ask Phil. Ask Harry. No. I think

your best bet will be Charleston. Our boys in South Carolina have come up with several good leads. If you two are hot for a cold night's exercise, try Charleston.''

Sam's first real thought struck pay dirt: they should have listened. If they had, Pete wouldn't be walking toward them, a suspected gunrunning boss, his hand gripping a .38, his mouth set against trouble. If they had listened, Sam and George might never have seen him here on a lonely pier where Pete should never have dared show his face.

This volume of imagery and thought flooded him in less time than the quick intake of one breath, and wrestled with Sam's protesting mind. It wasn't possible, he thought, not *Pete,* not the man who had trained him, encouraged him, spurred him on in his quest for curbing one corner of the world's madness. Yet the chief was here, close enough to see that, despite the distance from the street lamps, there was a gun in the old man's hand and its single, dark eye was trained on Sam's heart.

''This is unfortunate, gentlemen,'' the chief said slowly, almost as if he truly meant the words. Perhaps, Sam thought half-wonderingly, he did.

George stepped forward slightly. ''What the hell are you doing here?''

Though Sam didn't dare take his eyes from the chief, he wished he could turn and stare at George. How could a man as sharp-witted as Shindowski have missed the implications of the chief's presence? Then, as the gun shifted and pointed toward George, Sam understood. George knew just as well as he did what was happening here. But he was already trying to distract Pete with seeming stupidity. Or at least to make it appear they didn't get the connection.

That it hadn't a chance of working was obvious in the chief's next words. ''It's too late for heroics, George.'' His cold eyes flicked to Sam. ''Why didn't you listen to me? This need never have happened.''

"Right," Sam said. "Do you mean catching you? Or killing us?" Their only hope was to get the chief off guard long enough to disarm him, or barring that, make for the water. Inwardly he cursed the quixotic impulse that had led him to persuading George to leave their weapons behind. And he cursed the book signing he'd planned on attending, an event that made this night an excuse for being in Virginia Beach, an excuse that now looked likely to be the last excuse he ever tendered.

"Both, really," the chief answered. Sam had to grapple with his memory to remember what he'd asked. Something about killing them, he thought.

Pete Sorenson continued. "But it's irrelevant. You *are* here. And you did see me. I don't have much choice now."

"Oh, you have lots of choices," Sam said. He felt a grin twist his lips. Only Devra, and possibly George, would have known how falsely that grin rested there. "You could turn yourself in. I can see that from your standpoint it may not seem the best option, but, what the hell, chief, it would be the right thing to do. Who knows? We might even back you up."

The gun barrel shifted a fraction so that the dark eye again focused on Sam's chest.

"On the other hand," Sam said, "you could kill us and they'll get you for murder one...a sudden raise in status from slime bucket to murderer."

"You've always had a nasty tongue, Sam," Pete said. A rather wistful expression crossed his face. "It's a pity. I've always enjoyed it."

The chief's words reached into Sam's subconscious, dragging out a memory of something Devra had said just prior to her death, something about having missed his acerbic tongue since she'd become ill. He shook the memory, the hundreds of memories, away.

Sam's eyes cut to George in a swift, silent exchange of intention. Without expression, without so much as a nod from George, he knew his partner was with him, was thinking on the same wavelength. Fourteen years of surveillance, chases, football games and cold cups of coffee had rendered much of talking unnecessary.

Sam leaned back against the post he'd abandoned at the first forward movement by the chief. "Yeah?" he asked, not bothering to look at the gun any longer. George would be taking care of that. "It's funny, chief, I'll miss you, too. George and I were just talking about that very thing. So were the boys back on the beach."

Pete smiled, a wintry, chilling effect. "Nice try, Sam. No cigar."

"Have it your way," Sam said, straightening. He drew his lips back against his teeth and let loose a shrill, piercing whistle.

As he'd hoped, the chief flinched and half crouched. At that instant, as if George had been reading Sam's mind, George leapt forward, hands curled for the chief's arm, his body between Sam and chief.

Unfortunately he wasn't quick enough. The chief's responses were as fast as ever. So near the water, the gun's report was deafening and seemed to echo and ricochet. The sound swelled like a wave and crashed into Sam's ears and into the deepest places of his heart. George, already in full flight, stopped as though he'd rammed into a brick wall, then was propelled backward again, his neck snapping forward, arms flailing. He careened into Sam with the force of a runaway car. Sam heard another shot echo across the pier, and George's body jerked yet again. He took the full weight of his long-time friend's body almost gratefully, wrapping his arms around George, falling backward, cursing a third shot, cursing a sudden burning pain at his temple and cursing the screaming ache in his heart.

He hit the wooden pier with the combined weight of himself and George and heard a plank crack in protest. His head struck the pier once, then, as if in slow motion, they rose from the ground, defying gravity, only to be sucked back into that force a second time, causing Sam to groan as his head made another rough contact with the boards. His temple seemed to have a mind of its own, screaming protest after protest. One of his legs dangled over the side of the pier, touching nothing but feeling the chill rising from the dark water beneath him.

His hands, tightly wrapped around George's broad chest, were wet, sticky and hot. The clean salt smell of the sea was overtaken by the sharp coppery tang of blood.

"No!" he yelled, knowing no words, no prayers, nothing he could say or do would bring George back. Nothing he'd done had stopped the cancer from slowly, painfully consuming his wife, and nothing he could do now would heal the bullet ruptures in George's battered chest. Yet, as if his very soul had to scream this protest, he yelled again, *"NO!"*

Dimly, as if in answer to his shout, he heard another report of the gun. He flinched automatically, recoiling from the shot, pushing George from him, half in an instinct to protect George from further abuse, half in horror that George's hapless body was serving as a shield. He felt the heat of the bullet as it grazed near his cheek.

A shout from somewhere, perhaps the younger gunrunner, handed Sam his last chance for survival. As the chief whirled to bark some answer, Sam rolled from the pier, and down the ten or twelve feet to the dark, icy water. Falling blind, the chill wind pulling at his new jacket, Sam bit his lip to hold in a curse. He landed with a splash that sounded thunderous to his ears.

The impact, the pain in his temple, and the almost atavistic instinct for survival, sent him lunging for the protective cover of the pier. Only moments before he'd been standing on it with George. Now it contained a murderer and the bleeding body of his best friend, his partner. Now this pier above him was the only thing between Sam and certain death.

He couldn't seem to think. He was conscious only of his tremendous sense of loss, the terrible betrayal and a nebulous gratitude that the tide was in. He dove and moved farther back beneath the pier.

As he surfaced, keeping well under the canopy of the pier, careful to make no sound, he strained to hear what was going on above him. He could hear nothing at first but the restless boats now flanking him. Then he could make out the chief's footsteps. The wood creaked as the chief walked the length of the pier. The water some five feet from Sam spumed upward before Sam heard the report of the gun. He slid beneath the surface, the water seemingly made thicker by the cold, and swam under the pier, silently inching his way toward the shore.

He fought a wave of nausea that swept over him as the salt bit at his temple, telling him that he too was wounded. Somehow the notion that he had a wound steadied him slightly, but only served to underscore his feelings about having left George's shattered body atop the pier.

He felt disoriented. Everything had gone wrong, and the pain, the anger, and the cold water eddied around him and in him like a miasma of betrayal.

Beyond the horrifying notion that Pete Sorenson was not only a gunrunner but a murderer, that he had killed George, was the tormenting thought of never seeing George alive again. He would never again swap old stories, never see one of those gooey chocolate bars, never cheer for the Skins, never do any of these mundane, everyday things without thinking of George, without remembering the fourteen years, without feeling the loss of the best friend a man could have. Without remembering how George had stood by him through those dark days when Devra died.

A shudder worked through him. No, he thought, he could never pass another day of his life without remembering how

George was shot and killed on a godforsaken pier without farewells, without goodbyes, without Sam ever having once told George how much his friendship, his loyalty, his presence had meant to him.

Slicing through his agonized thoughts was the dull roar of a perfectly tuned engine. A brief flare of light and the wide, white spray of the backwash told Sam the sweetheart of a boat was gone, rushing headlong into the ocean, like a large fish that manages to escape the fisher's net.

Overhead Sam heard the clunk of the chief's footsteps, traversing back and forth, stopping here and there, then continuing, searching the water below, looking for evidence that Sam was alive. Or proof that he was dead.

Sam pushed silently free of the water's hold and crawled onto the rocky and dirty sand that characteristically collects beneath piers. He didn't stay there long, moving from shadow to shadow, until he'd cleared the pier and had no choice but to drag himself into the daylightlike glow from the nearby parking-lot street lamp. A glance over his shoulder told him that he was safe for the moment; the chief's eyes were still on the water below, probing the depths of the dark, lapping sea.

For a long moment, Sam stayed there, just watching the chief, watching the pier. It was only when he realized that George's body no longer lay upon it that he knew why he'd been staring.

A rough structure, a booth of some sort, marked the edge of the parking lot. George's car wasn't here; they had parked some four blocks away, down a Virginia Beach side street. The chief's car was there, however. For a moment, Sam toyed with hiding beside the chief's car and ambushing the murdering traitor as he approached. He rejected this thought without too much of a struggle; he was in no shape to tackle a man with a gun.

He raised an unsteady hand to his temple, and when he looked at his fingers and saw the bright red spillage glisten

in the street lamp's diffused glow, he felt as if he were looking at someone else's hand, someone else's blood. He moved
toward the parking lot, staggering slightly, clinging to rails,
rough planks of the small booth, anything that held him
upright and in shadow.

It seemed hours before he reached George's car. He'd
stumbled through five or six dark alleys, knocking against
dumpsters, clanging into metal cartons and piles of trash.
But he saw the car with the gratitude of a dying man seeing
the doctor's face bending over the hospital bed. There had
been no need for him to strive to get there; he had no keys
for the ancient and battered Oldsmobile, the keys were with
George. But seeing the car sitting forlornly on a dark street,
he dimly understood that he'd come to it as if in confirmation, as if to prove to himself that George was really dead.
Really gone.

Leaning against the front bumper of the Olds, Sam felt
the full impact of George's death. The metal he rested upon
had been the source of many a surveillance, the repository
for many a confidence, the place of a thousand talks.
George would never sit in it again. He would never sit in it
again, because George was dead.

The single thought went around in Sam's mind like a spi-
ral, over and over, in ever-tightening circles, the emphasis
changing each time on the three words as if he could make
sense of them by such a ruse: *George* is dead. George *is*
dead. George is *dead*.

Operating solely on instinct, Sam pulled a sodden handkerchief from his equally sodden pocket and wrapped it
around his head, grimacing against the salt water plunder-
ing his wound, tying the ends with shaking fingers. The
makeshift bandage only exacerbated the throbbing in his
temple, the pain in his head. It did nothing for the scream
of rage and pain in his heart. He leaned against George's
car, fighting a weakness of spirit, a weakness of body. His

eyes stung and though he tried to tell himself it was from the salt water dripping into his eyes, he knew better.

His mind wrestled with logistics—Who should he contact? What had the chief done with George's body?—while his heart grappled with the intangible, the too-much-to-be-borne grief at the loss of his partner.

He knew the chief wouldn't rest until Sam joined George. The reality of having surprised his boss at gunrunning, of having witnessed the murder of George Shindowski, of having narrowly missed his own death, all told Sam that his life wasn't worth a plugged nickel.

He could scarcely keep standing, even leaning against George's car. He'd rest for a few minutes, he thought, then he'd figure out what to do. What authorities to call—since the chief was one of the biggest? It would be Sam's word against Pete Sorenson's. So, who could he inform? He tired with the effort to think clearly and now all his mind could do was wonder what the chief had done with George. The grieving part of him wondered what he would do without George.

He slumped to the sidewalk beside the old car, and he dimly knew that had anyone seen him, he would be pegged another misbegotten derelict, wet, disheveled, and eyes blazing with quick fever, lips moving in inchoate words.

Sam McDonald's last conscious thought was that even his namesake couldn't write himself out of this one.

Chapter 2

Katherine McDonald raised a hand to wave at an acquaintance across her cousin's crowded bookstore, but her mind was elsewhere. This book signing would be over in just a few hours, and she'd be home, dressed in slacks and a sweater, her Irish setter, Max, loping ahead of her, chasing ducks, startling roosting egrets and herons.

She glanced at the tidy stacks of the latest "Sam" and Katherine McDonald novel, *Shadowman,* waiting for the public "half" of the writing team to sign, and lifted her eyes to the front door of Andrew's waterfront store, as if night would magically advance and this evening of publicity would be over before it really began, or at the least as if Sam could equally magically appear and, for once, do this for her.

She sighed. He wouldn't be there; he never was.

"Any chance he'll make it?" asked a woman she'd once met at one of Andrew's parties.

Katherine smiled and shook her head. Even to herself the smile felt wistful. A shadow of sympathy crossed the wom-

an's features. *The tangled web we weave...,* Katherine
thought, wondering what this woman's name was and why
the woman's evident sympathy should make her feel resent-
ful, restless.

Someone else stepped up then, asking about Sam, about
the next novel, asking questions that only produced another link in the endless chain of lies. Today she all but
hated this husband of hers. He had never stood beside her.
He couldn't. But if she were perfectly honest with herself,
his lack of appearance was certainly her fault, not his. She
answered smoothly, so easily that she felt her words came
from some part of her that was only habit; the real part of
her remained home with Max, her eyes focused on a scene
playing in another land, her heart beating to the rhythm of
dimly heard computer keys.

"Because of the years he spent as an operative with the
CIA, it's still somewhat dangerous for him to make public
appearances," she answered softly, dully. She'd said it so
often it almost felt like the truth.

"Are you ready, dear?" Her cousin Andrew Deering's
voice penetrated her momentary fog. "People are waiting." He gestured toward the book table.

Katherine smiled at him, a relaxed smile, taking in the
sparkling eyes, the gamin smile, the perpetually moving,
narrow fingers of her cousin. Andrew never tired of the
game, was never bored by the lies, by the stratagems.

"Ready as I'll ever be," she said, stepping forward and
edging through the group by the table to stand behind the
chair waiting for her. Her eyes met Andrew's. He smiled and
gave her a rueful look of commiseration. He knew how
nerve-racking she found all the publicity, especially since it
was compounded by a never-ending string of lies. Yet it was
the very lies that made book signings possible for Katherine, that made the McDonald novels sell.

Andrew cleared his throat and, waving his hands for attention, introduced Katherine and, after a brief round of

applause, told the people assembled the standard line about Sam, the reasons he wouldn't be there, the oft-repeated excuse. He wound up with, "And we wouldn't want anything to stop our Sam from writing, now, would we?" He laughed, and the people listening to him smiled. No, they wouldn't want that.

Katherine watched the crowd exchange knowing looks. They all understood about Sam. They all knew *about* Sam. She shook her head wryly. None of them knew him at all. She knew him better than anyone on earth, and what she really knew about him wouldn't fill a thimble.

"Besides," Andrew added before Katherine could even sign the first book, "we all know who really writes these thrillers." Self-conscious laughter broke out in spurts between she and Andrew. Self-conscious because not one person in the room knew Sam, and all wanted to act as if they did. Laughter because they all wanted to feel they shared in an inside joke.

"Your husband's so *very* exciting," one fan murmured to Katherine, taking back the now-inscribed book. "You must be so happy together."

"Very," Katherine replied automatically, though a part of her wanted to correct this misconception. Her eyes again strayed to the door that would never be filled with her husband's frame. For some reason, today this notion filled her with a strange sense of regret.

"He's a lucky man," a man in a checked sports coat murmured in her ear. His eyes roamed over her body with a knowing, suggestive leer. He actually licked his lips as his eyes lingered over the curves evident underneath her cream-colored silk blouse. "Very lucky."

Katherine took the book he was loosely holding out in her direction and stepped back a pace, lifting the book to breast-level, blocking the obnoxious gaze. "I'm the one who's lucky," she said with a bit more determination than usual.

She finished signing the book and averted her eyes. "Sam's everything a woman could..." She trailed off. Her voice seemed snared in her throat, her eyes on the tall, dark-haired man just to the right of the door. How long had he been there? How had she missed his entrance?

He wore the latest style in rumpled linen, but without the shoulder pads—this man didn't need any padding. Around his head he wore a stained handkerchief, raffishly knotted on the side, dipping low to hide his left eyebrow. The visible eyebrow was dark and slightly winged, lending a somewhat devilish look to him. His eyes, scanning the crowd, were a dark, almost cobalt blue, and they gave her the impression he was seeing something she couldn't. Whatever it was he saw, Katherine could tell it was profoundly confusing to him, and somehow childishly delightful.

The newcomer raised his hand and ran it across his beard-shadowed and roughened cheeks and on down across his hard, square jawline. Then he lowered his hand and stared at it as if it belonged to someone else. Despite the wondering look on his face, he somehow conveyed an impression of looking nothing shy of dangerous.

Katherine cut a sharp glance toward Andrew, who, like she had been, was staring at the man inside the doorway of his store. Andrew wore the expression of someone having seen a ghost. A hint of the stranger's delight curved Andrew's mouth upward in a grin. *A friend of Andrew's?* Katherine wondered in sharp dismay. Something about the man had caused an unaccountable churning in her stomach. But if he was a friend of Andrew's...he wasn't likely to look her way. Besides, she thought with unaccustomed bitterness, she was supposed to be married.

The man moved forward then, recapturing Katherine's attention, and that of the crowd. Heads turned and on seeing the stranger, several women seemed to sigh without expelling breath. It was more a softening of expression, as though they'd seen something they'd often dreamed about.

The men in the bookstore seemed to stand a little straighter and stomachs pulled in while chests seemed to swell. Eyes danced from the stranger to Katherine and back.

Katherine heard a man's voice say, ''Looks like he made it this time,'' and she turned to locate the voice in some dismay.

The stranger caught the speculative atmosphere and looked up, first at the crowd, then following their curious gazes, directly at Katherine. His eyes widened slightly and a strange look of relief crossed his face, softening it, making the hard features seem warmer, kinder. His full lips parted and mouthed her name. Recognition lit his blue eyes.

''Katherine,'' he mouthed again, a smile easing the tension on his face.

She was there, he thought. He'd known she would be. It was dangerous for him, coming here like this, but it was worth it just to see Katherine again. To see her honeyed hair, to drown, for just a moment, in the incredible wells of her rich hazel eyes. Yes, she was there, surrounded by people, out in the places he could never go, doing things he could never do, because his past always clouded his present.

At the moment, he felt everything was cloudy. Time, life, present, past and even future, all obscured by some mental fog. Everything except Katherine. He wasn't even sure how he'd gotten here... and into his mind flashed the image of a lonely pier and a bobbing, sleek boat, and the copper smell of blood. The despair that seemed to haunt him today welled up and threatened to overtake his mind again. And the pain in his head, the steady sledgehammer pounding at his brain, drove thought away, pushed all linear sequence of time from his mind. He'd been involved in some kind of accident, he knew that much. A boating accident? But he wasn't sure of anything else. Except of his love for Katherine.

Here, with her standing just across the room, he felt real relief for the first time in days. Or was it weeks? In this room, this wonderful place filled with books, fans, and camaraderie, Katherine stood there, her generous lips parted, her gentle eyes wide with the shock of seeing him, looking as he so often dreamed of her. And as always, whenever he saw her, thought of her, she served as his anchor, the one person on earth he could truly trust. Hers was the only face he saw, the only face he recognized as belonging to him. For Katherine had always been there, in his heart, in his mind. She had stood by him through all the good times, and the bad. Katherine said so publicly, each interview, each appearance.

Katherine, he whispered, and her name felt like velvet on his lips. He smiled, feeling it was the first time he'd smiled in such a long time, happy again, not knowing and not even questioning why he felt like he was home for the first time in years. All because of Katherine, the constant companion of his dreams, the sole keeper of his heart.

God, it was good to see her now. It seemed a lifetime since he'd kissed her soft lips, forever since he'd touched her skin, told her that he loved her. When was the last time he'd told her how beautiful she was, how talented, how lucky he was to have her?

"Katherine," she murmured, as if saying her name could pull her across the room and into his arms. Because that's where he wanted her to be. That's where he *needed* her to be.

He started toward her, all the love he felt for her pouring from his eyes.

Katherine felt the impact of the stranger's gaze, of the gentling of his features to her very core. Who was this man? Obviously he was no friend of Andrew's. Why would he stare at her so, whisper her name as gently as a lover, as if he knew her, and knew her oh, so very intimately? The very fact that his gaze drank her in like a man who hasn't seen liquid for days made her tremble. Because his lips eased into a crooked—*and relieved?*— smile made her feel oddly vulnerable, made her wish for just a moment that she could really be who or what he wanted her to be.

He raised a slightly unsteady hand toward his head and gestured at the makeshift strip of stained bandage around his brow. He shrugged and his grin broadened, showing a flash of white, straight teeth, then he stepped another cautious pace forward. Toward her.

Her heart pounding, her thoughts suddenly chaos, Katherine involuntarily stepped backward, her hips bumping against a stack of the new *Shadowman* novels ready to be signed, sending them sliding from the table. Someone behind her caught and righted them. Katherine cast that aide a quick look of gratitude and turned back to the stranger.

He wasn't looking at her now. He was staring at the righted stack of *Shadowman* novels, glossy black covers seeming to absorb the light, the title's electrifying shock of white and red compelling a buyer's touch. He blinked two or three times, as if his vision had blurred, and then, to Katherine's consternation, his face split into a wide grin of relieved recognition. As if he were hypnotized by the books, he walked toward the stacked table. The crowd parted easily, almost gratefully.

A horrible suspicion crossed Katherine's mind and her eyes flew to find Andrew. Had he dared carry their deception, their protection of Sam, to another whole plateau? He was watching the man with that same look of awed wonder he'd been wearing earlier. His usually drawn-bow mouth was slack with fascination. From his expression, Katherine had to conclude that he hadn't hired this stranger to make an appearance on behalf of the elusive author. Or if he had, she amended wryly, he was happier with the results than he'd anticipated.

The stranger's hand reached out to softly stroke a *Shadowman* cover. His touch was almost reverential, his expression guarded, yet painfully so. Katherine could see that he was intensely moved by the slick surface, the experience of touching the book. It was a lover's touch and her skin drew tight in response. Either he was an excellent actor, or the truest fan she and the elusive Sam McDonald could ever hope for.

Katherine dragged her eyes from the bent head of the stranger and signaled Andrew, who was still watching the man as if transfixed. When he turned wide eyes in her direction, his expression was nothing short of a question mark. "Who?" he asked silently, his thumb pointed at the stranger.

The man wasn't some hired ringer then. At least, he hadn't been hired by Andrew. Then who was he? Why did she have the odd sensation that it was important that she know?

The stranger lifted his hand from the book as if the cover had been too warm and met her gaze again. A thousand questions hovered in his eyes, and more than a few answers. Katherine's breath caught. What did he want? And what was it about him that made her harbor a vague desire to give it to him?

Katherine slowly shook her head, whether in answer to his unspoken questions or to the questions inside her, she couldn't have said. She ran the tip of her tongue along her suddenly dry lips and lifted her hand to weave in a tickling strand of hair that had come loose and was trying to dance on her too-warm neck.

Katherine, he mouthed again. Katherine swallowed heavily. What was it about this man that a simple whisper of her name on his lips made her feel weak and defenseless, as though he'd said the words against her bare skin?

He closed the distance between them, aided by the silent crowd. He raised a slightly unsteady hand to her shoulder, then to her cheek.

"Ah, Katherine," he said aloud. His voice was rasped, as though he hadn't spoken in a long time. And its very graveled, raw quality made her shiver.

Unable to move, mesmerized by his warm touch on her cheek, by the desperation in the confused eyes, caught by a choking desire so strong that it momentarily robbed her of thought, Katherine stood gazing into his eyes, feeling, yet not truly conscious of, his free hand grasping her shoulder.

His arm slid around her back, and though she trembled at the touch, at the heat, she remained still, her senses reeling. *Help me,* she pleaded silently, but she knew the plea wasn't directed at Andrew or the crowd eagerly watching the strange tableau. It was directed toward this disheveled stranger who so easily held her in his loose embrace.

Slowly, as if answering her plea, his head bent and his lips lowered to hers. He kissed her gently, almost with reverence, with gratitude.

Katherine raised her hand to push him away, but instead, as his warm lips, tasting of salt and sea air, covered hers, she found herself clutching his lapel. As the kiss deepened, the stranger's fingers slid to the nape of her neck, drawing her closer. For a shocking, absolutely shattering moment, Katherine gave in to the kiss, absorbing his scent, his need, his want, knowing it matched her own.

Someone clapped, and someone else chuckled nervously, and the strange spell was broken. Katherine pulled back, bemused by what had transpired, afraid of the fire he'd started deep within her.

His eyes, darkened by desire, searched her face, plundered her gaze, as though his only contact with humanity was through her.

"Help me, Katherine," he murmured so softly she knew only she could hear him. His warm hand took her too-cold fingers and gripped them tightly.

Who was this man? Why was he asking her for help? And what was it about him that made her want to help him? Made her feel as though she *had* to? That she couldn't do anything else?

A woman Katherine had never seen before stepped up to the stranger. She tentatively touched the man's rumpled sleeve. "Sam?" she asked. "Sam McDonald?"

Katherine's heart seemed to stall for a full beat. She started to murmur a denial, but the stranger half turned, presenting his profile to Katherine, though not releasing his easy grip around her.

"Yes?" the stranger asked the woman in that rasped, rich voice.

Katherine's hands trembled and her knees threatened to buckle. She pulled out of the man's embrace. She had the shaken sensation that she was dreaming, or perhaps in the throes of a nightmare. What on earth was going on? This stranger was certainly not her husband. Not Sam. For a split second the wish that her Sam could be someone like this threatened to overcome the rational need to get him out of the bookstore.

She drew a deep breath as the woman handed the impostor a copy of *Shadowman*. Katherine had to dig her nails into her palms to keep from leaping forward and snatching the book from the stranger's hands. But the crowd around him stopped her, her own shock held her still.

Whatever he was, whoever he might claim to be, the stranger, the *impostor,* spelled trouble, she thought, with a capital T. Because he'd held her in a spell with his warm smile, had stilled her with his soft and purposeful kiss, the people in the bookstore obviously had mistaken him for the novelist they were certain they'd never see. But Katherine knew—who better?—he wasn't Sam, knew Sam could never show his face at a book signing.

He made no move to sign the book. He turned it over in his hands and read the back cover. She studied him with a stab of fear, a frown of perplexity. Now that he wasn't looking at her, now that his warm lips and gentle hands didn't hold her captive, she took in the full extent of his unkempt appearance. The stains on his handkerchief bandage looked remarkably like bloodstains, his jacket had felt slightly stiff, as though it had been dried upon him, and he carried the scent of the sea. And his eyes, dark and filled with warmth when he looked at her, now spoke of evident confusion. All of this settled in Katherine's nervous system and triggered a massive alarm.

She raised a trembling hand and beckoned for Andrew to join her. She looked pointedly at the impostor, subtly tapping a forefinger against her temple. To anyone watching her, she would only be taken to be rather thoughtful, but Andrew knew her well. She felt vaguely guilty for the gesture, for the slur on the stranger. And as she lowered her hand she felt a hitherto unexplored sorrow settling in her heart. This wasn't the kind of man who should be suffering some mental aberration.

She drew a steadying breath. *Do something!* she mouthed at Andrew.

Unseen by the people in front of him, her cousin held his own forefinger against his chest and raised his eyebrows high. "Me?" he pantomimed histrionically.

Katherine nodded, decisively.

With a shrug and habitual smile of complicity Andrew deftly made his way toward the stranger. Andrew was within three fans of them when another woman approached the man and curled her plump fingers around his forearm. Andrew paused, eyes alert. Katherine didn't move.

"Hello," the stranger said calmly. He handed the book he still held back to the first woman, his elbow brushing Katherine's arm, and turned to the other one. In doing so, he missed the slightly shocked, somewhat affronted frosty glare from the first. Katherine took her book swiftly and, without waiting to find out who the woman wanted the book made out to, signed it and handed it back.

The stranger—the *impostor,* Katherine reminded herself firmly—smiled down at the second woman. She visibly reacted to the warmth of that smile, a reaction Katherine understood all too well, though it didn't make her feel much better.

Katherine could see no more than the impostor's profile. Even there, she could read nothing but sincerity on his tanned face. Nothing but sincerity and this great, vast well of dislocation. He stared at the book the woman was holding out to him, then took it with a look that Katherine knew well, surprised wonder, a slight awe and a great deal of pride. She knew she'd worn that expression the first time she'd ever signed a McDonald novel. He turned and handed it to Katherine with a slightly rueful grimace, then looked at the woman eyeing him with fascination.

"I'm sorry," he said. "Katherine has the only legible handwriting in the family. She always signs our books."

A hand came down on Katherine's shoulder, making her jump. "Am I to take it that you *didn't* hire him, dear?" Andrew's high-pitched whisper breathed into her ear. Katherine shook her head, eyes still on the impostor. "Well, if *I* didn't, and *you* didn't, who did?"

"There isn't any one else," Katherine whispered.

"What about that psychiatrist friend of yours . . . the one who's always trying to get you to *divorce* Sam? Jason Woodard?"

"It couldn't be him. He disapproves of the whole thing. He wouldn't hire a ringer."

Andrew sighed. "I suppose not. But really, dear, it is perfectly brilliant. I'm only sorry I didn't think of it."

"Brilliant!" Katherine exclaimed aloud, causing one or two heads to swivel in their direction. She lowered her voice and turned her head to his ear. "The man is claiming to be my husband! He's acting like he really wrote my books!"

"Sam's books, too," Andrew murmured. When she jabbed a finger in his arm, he dropped the quizzing expression and whispered in a tone as close to serious as he was capable of producing, "I'm not blind, dear. I can see he's a problem." His eyes flicked back to the impostor and a wicked smile curved his lips. "But really, you must admit, he looks the part!"

"He doesn't look a bit like Sam McDonald," Katherine breathed in Andrew's ear.

"No? Pray tell me, dear, how *does* your husband look these days? From what I remember, his eyes are blue, his hair is black, and his shoulders are broad." His eyes rested on the stranger with sardonic humor. "This fellow seems to have all of that and more. I can't seem to recall any other details about Sam." He studied the stranger, then turned to Katherine and said aloud, "I wonder why that is?"

Katherine shot Andrew a withering look, a look that failed to impress her cousin. "Do something," she said.

"Such as?"

"Stop him," she answered, calmly, turning to smile at a woman eyeing her curiously.

"If you haven't noticed, he's considerably larger than I am," Andrew whispered.

"Then call the cops," Katherine whispered back.

"Think of the publicity."

"Well, do *something!*" Katherine turned her gaze rather wildly back to the impostor who had been pulled by the crowd until he stood two or three paces away. He was standing stock-still, his eyes on her, his expression that of longing and confusion, and again, this indefinable hint of relief or joy.

"You're the one who kissed him, dear, not me!" Andrew said. "It seems our mystery man knows you." His eyes met hers in reproach and speculation.

"I never saw him before in my life," Katherine said faintly, then pressed her lips tightly together. The impostor's pleading eyes thoroughly rattled her. She didn't need this, didn't deserve it either. Something was obviously wrong with the man; why did it make her feel guilty to have to get him out of the bookstore?

Katherine could only shake her head. She felt numb, as though this really were a nightmare and she couldn't wake. "Please, Andrew, get him out of here," she pleaded quietly. She felt a wave of pity for the stranger shake her, forcing the guilt she felt to the surface. The man was obviously ill and confused. Would he be all right? Should she call the police just to get him help? Or had his kiss so thoroughly confounded her thinking that she was mistaking some nutcase for something more?

The man took a step toward her, his eyes alight with intention. Though she backed away from him, a curious idea formed in her mind. What if he weren't merely confused, slightly disoriented? What if he really believed he was Sam McDonald, her husband? What if it weren't some kind of strange act? What if he were truly crazy? Someone claimed his attention and he turned politely, if somewhat vaguely, toward the man.

Oblivious to her thoughts, Andrew added in a soft voice, "I wonder if someone finally figured out your game and hired him to blow your cover—so to speak, dear—sky-high."

Slowly, almost inaudibly, she said, "Andrew... I'm beginning to think no one *hired* him. I think we may have a real problem on our hands. I think you'd better try to talk to him. If he's not reasonable, then call the police."

"Your wish is my command, Cousin, dear, but only if you'll tell me what you constitute as 'reasonable.' Have you considered the size of that man's muscles? When I'm tossed through my own plate-glass window by your unusual guest and have to be dragged out of the bay, remember that you owe me, positively *owe* me one. I'll put it on your tab.''

Andrew lightly stepped away from her, his delicate hands tapping a shoulder here, a backside there, until he stood on the far side of the stranger, gently drawing him away from the crowd at the table.

Anyone not knowing Andrew well might have assumed the fluttering of his expressive hands was just another of his dramatic gestures, but Katherine could see that he was truly nervous. The stranger leaned closer to Andrew. After a few moments' conversation exchanged mouth to ear, Andrew drew back to look over his shoulder at her. His eyes were filled with warning. Katherine frowned a question at him, but he shook his head, leaning closer to the stranger to hear his next words.

The men shook hands, and presently Andrew, with a hand at the impostor's elbow, guided the man through the bookstore, and on out through the back offices.

Katherine, though wanting to follow them, was caught by the swiftly encircling crowd. She felt as if she were only going through the motions of attendance. She signed several books, forced smiles to her lips and numbly deflected the speculative questions, but she couldn't help but keep glancing at the back of the bookstore. When a couple of the people present tried directly asking her about the man, the man who had claimed to be Sam McDonald, the man who had kissed Katherine without a single protest on her part, Katherine only shook her head and smiled slightly.

To her relief, Andrew finally reentered the main room of the bookstore. He nodded, but his face was grim. Katherine closed her eyes for a moment, as much to school her thoughts as to quell the urge to abandon this book signing and go outside to discover what happened to the man who had claimed to be her husband.

Andrew pulled her aside several minutes later, during a lull in the book signing. "I think he's gone, dear," he said softly.

"What did he say?" she asked. "Where did he go?"

Andrew shook his head. "I don't know where he went, and believe me, I didn't ask. But as to what he said, he said he'd . . . just go on home and wait for you."

"What? You didn't tell him where we live?"

Andrew gave her a look filled with reproach. "I live there, too, dear. Do you really imagine I would give out our address to any handsome stranger?"

Katherine withheld her affirmative but couldn't hold back a raised eyebrow.

Andrew looked affronted, but grinned to show he wasn't. "Especially when he's obviously too terribly attracted to my female cousin?"

"What else did he say?" Katherine asked, ignoring the implications.

"He said he knew he shouldn't have come, but he couldn't resist it. And get this, Katie dear, I think you're right about this guy. I think he really does believe he's Sam McDonald. Could anything be more outrageous?" He grinned, the strain of the past hour erased as his ready, gamin humor rose to the surface.

"It couldn't be much more outrageous, no," Katherine agreed.

"Unless the real Sam walked in."

Katherine shot him a withering glance. He ducked as though her glance had sent a physical weapon in his direction. "I know, I know. My sense of humor is warped."

"And you think he's gone?" she asked, ignoring his wit.

Andrew shrugged. "My alleyway isn't all that enticing. The delicatessen behind me positively delights in noxious odors. I wonder if rotting garbage constitutes toxic waste? That would certainly put a kink in that—"

"Andrew!"

"Okay. No, dear, I don't imagine he'll stick around for long."

"What if he comes back?"

Andrew took on the head-of-the-class look of brilliance as he said, "I told him I thought it would be better for you if he didn't. That seemed to register with him. He said he wouldn't do anything that might cause you any trouble."

Katherine again felt that odd pang of guilt over this strange man.

"The really funny part was that he didn't know me from Adam. But when I told him who I was, he greeted me like a long-lost brother. He says he had a boating accident or something. It's apparently making him feel a little 'off-balance.' His very words." He glanced at the few people converging on the table again. "Show time, Katie."

"It was very weird, Andrew," Katherine said slowly. "He looked at me as if he really recognized me."

"Of course, dear. You're famous."

"No, I mean *really* recognized me. As if he *knew* me."

"Well, I know you, too, dear. *And* I know how you collect strays. Look at Max. Look at *me* for that matter."

Katherine shot him a warning glance. Andrew raised his hands in mock surrender. "Okay, I'll let you wallow in your myth that I'm the one helping you, but I know the truth, Katie." His hands dropped and his face grew serious. "But this is a crazy, not a stray. Don't even think about it." He took her arm and shook it slightly. "If he comes back, I'm calling the police."

Slowly, though she felt it was the last thing she agreed with, she nodded.

The rest of the book-signing event passed slowly. Katherine knew that her mind was really on the odd stranger and the even odder sensations of sympathy he stirred in her. She still seemed to feel the warm pressure of his lips against hers. And she had the bizarre and wistful impression that he had really looked at her as Sam McDonald might have done. . . had there been a Sam McDonald.

When Andrew finally escorted the last of her fans through his front door, Katherine experienced a deep sense of relief instead of her usual letdown. She couldn't seem to shake the encounter from her mind. Andrew cleaned up without speaking, as though sensing her preoccupation. A glance at his face told her he'd shrewdly guessed the reasons for it.

"Come on, Katie girl. It's time to go home."

"Okay," Katherine said dully, rising to her feet.

"I'll whip you up one of my famous omelettes and a manhattan the size of its name."

Katherine smiled, and felt it was a ghost of her usual broad grin. Andrew, as he usually did, remained in tune with her mood and kept up a light running patter as he ushered her through the stacks and the clutter of the back rooms. He pushed open the heavy rear door and Katherine inhaled the moist night air gratefully. She leaned against the brick wall of Andrew's store, almost smiling as a whiff of the deli's "toxic waste" met her nostrils. She felt her real mind, maybe her soul, was a thousand miles away while she waited with her eyes closed as Andrew locked the many dead bolts on the back door.

"The car's right over here," he said, touching her arm, then gesturing at the five-year-old Mercury gleaming in the faint glow of a distant street lamp. Together they crossed the night-darkened alley, Andrew escorting her around to the passenger's door. It was a step too close to the deli's bins and Katherine turned her head to get away from the terrible odor.

Her cousin inserted the key into the lock and the button flipped up with an audible click. At the same exact moment, Katherine heard a crunch from the shadows behind her, a scrape, like the sound of a shoe grinding gravel. She whirled to see what caused it, her heart pounding in sudden fear, adrenaline shooting through her veins.

A tall, shadowed figure stepped from the dark. His hand, made huge by the distorting light, reached for her. Instinctively she jerked back from that terrible hand, a small, high-pitched negation escaping her lips.

The hand closed around her upper arm.

"Katherine?" a deep voice asked, and her assailant stepped into the faint light in the alleyway.

Chapter 3

Even as she strained to get free of the danger, Katherine realized who he was. His curiously rich voice seemed to play upon her spine and his hot, hard grip triggered the memory of his deeper embrace. Dear Lord, what did he want from her? And what did he make her want from him?

She could see him no better than a few seconds earlier, had no greater clue what his intentions were, but at least she recognized him. And while she certainly had no assurance that his mind had cleared, she nonetheless stopped struggling for freedom. The warmth in the gaze was evident even in the dark, and his grip on her was a gentle question, nothing more.

"Hey! What do you think you're doing?" Andrew demanded. The fear he must have felt for her, the unexpected second encounter with their "crazy" of the evening, made his voice sound peevish instead of forceful.

"Katherine," the man said again, his voice raw and harsh with some unspoken emotion. He stepped forward slightly. The dim light etched his face, reflected from his startlingly blue eyes. He was too close, too tall, too frightening, and yet, perversely, Katherine felt no fear of him, nor fear of what he might do to her. Any fear she felt was all due to the strange affinity she felt toward this impostor.

Before Katherine could pull her arm free, she heard the squealing protest of a car's tires and the alley was suddenly flooded in the bright lights of an oncoming car. The stranger's head whipped sideways and his eyes narrowed in a pain-filled wince. But Katherine's overall impression was that he changed; he wasn't the same man he'd been seconds before.

He swore, a sharp, bitten-off phrase that was drowned out by the roar of the car. But Katherine could see that he recognized something, either the car or the reason for its presence. And the recognition held nothing of the warm knowledge he seemed to feel toward her. No, he didn't much care for whoever was behind the wheel of this car.

Headlights strafed the alley, pinning the three of them in grotesque silhouette against the deli's brick wall and the overflowing dumpster. Katherine had the odd feeling that the car was somehow preternatural, that the engine's scream was really that of a living thing, as it echoed in the narrow strip of alley.

"Hey!" Andrew cried again, this time at the oncoming vehicle, lifting his hand up and down, palm flat, in a futile slow-it-down gesture.

"Get in the car!" the stranger yelled, his voice as cold and hard as it had been warm and strangely hypnotic earlier. "Hurry! This isn't a joke!"

Katherine felt as though time stopped and she could see everything terribly clearly. Tiny details, all separate, yet inextricably intertwined, shot into her mind as if catapulted there. She saw Andrew's hand wagging up and down, saw his other hand dangling the keys from that ridiculous blue fuzzy ball he called a key chain. She saw the lighted interior of the car yawning before them, the door held open by Andrew's leg. She felt the sharp grip of the stranger's hand on her arm, and though the long fingers bit into her skin even through the material of her dress jacket, she knew a moment's gratitude that the big man stood so close to her.

His command to get into the car seemed to come in verbal slow motion, echoing hollowly, as voices did sometimes when she had a bad cold. *"H-u-r-r-y...!"* And equally slowly, equally distorted, the roar of the intruding car penetrated her ears. And for a long, spiraling moment it seemed she could almost feel the heat of the headlights.

Then insanely, irrationally, as if she were sitting behind her computer working through a shoot-'em-up scene, she heard the unmistakable sound of gunfire. While she instinctively ducked, her mind told her all this was crazy. That it was some kind of prank.

The grip on her arm became a painful wrench, and she forgot about the notion of a prank. Now she wondered if it could be a kidnapping. The next thing Katherine knew she and Andrew were being shoved, sardine-fashion, into the car. The impostor pushed at her without the slightest hint of the gentleness he'd employed during his kiss earlier that evening. Her notion that he seemed a different man returned. He swore at Andrew to get the lead out of his pants and *move it!* and roughly urged Katherine to do the same.

Katherine stumbled over Andrew, twisting painfully, cracking her shin on the door ledge of the Mercury, and she heard Andrew groan as her elbow pressed heavily into his chest. But these were forgotten as the stranger crawled over her, not caring where his knees landed, ignoring items that fell from his jacket pocket, not noticing what parts of her he intimately crushed in his progress. She whipped aside and rolled to the floor of the Mercury. As she pressed her body beneath the dash, scrunched between Andrew and the swearing stranger, she barked a protest. She drew a deep breath to vocalize this further, but she heard, as though from inside her head, the other car's tires screech, and winced as Andrew's car once again lit up as brightly as midday.

"Give me the damned keys!" their stranger—their kid-napper? their rescuer?—yelled, sliding awkwardly behind the wheel. He was so much taller than Andrew that his knees winged out on either side of the steering wheel, one pressing sharply into Katherine's cheek. And somehow this simple contact steadied her, as if by touching him, she also touched his mind. He was trying to save them.

"Give him the keys!" Katherine yelled at Andrew, her eyes on the stranger's face. He flicked her a glance she couldn't read—gratitude? amusement? acknowledgment?—and when Andrew still didn't move, the stranger swore viciously and reached out to jerk them from Andrew's nerveless fingers. He stared at the fuzzy blue ball for a second, his expression that of a man who had inadvertently stumbled into a madhouse. Katherine knew exactly how he felt.

Then he lifted his eyes from the handful of keys and leveled a hard glare at Andrew. "Which one is it?" he growled.

"Th-the silver one. The s-square silver one. Third in."

Their stranger didn't waste any time with thank-you's. He merely shoved the appropriate key into the ignition, pumping the gas pedal at the same time and with a swift turn of the key to the right, fired the engine.

"Stay down, darling," the stranger said, lightly touching her hair, then dropping his hand almost immediately. Katherine had no doubts what the gesture had been: a reassuring caress. It was the gesture, the offhand familiar gesture of a lover, of a *husband*. And it made her feel hot and cold at the same time.

"I've had enough of this," Andrew said, though his words were scarcely audible over the whine of his own car. The car leapt forward, almost stalling, then roaring into action.

Andrew yelped as his head made contact with the glove compartment. He struggled against Katherine, against the seat, against falling out the still-opened passenger door.

"Get *down!*" the man at the wheel snarled. "And for God's sake, shut that door."

Andrew's struggle to right himself had unintentionally served to do the trick for Katherine. It was she who reached across her cousin to grab hold of the swinging passenger door and pull it closed. She groaned at the sudden wrench of her shoulder.

Without a word the stranger reached out a hand and shoved Katherine back down to the floor, pressing her face tightly against his well-muscled leg, and stroking it once, a firm, strong massage that raised questions rather than served as the assurance he apparently intended.

As the car spun sickeningly at a sharp turn, one that presumably took them out of the alley, Katherine lurched against her cousin. His wide eyes met hers. Despite the discomfort, despite the fear of the past few minutes, Andrew's dry wit surfaced. "Don't worry, Katie. I've got insurance."

An almost hysterical chuckle caught in Katherine's throat. She searched her cousin's face for any sign that this was all some sort of elaborate practical joke. It had all the makings: both of them huddled on the floor of Andrew's car while a man claiming to be her husband was careening down Virginia Beach streets after having rescued them from a mysterious car loaded with an unknown number of bad guys shooting at them.

But the gunfire had been real enough. She'd heard it striking the Mercury, had felt the car rock with the impacts. And before she had jerked the door closed, she'd seen the bullets blistering the brick wall that had shadowed the stranger just before the nightmare began.

Katherine felt an odd dislocation of time and events, which seemed endless in its terror, infinite in its sheer irra-

tionality. And yet she knew it had only been seconds in du-
ration, only minutes since she and Andrew had
unsuspectingly left the bookstore.

What would have happened if the man hadn't been there?
They would have been killed, she thought, and was almost
surprised to discover that the thought didn't terrify her. She
felt almost beyond fear now. The situation was completely
out of her hands. Their fate lay in the hands of the stranger
uncomfortably straddling Andrew's steering wheel.

Katherine raised her head slightly, and this time the tough
man behind the wheel didn't react, didn't shove her face
back to his thigh. The ghostly green glow of the dashboard
lights illumined the rough planes of his unshaved face, giving him a severe, almost tortured look, a look in no way di-
minished by the occasional flicker of yellow light from street
lamps. His jaw was clenched tight and his eyes were narrowed, his mind obviously focused on the car from the alley,
eyes flicking from the road before him to the rearview mirror.

"Who are you?" Katherine croaked, her throat parched
and her tongue made thick with fear.

His lips jerked left in quick amusement. The expression
on his face lightened dramatically and his eyes dropped to
hers in tender humor. "Been gone so long you've forgotten
my name, Katherine?"

Slowly Katherine shook her head, an odd, skipping beat
taking over the already heightened rhythm of her heart.
He'd called her "Katherine," but he might as well have
called her "love," for that's what his tone implied. She
looked up at him, half expecting to meet that burning gaze,
but he'd already trained his eyes back on the road and the
rearview mirror.

"You always did have the damnedest sense of humor," he
muttered, the smile still thinning his lips.

Clutching the seat of the car against its furious sway,
Katherine turned slowly to look at Andrew. He frowned

heavily, obviously sending her some mental message, but she wasn't getting it. He gazed at her pointedly for several seconds before slowly lowering his eyes to the vinyl seat. Following, Katherine saw a battered, water-crinkled paperback and a slim leather pouch no longer than a cigarette pack but only as thick as a folded handkerchief. She glanced back up at Andrew and almost smiled when he nodded very slowly, eyes eloquent with speculation.

The stranger paid no attention as Andrew reached a trembling hand for the small leather folder, though Katherine almost screamed when the man's leg pressed between her shoulder blades as he shifted from gas pedal to brake for a turn, then once again crushed the gas pedal to the floor.

Andrew flipped the folder open, and, after angling it for the best light from the street lamps whizzing by, nudged Katherine with his elbow. But Katherine had already seen. All that was in the folder was an official-looking badge tucked inside a thin sheath of protective plastic. Across the brass badge, the words U.S. Department of Treasury had been etched in black.

She met her cousin's eyes and shrugged even as he frowned.

A muttered curse from the stranger demanded their attention. He swerved the car sharply to the left, sending Andrew tumbling into Katherine and Katherine back against the stranger. Another swerve flung her back toward Andrew.

Adrenaline once again surged through Katherine. After a close look at their driver's face, she realized he wasn't swerving the car to escape the assailants. He had simply, and quite terrifyingly, lost control of the Mercury.

"Are you okay?" Katherine asked, but as dry as her throat felt, she was sure he hadn't heard the scarcely voiced question.

"I think I lost him," the stranger said, his voice harsh and low.

At the relieved note in his voice, the night's events seemed thrown into sharp contrast. While there was still a rough tone to his low-pitched voice, it carried the same note of bemusement as earlier in the bookstore when he'd spoken her name, when he'd drawn her into his arms.

Danger was here in the car, certainly, but to Katherine, it seemed all the danger emanated from and around the man above her, the man who had pushed her and Andrew to safety while he remained a target behind the wheel. She looked up at him, feeling ridiculous crouched at his feet, and bemused by the strange sensation of being safe amid chaos. Then she looked closer.

The stranger's face was strained, his eyelids heavy, a frown wrinkling his broad brow. And though the street was dark now, street lamps less frequent, the light from the few they passed seemed to bother him. He raised an unsteady hand from the steering wheel and rubbed at his forehead, wincing when his fingers probed too near the handkerchief bandage.

"Who?" Andrew asked.

"What?" the stranger asked back, not glancing at Andrew.

"You said you thought you'd lost him. Who are you talking about?"

The stranger shook his head, and to Katherine the gesture seemed more a sign of weariness than of negation.

"Are you driving us to the police?" Andrew continued.

"Of course not!" the man barked. He drew a deep breath and said in a much more reasonable tone, though it was an obvious effort, "You don't understand what's involved here."

Katherine turned to meet Andrew's half-affronted gaze. She held up a finger to keep him silent. She drew a deep, steadying breath. "No, we...don't...understand what's involved here. You're right." She felt Andrew nudge her beneath her shoulder blades. "But we'd like to. We'd like to know what's going on."

After a long pause, the stranger sighed. "Pete has a long arm," he said so quietly that Katherine almost didn't hear the words.

When he didn't elaborate, Katherine asked softly, "Pete? Pete who?"

But the stranger didn't answer.

"Who's Pete?" Andrew asked, stepping his voice up a notch.

The stranger turned then, shooting Andrew a dark look. "Just be glad you're not involved in this."

"Involved?" Andrew squeaked. "I'm sitting on the floor of my own damned car while a perfect stranger takes us on a high-speed chase and somebody I don't even know is shooting at us."

"Was," the stranger said.

"What?"

"Was shooting. I lost him about three turns ago."

"Oh, that makes it so much better. Excuse me." Andrew's voice was sharp with sarcasm.

The stranger's lips quirked again, but he said evenly, "Look, if I told you what was coming down here, and he somehow got hold of you, you wouldn't stand a prayer, and I can guarantee you that he knows every trick in the book that would make you talk. You would tell him everything you ever knew."

Katherine felt as if someone had slammed a huge fist in her stomach.

"What...what did you just say?" she asked. She held her breath waiting for his answer. Behind her she felt Andrew doing the same, and his arm against hers was rigid with shock.

"I'm only saying it's better this way," the man answered.

Slowly, Katherine released her pent-up breath. It had to be a coincidence. A crazy coincidence. He couldn't possibly have just quoted—exactly quoted—a paragraph from one of her books. His answer hadn't followed the lines her main character had said in, which one was it? *Daylight's Shadow? The Edge of Madness?* but the fact that he'd said it at all lent weight to the notion of an elaborate joke.

She cleared her throat. "That sounded right out of a novel," she said leadingly.

The stranger glanced her way, amusement again dancing in those amazing eyes. "Life imitates fiction," he quipped and again dropped his hand to her head in that caress she was already beginning to find familiar. This time, however, the hand didn't rise, and Katherine instinctively turned toward his palm, like a cat seeking stroking.

"This is ridiculous," Andrew sputtered. "We don't even know you."

The hand lifted and Katherine had to press her lips together to contain the involuntary protest. The stranger was eyeing Andrew with that same amusement he'd displayed earlier. "'Et tu, Brute?'" he said and quickly jerked his eyes back to the road as he lost control of the car again. "Damn."

Against Katherine turned to meet Andrew's shocked gaze. She was feeling a little shocked herself. The situation was getting more and more bizarre. The fact that the man had been in Andrew's bookstore could explain his knowledge of the store, but he seemed to know much more than that; his amused quip implied he knew about Andrew. Did he, or was his mind so confused that things he said made a certain macabre sense? Who was this man? What did he want from them? And who was in that other car?

The car wove to the left and the stranger corrected it too abruptly, causing it to swing too far to the right.

"Are you all right?" Katherine asked again, louder this time, more certain that he wasn't well. Somehow the notion that he might be ill sat easier with Katherine than the idea that he was crazy. If he were ill, might he then get better and . . . ? And what? That was the question. If he were well, he wouldn't think she was his wife and lover. The thoughts accompanying this realization sent color sweeping into her cheeks.

A brief smile flitted across the stranger's face and he looked down with a tender expression. His face was so filled with easy, gentle recognition that Katherine found herself smiling back. Even as his eyes went back to the road, he lowered a hand from the steering wheel and again rested it on Katherine's hair. The gesture, already familiar, carried a new quality this time, and she froze, her heart beating unaccountably painfully as the large hand shifted to deftly release the catch on her hair clasp. He fluffed her hair almost absently, gently sifting strands of hair as if memorizing the texture. The touch was a lover's touch, and was performed casually, as though he'd done this a thousand times before.

"I'll be fine," he said.

Katherine fought a shiver as the gentle hand continued to play with her hair, dipping to the nape of her neck, to lightly caress the sensitive skin beneath her earlobes, her jawline. The shiver could have come from the peculiar course of terrifying events or from the warmth emanating from his palm, the tenderness of his touch. But she knew its source: his touch.

Andrew nudged her and whispered *hospital* in her ear.

"Are you sure you don't need to go to a hospital?" she asked the man who had answered to her false husband's name.

The hand against her hair stilled abruptly, then lifted. Katherine bit her lip to prevent an instinctive objection at the loss of his touch.

"I'm sure," he said curtly. "No hospitals. That's the first place he'll look."

"Who?" Katherine asked incautiously.

But the stranger only shook his head. The action made him wince. He closed one eye as if his vision was blurring.

"That's it," Katherine said, meaning her words in every sense possible. She'd had enough of chases through dark streets, being shot at, not knowing what was going on, and above all, watching the pallor steal across the rigidly set face.

She pulled herself stiffly onto the seat and turned to face the windshield. What she saw there made her own color drop: the window had been hit at least twice, a spiderweb of cracks filling the space where the road should be. No wonder their rescuer had difficulty keeping the car to one lane.

His hand shot out to grip her arm in an apparent protest, but when she didn't move or speak, the hand relaxed and dropped from her arm to lie casually on her thigh. Katherine swallowed heavily as the stranger looked in the rearview mirror another time, then slumped against her, his unfocused eyes on the road in front of them. He seemed unaware that his fingers were digging into the soft flesh of her leg.

Closer now, Katherine saw that his lips were almost white with suppressed pain and that his face was too pale and, where there was no dark beard, was filmed with a shiny layer of sweat. Fever, she thought. He's running a fever. What sort of wound did the makeshift bandage cover? How long ago had it happened? Long enough for fever to set in.

The car veered into the left lane again. And this time it had nothing to do with the cracks in the windshield. He corrected it at her gasp.

"Pull over," Katherine commanded firmly. When he ignored her, she raised a hand that only trembled slightly now and laid it upon his arm. "Please. Pull over. Let Andrew drive now. You've lost them."

He glanced at her long enough that the car started to swerve again. This seemed the winning argument that her

hand on his arm had begun and he pulled to the right curb
and put the car in park.

"God, I've got a headache," he murmured, but he didn't
move from behind the wheel. He rubbed his eyes with his
free hand while the other massaged her leg. His mouth
screwed to a grimace of pain.

Katherine didn't take her eyes from him, nor her hand
from his arm, but knew that behind her Andrew had opened
the passenger door and was all but silently exiting the car.

The stranger lifted his head and stared through the
cracked glass at the night-darkened street in the two narrow strips of light from the Mercury's headlights. Andrew
materialized at his left shoulder, startling Katherine slightly,
but the man didn't see him, didn't so much as look that way.

"Where are we?" the stranger asked, frowning heavily.

Katherine looked out the passenger window. "Somewhere near Cape Henry, I'd guess," she said, referring to the
large, historic base at the Bay's point. "But it's dark and
we've driven so fast that I—ouch!"

His hand upon her leg gripped so tightly that she was unable to restrain the involuntary cry.

"Sorry," he said absently, immediately relaxing the pressure and patting her leg in apology. The very casualness of
it, the very familiarity drove a chill down her back even as
her leg seemed to burn with the contact.

"What…?" she began, but trailed off as she turned back
to him. His hand on the steering wheel was white-knuckled,
so fierce was his grip.

"I'm lost," he said bleakly, his voice filled with self-
condemnation, and something else, something that sounded
a great deal like a plea for help. *Help me, Katherine,* he'd
said in the bookstore. Had he been lost then, too? Did he
mean lost in a larger sense of the word?

Katherine could see Andrew pointing at the door and
nodded absently. "If it's any consolation, so am I," she
said. She glanced at Andrew's hand again. "But Andrew

won't be. He's never lost. He could find his way out of a coal mine at midnight.''

The man beside her didn't smile. If anything he frowned even more. ''Katherine...?''

''Yes?'' she asked warily.

When he spoke again, his voice sounded far away, distant. Lost. ''I can't remember how to get home.''

Katherine's heart wrenched at the simple phrase. Part of the pang she felt was because his words were so at odds with his looks; the words were forlorn, confused, even lonely, while his looks were hard, tough, utterly capable. But for the most part the words struck some chord deep inside her with such uncanny precision that she felt her entire body vibrate in reaction. *I can't remember how to get home.*

She opened her mouth to answer, then closed it again, thinking, do any of us remember how to get home? Is it something we lose at birth, the knowledge of how to return? Unable to resist the desire to share her empathy with him, she dropped her hand to the large one on her leg. She wrapped cold fingers around his warm hand and applied soothing pressure.

He turned to face her then, an odd expression on his face. It was partly comprised of bewilderment, partly recognition, and this odd look he'd worn in the bookstore, that of sheer wondrous joy. His hand on her lap turned and gripped hers fiercely, while he lifted the other from the steering wheel to lightly cup her face.

''You're so beautiful,'' he said slowly. ''Thank God you're with me, Katherine. I couldn't make it without you.''

Katherine's heart jolted at the touch of his hand, then began to beat in a heavy, irregular rhythm as his words reached deep inside her. He seemed to make all the sense in the world, more sense than anyone had ever made before, yet his words might as well have been uttered in Latin for all the actual logic they held. As she had in the bookstore,

Katherine experienced a tinge of regret that what he said wasn't—couldn't be—real.

She gently patted the hand on her cheek, then drew it from her face and lifted both of his rough hands to her chin, shaking them a little, wondering what to say or do next. What could she say to his statement? I wish it were true?

She shook her head somewhat sadly, wondering what was wrong with this man. Who was chasing him—them? How did he know her and why had he answered to her fictitious husband's name? This was more than a pose; he was still staring at her as if she were the sun and moon all wrapped up in a gold-ribboned package.

And she couldn't help but smile at the sheer simplicity of his bemusement. And at her reaction to it.

Andrew rapped on the window then, making her jump, making the man tenderly holding her hands whirl suddenly, his face transforming into a cross between hunted and hunter, switching from fear to anger in less time than a single beat of her heart.

"Unlock the door and scoot over," Andrew called through the window. He pointed at the depressed lock.

For a long moment the man stared at Andrew as though he'd never seen him before. Then he slowly nodded, and twisted with a grimace to pull up on the lock. Andrew opened the door swiftly, and after an awkward pause, as if reluctant to proceed, he gestured for Katherine and the man to move over.

After she'd shifted to the far right side of the front seat, and, with a slight smile at the irony, fastened her seat belt, Andrew asked in a carefully blank voice where they should go.

"What?" Katherine asked at the same time the stranger answered, "Home."

Katherine ignored the impostor and closed her eyes in brief escape. Where should they go? It was a logical question. And a telling one. He'd said no police, and he'd argued against a hospital. Where should they take this man who had obviously rescued them from a dangerous situation? And what should they do about a man whose act of bravery only marginally overrode the strong possibility that he was the actual cause of the danger?

His warm hand covered hers and drew it into his lap, a gesture too easy and intimate for Katherine's peace of mind. If she closed her eyes and shut her mind to the insanity of the evening, she almost could convince herself he really was her lover, that she really could have a husband who would be so affectionate, so nonchalantly tender. But when she opened her eyes she saw a total stranger with a bandage on his head and eyes that looked as lost as a runaway puppy.

She felt the color rise in her cheeks, held her hand perfectly still, all too aware of the need in him, the heat radiating from him, the answering spark in her. When his hand tightened around hers she had the feeling that he was clinging to her like a drowning man clings to a life raft.

"Katherine," he said raggedly. "I'm so tired. Can't we go home?"

"Katie..." Andrew said warningly.

"Home," Katherine decided finally and was rewarded by a firm squeeze of her hand.

"I don't think this is such a hot idea," Andrew said.

"Take us home, Andrew," she replied, quietly.

"God, yes," said the stranger holding her hand, "take us home. Oh, please...get me home, darling."

Chapter 4

"Strays," Andrew muttered caustically, but he put the car in gear and maneuvered it to the left for a U-turn.

Katherine didn't answer; her throat was constricted by the pressure on her hand resting so snugly at the apex of the stranger's thighs. There was nothing *stray* about her feelings at this moment. But there wasn't anything particularly comfortable about them either.

Despite the shattered windshield, Andrew deftly wended the ill-used Mercury through the main streets of downtown Virginia Beach, gaudy neon lights flashing over doorways that spewed out loud music but little else; the summer crowd had flown back to colleges, jobs and marriages.

Beside her the stranger spoke suddenly, his graveled voice making her start, but his words were an odd extension of her thoughts. "The pretty girls slip away like the season."

Katherine finished his thought—hers—for him. "And now, like it happens every year, it seems all you see are streets filled with uniformed men who transform, almost like magic, into boys."

The stranger sighed. "And there they are, all those boys, standing in brightly lit phone booths calling home for the first time in months." His voice was etched with sorrow, as if he'd seen this before or had experienced it himself.

Katherine forced her eyes to the window again. On a few corners, small groups gathered, but their faces looked too tanned, too robust for these waning days of autumn, and even a newcomer to town knew these were the stipended beach lovers, those with just enough money to roam from summer to summer, never waiting for the bite of winter.

Slewing her eyes to the left, Katherine saw "Sam" frowning at the street scenes. His tongue slowly moistened his full lips and withdrew. He swallowed, his eyes lingering on an ambulance parked outside the theater, at a couple laughing, getting into their car. And, at a sudden break in the city lights, a dark expanse that promised water, that hinted at the ocean lapping just beyond, he turned his head to maintain the contact, something both yearning and fearful in his eyes.

Katherine pulled back slightly, and his eyes met hers and suddenly focused. "Witch Duck Point," he said and smiled, squeezing her hand.

This Sam seemed to have just remembered something, but what he'd remembered was where Katherine lived. And he had no business remembering that.

While it was no secret she lived at the place where the Puritan sanctimonious had ducked witches beneath the inlet waters—those who lived were burned as witches, those who didn't were buried in consecrated ground—his knowledge unnerved her nonetheless.

But instead of pulling away from him, hoping he might reveal some clue as to the strange events of the night, Katherine leaned against him slightly, as if she really were the wife he apparently thought her to be. She was catching more flies with honey, she told herself, but a little voice deep within her seemed to sigh in contentment; this is where I'm supposed to be, the voice murmured.

"That's right. What about it?" Katherine asked, her voice soft, unthreatening.

"That's where you live," he said. He frowned and his hand tightened around hers painfully, then relaxed. "Where *we* live," he corrected. He leaned back against the seat, resting his head, closing his eyes.

Katherine glanced across at Andrew's stern profile. As if aware of her regard, he flicked her a look that spoke volumes of his censure of her decision to take the man home. If he knew one quarter of what was going on inside her, he wouldn't confine his worry to mere looks.

"Well, do you have a better idea?" she asked softly.

Before Andrew could reply, "Sam" answered, "I think I must have hit my head on the boat. It hurts like hell."

"What boat?" Andrew asked.

"I lost my wallet in the water."

"Did you fall in?" Katherine asked gently.

"Sam" frowned and shook his head. "No. Yes. I don't know. I can't seem to think clearly."

"Here's a switch," Andrew murmured. He waved a hand at Katherine's quick shake of her head.

The man closed his eyes and Katherine leaned forward to study him again.

"I think he has a concussion," she whispered to Andrew.

"That's a kind way of phrasing it, dear."

"Oh, Andrew."

He chuckled, but heaved a long sigh. "For once, Katie, I'm inclined to agree with you. The question is, what are we going to do with him?"

"Take him home, let him rest. Call Jason."

"Ah-h-h, signs of sanity at last. And you'll do whatever Jason thinks best?"

"Of course," Katherine said, turning her eyes back to the road.

"Katie..."

"I said, of course."

"That's what you say when you're on deadline and I tell you to stop for a bite to eat. And you don't."

"I promise," she said with a wry smile.

"Tell me something," Andrew began, but before he could finish, their passenger broke in.

"Thousands, maybe millions, of stars lit the night sky, until their pulsating glow seemed a living presence."

Andrew glanced at his passenger, his eyebrows raised, his mouth half-opened. The man between them continued to speak, muttering as though to himself, oblivious to the sudden swerve of the car or the stiffening chill that washed through Katherine.

"When we wish upon a star, are the wishes out there somewhere in amongst those millions of pinprick lights? And if they are, and we could see them, would we even recognize our own dreams?"

Andrew started to say something, but without looking his way, Katherine held up her free hand. "Wait," she said, leaning forward, closing her eyes, as if by not seeing the impostor, she could understand his words.

"Katie—"

The stranger continued. "Are our dreams like the stars themselves? One day we recognize one, perhaps even a whole constellation, and another we discover a different one. Are our own dreams like that, too?"

"Katie...?"

Katherine looked up to meet Andrew's eyes. He nodded before turning his eyes back to the road. "He's quoting *you*, dear. *The Edge of Madness*, I think."

Katherine leaned back, her heart pounding uncomfortably. Andrew was right, she had been right before; "Sam" was quoting her work. She remembered the battered copy of a paperback book that had lain upon the seat of the car. She felt around behind her and pulled it free. Even in the garish glow from the dashboard, and despite its waterlogged condition, she recognized the cover: *The Edge of Madness*.

Without the aid of hypnosis, even she probably couldn't have quoted her book as accurately as this man had done. What kind of special madness did he possess that he could quote her own books to her, that he called himself by her fictitious husband's name, that he held her hand so tightly, believing that he was her loving husband?

And what kind of magic did he weave that made her feel as though she would be committing a crime to hand him over to some sort of authority? But, worst of all, what kind of magic, what kind of madness, did he weave that made her return that pressure between hands, palm to palm, fingertip to broad plane of flesh and bone?

The badge, she told herself, firmly, stilling her response; the magic was simply a badge. He *was* some sort of authority himself. It had to be his; its case was as waterlogged as the book, as the man's clothing. And the rest of the magic came from this stranger ignoring his pain, his wound, and his evident disorientation, in order to rescue them. He might be confused and probably was that trouble with a capital T she'd thought him at first glance, but he was also an agent of some kind and in real danger. The very least she could do was see that he got some medical attention and a good night's rest. Wasn't it?

He continued to mouth random quotes from her books, sometimes the more obscure references, others direct action scenes, and while his words—her words—added to her general sense of unreality about the night, she didn't really listen to the recitation. She didn't have to, she knew them. She *wrote* them.

Almost gratefully Katherine turned to thoughts of calling Dr. Jason Woodard, her psychiatrist friend and neighbor. He might disapprove of her fictitious husband, calling it "a perfect excuse to hide yourself from men," but he'd never once chided her about her drive to collect strays. Would he feel the same insouciance about an unknown Treasury department agent who called himself Sam Mc-Donald?

"It's all your fault, Katherine," the unknown Sam McDonald said clearly, as Andrew steered his battered car down the winding drive leading to Katherine's home and his guest house at the very tip of Witch Duck Point.

"This ought to be good," Andrew said, sotto voce.

"If I hadn't wanted to see you so badly..." their passenger slurred, then stopped.

Katherine shivered. She couldn't have said whether the goose bumps on her arms spoke well or ill.

Andrew drew up in front of the entry to Katherine's house, cut the motor and doused the headlights. The darkness and silence were complete. Mist rolled across the lawn adding to the sense of quiet, and in some vague way, Katherine thought, creating an illusion of safety, as if nature itself were folding a protective cloak around her home, a wall of fog around them.

"We're here," Andrew said unnecessarily. He threw open the door and walked, somewhat stiffly, around to her side of the car. He opened the door and held out a hand to her. "Let's get your hero inside, dear. He looks as though he's freezing to death."

Katherine saw her cousin was right. While the man's hand was warm and a heat emanated from his body, he was shivering.

"Fever," she whispered. "Maybe shock."

"Probably. So let's get him inside."

Katherine looked up gratefully at her cousin. Half of the reason she never missed companionship was Andrew's doing. He cooked for her most of the time, told outrageous stories with dry wit and supported her unfailingly on any writing project she undertook, up to and including the fabrication of one husband. It seemed he was involved in almost everything she did, and though he usually punctuated every action with some caustic remark, he steadfastly adhered to her side.

"I know this is crazy," Katherine said, wrapping an arm around the stranger while Andrew did the same on the other side of the man.

"As long as you know you're doing something nuts, that makes it all right," her cousin said, straining to take most of the stranger's weight. "That's always been *my* motto, dear."

"Sam" chuckled between them. The laugh was infectious enough to draw a smile from Katherine, and Andrew gave him a speculative glance. "He's crazy, but he has the wit to appreciate great humor."

"That only proves he's running a fever," Katherine said, her breath expelling in puffs of white at the exertion and the cold.

Between Andrew and her, they managed to shepherd the man to the front door. Andrew supported him while Katherine fumbled with the door keys. Just as Katherine managed to push the door open, and turn to signal Andrew to lead him forward, "Sam" raised his head and met Andrew's gaze squarely.

"Thanks, pal."

"Anytime," Andrew said, but Katherine could see his barely suppressed humor.

"No, I mean it. I don't say these kinds of things very often, but you're really a great guy. I should have told you before. Years ago."

Andrew's mouth opened, then closed again. His eyes met Katherine's a little wildly. She clicked on the hall lights and reached for her side of the stranger.

"Well, you really know how to take the wind out of somebody's sails, don't you, big guy?" Andrew muttered.

"Sam" didn't answer.

Feeling the weight of a heavy arm across her shoulders, her arm around a narrow, muscled waist, Katherine couldn't have agreed with Andrew more. This man took more than the wind from her sails. Much more.

As she and Andrew deposited the man on the sofa in the living room, she knew that the feelings he inspired in her had something to do with the recognition she saw in his eyes; the odd something that made her feel as if he really did recognize her, knew her perhaps better than anyone else did.

"You changed the furniture," he said now, looking about him through squinted eyes. He looked at the rustic, American primitive pieces as though they were objects from another planet. He frowned heavily when his gaze lighted on a half-read novel by a leading thriller competitor and friend.

"I—yes," Katherine stammered, lying about the furniture, deciding the truth was one thing she didn't feel like arguing about at the moment.

"Where are you in that book?" the impostor asked easily. "It was pretty good. Almost as good as ours."

"I'm calling Jason now," Andrew said, and to Katherine's ears, his words carried a warning. She nodded, then sighed and sat down beside the unknown Treasury agent, draping a rich-colored, hand-crocheted afghan over his shoulders and drawing it loosely around his neck. She wanted to push back the handkerchief on his head, but was afraid of hurting him ... and of what she might find.

He closed his eyes and leaned his head back against the loose cushions of her square sofa. "I'm so tired," he murmured.

"Oh, no. You can't fall asleep now," Katherine said, taking his hand swiftly and patting it. "I think you have a concussion. You shouldn't go to sleep."

"Please, lady ... I'm so very tired."

Before she could stop him, he slumped left on the sofa, curling easily into the embroidered pillows Andrew had brought her from Mazatlan.

Katherine sat staring at him for a few seconds until the full impact of his words hit her. He hadn't called her Katherine that time, nor even one of his abbreviated endearments. He'd called her "lady" as if he'd never seen her before. Perhaps whatever had happened to him was wearing off. And perhaps in this lucid moment, she could find out who and what he was, who had chased and shot at them that night, and what they should do now.

Even as she reviewed possible questions to ask him, she was all too conscious of a stab of regret; there had been something about his absurd delusion that hadn't seemed so absurd at all.

"What's your name?" she asked softly.

He frowned and opened his eyes a crack. "Cut it out, Katherine. The joke's stale."

"Please tell me," she asked, and when he only scowled at her, she persisted with logic. "Look. First, you've been hurt. Second, you yourself admitted to being lost, then you couldn't remember where...home...was. So tell me, what is your name?"

"Okay, okay. I'll play, Doctor," he slurred. "I'm Sam McDonald. And you're Katherine. And we've been married ten years and I've loved you every single day of that time. Satisfied?"

No, she wasn't satisfied. She was stupefied. It was almost as if he had created her fictitious husband himself. That or somehow or another she and Andrew had actually made a fictional character come to life. She shook her head ruefully; whatever this man with his strange delusions had seemed contagious.

A noise at the far door, the door leading to her study, made the stranger tense, but Katherine knew it was only Max. Andrew must have used the phone in the study and now Max wanted in to Katherine. She rose from the sofa and opened the door, wincing at its persistent creak.

"I'll oil that door one of these days. I promise," Sam muttered.

Katherine felt a little dizzy at the casual note, the husbandly type comment. But she pulled the door open the rest of the way only shaking her head. As usual Max bounded into the room with typical Irish setter enthusiasm, polite enough—and well-trained enough—not to jump up on her or anything else, but excited enough that his huge, feathered tail dusted two end tables and a floor lamp.

To Katherine's amazement, Max only wasted a few seconds' greeting on her, passing her up for the stranger on the sofa. After the briefest of bristling assessment, Max plunked down beside the sofa and whined at the man lying there. When he didn't receive the response he wanted, he nudged the stranger's cheek with a cold nose.

Sam opened his eyes and met the curious, worried brown eyes of an Irish setter. Katherine's dog, he thought, and was vaguely pleased he knew this, and vaguely disturbed that he was pleased by it. Why did he feel so out of touch? If only his head didn't hurt so. If only Katherine would let him sleep. If only he could remember the dog's name. If it was Katherine's dog, it was his dog too. Lord, he even knew the brand of dog food they fed him. And as he thought this, the dog's name came to mind.

He felt a smile curve his lips and reached a hand for the soft fur beneath the dog's ears.

He concentrated on petting the dog, calling him by name, grasping at mental straws, doing all of this to avoid meeting Katherine's eyes. He didn't want to scare her, didn't want her to worry. Something was very wrong, and Katherine knew it; he'd seen the wariness in her eyes, heard the reticence in her voice. If he admitted how little he really remembered . . . and yet, he remembered all that was really important—he loved her, she loved him.

But where was the rest of his life? Where had he been that it seemed he'd been away from her for years? He hadn't recognized Andrew, hadn't recognized anything about Virginia Beach . . . except the water. And that he remembered with a shiver of fear and disgust. Why?

And why did Katherine seem so aloof, so scared of him?

He was here now, with Katherine, and that was all that mattered. He remembered her.

He told himself the rest would come with time. He closed his eyes, still stroking Max's silky head, wondering why his heart was beating faster, wondering why he had the disturbing feeling that time was something he didn't have. Dimly, in the recesses of his mind, he heard a voice telling him that Sam McDonald's life wasn't worth a plugged nickel.

Katherine watched as the stranger caressed Max's ears, relief and recognition commingled in his gaze, in his fingers. He'd looked at the dog blankly at first, she was sure of that, then, as he'd done with her, as he'd done with his sudden awareness of Witch Duck Point, the light had dawned in the man's blue eyes.

"Max!" he breathed. "Oh, Max!" His long hand raised and drew the sleek red head close. "How are you, boy? Miss me?"

For a terrible second, Katherine thought she might faint. He knew Max. And amazingly, Max's tail was wagging. Max, who hated or feared most men, was happily basking in the stranger's attention.

What kind of dream was all this? Was she asleep and didn't know it? Surreptitiously she dug her nails into her palms. She felt the sharp bite. She was awake and she had to think. But watching the impostor stroking Max with every evidence of longstanding friendship, she couldn't seem to put her mind in order.

Katherine had found Max about two years ago, badly injured, and, the vet had said, judging by the condition of the paws, near starvation. The vet had done what she could, and Katherine had done the rest. The result was undying loyalty and a true friend. But other than Andrew, Max completely eschewed male company, except to leap and bark ferociously until the intruder went away.

Katherine had always assumed that a man had abused Max, but with this Sam, the big dog seemed right at home, even happy to see him. Was it because the man was so obviously happy to see the dog? Max yawned easily and stretched out on the floor beside the sofa, large head on large paws, for all the world as if he were protecting the nearly unconscious man on the sofa. Or as if he were waiting for him to awaken.

Like the dog, the man closed his eyes and sighed deeply. No matter what mysteries he represented, no matter how much he confused her, she still believed she owed him her life, and she wasn't going to let him slip into a concussed sleep. Didn't people die that way?

"Hello?" she asked, the false name unable to come to her lips. How could she possible call him by her fictitious husband's name? It would be like announcing her acceptance of his would-be role. But she couldn't let him drift to his uneasy slumber. She moved swiftly to the sofa, despite her legs feeling as shaky as a newborn colt's and her mind seething with conjecture. She edged Max aside and leaned over the sofa. Her heart constricted as she reached out a hand to lightly shake his shoulder and his blue eyes opened to gaze at her with dramatic focus. He mumbled something and she bent closer to listen.

He turned slightly, rolling onto his back. His hands lifted and slid up her forearms. Instead of making her start or pull back, his touch on her arms seemed to immobilize her, freeze her in place. The light touch on her arms shifted, becoming a compelling grip.

"I love you," he said, drawing her down.

"No," Katherine murmured, as much to herself as to put the truth to his falsehood.

"Oh, yes I do, Katherine. And you know it."

His fingers snaked up the sensitive flesh, drawing her downward, exhorting her response. Unresisting, strangely unable to withstand the certainty in his eyes, his touch, his words, she allowed herself to be drawn against his chest. The heat rising from him met her at the same time his full lips pressed up to meet hers. He groaned softly and his hands released their hold on her arms only to slide around her back and pull her tighter to him.

Dizzied, her body caught up in pure sensation, Katherine desperately sought for rational thought, but as with her ragged breathing, she seemed to have no control over her mind. He smelled of salt water and fever, his hands against her back were as hot as his tongue meeting hers. He tasted of dreams and fears and his kiss was both gentle and fierce, hinting at mysteries as intensely different as the man himself.

Her heart pounded against his, and the strong, irregular rhythm became matched. Her body felt liquid, molten, melted by the fire in his touch, his scarcely banked passion. Another groan on his part sparked an echoing moan from the deepest recesses of her throat, an almost animalistic cry of surrender.

A sound behind her, a sharp gasp followed by a loud, false cough, acted on her like a fall into an icy lake. She pushed back almost frantically, trying to gather the shattered pieces of her self-possession. She clutched the front of her blouse as though it had been unbuttoned, as if the heat in her could be held in check by such a ruse. She raised an unsteady hand to sweep her long hair from her face.

The man she decided to call Sam let her go without argument, his eyelids held at lazy slits, a soft smile playing on his lips, his chest still rising and falling with the force of his desire. His eyes were a darker shade of blue than before, deeper, almost violet.

"Well, he certainly won't fall asleep that way," Andrew said dryly. "Good job, Katie."

Katherine shook her head, feeling as dazed as her would-be husband looked, knowing no explanation existed for giving in to a kiss with a total stranger, a stranger who was obviously suffering some sort of mental aberration. To her relief, her cousin smiled somewhat crookedly and shot her a look of sympathy. Of anyone, she thought, Andrew would understand the complexities of human frailties.

"Jason's on his way," he said now, turning with only a sideways glance in the direction of the sofa, and heading for the bar. "He prefers Benedictine, doesn't he?"

"Yes," she answered absently.

"I'll have scotch," Sam said from the sofa, and, before Katherine could answer, Andrew stepped in glibly, saying, "None for you, hero. Head wounds and alcohol don't mix. Take it from me. I know."

Sam started to protest, but Max's quick leap to his feet and bound toward the front door, baying furiously, drowned anything he might have said.

"Quick, Katie, go stop your redheaded dragon. I don't think he likes the good doctor."

"Except for you—and—" she shot a glance at the recumbent Sam, again unable to name him, "—Max doesn't like many people."

"Now, I wonder what gave you that idea, dear?" Andrew questioned, with a hint of a smile.

"Doctor?" Sam sputtered, pushing to his elbow. "You called somebody?" His words were an accusation. Avoiding his suddenly glaring eyes, Katherine didn't wait to hear more; she escaped into the hall to halt Max's attack on the front door.

After safely securing her eager guard dog in the guest room, she glanced out the peephole and saw Jason Wood-

ard standing, heels apart, one hand holding a bright yellow
bag and the other hooked through a loop in his faded blue
jeans, his sheepskin jacket as open as the man himself. His
graying hair was swept back, his narrow face calm with that
wholly nonjudgmental expression that sat so well on his
youthful features.

A rush of affection for him, for their years of unfettered
friendship, his speed at responding to a distress cry from her,
his basic familiarity—a note of common sense in a night
gone mad—swept through her. She opened the door swiftly,
and after a brief tight hug, ushered him in, her words in-
audible over Max's assault on the guest-room door.

Jason stepped past her and would have gone on into the
living room had she not halted him. Quickly she filled him
in on what she knew about their guest. And what all she
didn't know.

Jason nodded, his eyes already on the living room. "Andrew told me," he said, then he chuckled. "How does it feel
to have a character come to life?"

This was a little too close to her earlier thoughts and she
colored even as she shot Jason a sour look. "You're here for
Sam, not me."

"Oh, you call him Sam, do you?"

Feeling the color spill to a full blush, remembering the
heated kiss, Katherine looked away, nodding at the living
room. "He's in there."

Jason ambled into the living room, and after a brief salute in Andrew's direction, he pushed aside a vase on the
coffee table and sat down on the polished surface. He met
Sam's distrustful glare with a bland expression.

"Don't worry," he said. "You know me—I'm the
friendly neighborhood shrink. Every neighborhood should
have one." He lowered his voice conspiratorially. "All that
it really means is that my nutty neighbors can call me anytime, day or night, and they know I'm so fuddled about

money that they'll never get a bill." He held out a hand and pumped Sam's once, then released it, saying, "I'm Jason."

Completely ignoring the bemused distrust on Sam's face, Jason dropped both hands onto the worn knees of his jeans and cocked his head, his eyes on the makeshift bandage. "But being a shrink also means I know how to look at the sight of blood without fainting." When Sam didn't respond, Jason continued easily, "Meaning, I know how to fix that head of yours. Physically."

"There's nothing wrong with me," Sam said, but his voice was tainted with doubt.

"Let's have a look, shall we?" Jason swung his yellow bag to the table and opened it.

Sam looked at the bright bag and over at Katherine. A frown creased his brow. She smiled faintly. "Jason says black's a gloomy color."

"Funereal," Jason corrected. "Who wants to be doctored by things coming out of a funereal pouch? Yellow's better. See, I usually treat children under puberty. And yellow makes them think of sunshine, daffodils, springtime, freshness. Those are things that yellow means to me, anyway.

"Okay, now, since Katherine won't let me show her how effective my nimble fingers can be—" he broke off, both in words and in the act of gently pushing Sam back toward the cushions as his patient turned angry eyes in his direction.

Katherine's breath caught as Jason pulled back, hands spread wide, his eyebrows raised. Sam's eyes were blazing, his lips compressed in a tight line, his jaw clenched with anger. Slowly, as he took in Jason's surprise, the ire faded from his face.

After the briefest of hesitations, Jason lowered his hands. "Kidding. Just kidding. Now, lay back and let me have a look."

Katherine's breath released in an audible sigh when Sam allowed himself to be propelled backward. Jason flicked her a brief inscrutable glance and turned to Sam.

"Now, if I promise to make no more risqué cracks, will you let me see that head of yours?"

Sam didn't raise so much as a protest as Jason leaned forward and lightly pulled on the handkerchief. When Sam winced, Jason stopped and asked Katherine to get him a warm wet cloth. Andrew held up his hand and disappeared down the hall for the kitchen.

While he waited for Andrew's return, Jason continued talking easily, asking Sam seemingly casual questions, but questions that Katherine knew would tell Jason a great deal about his patient. He was careful to avoid any direct inquiries concerning his patient's relationship with Katherine, though he alluded to several events that the four of them could have done together.

Katherine's heart did an odd flip when Sam frowned and looked puzzled. She tried telling herself it was pity she felt for him, but she knew she wasn't being completely honest; what she felt was sympathy. If there was any pity, it was for herself. For during that one moment, wrapped in his arms, his warm lips against hers, she'd truly believed in his fantasy, had wanted it to be true.

Jason's subtle probing and his doctor's sure touch only brought home the impossibility of such a fantasy holding any trappings of reality.

When Andrew brought the warm cloth, Jason continued talking, but he asked questions that only related to the external injury. How did it happen? Who bound his head? Where did it happen? To all the questions, Sam returned short, uninformative answers.

Jason applied the cloth to the exterior of the makeshift bandage and after a few minutes removed it and gently pried at the stained handkerchief until it came free.

Katherine had to bite her lips to hold in her gasp of horror. A jagged furrow ran from approximately an inch above Sam's left eyebrow, across his temple and disappeared into his hairline. It was angry and red, the flesh opened and ugly. Dried blood was matted in his hair and smeared across the high planes of his temple. So much had been hidden by the bandage, Katherine thought, and then wondered what else was hidden inside this man's confused mind.

She looked up and met Andrew's shocked gaze. He looked pale and was, like her, holding his lower lip between his teeth. His hand holding the drink he'd fixed for Jason was shaking badly. Swiftly Katherine crossed the room and pushed her cousin to a nearby armchair. "Don't look," she said. He'd never been able to handle the sight of blood.

It was only at that moment that Katherine realized the full extent of what she didn't know about the man Jason was so deftly treating. She didn't know his name, his address, or his likes and dislikes. But most of all she realized she didn't know if he had a family waiting for him to come home. She looked down at his hands loosely draped on either side of him and sighed in relief. No wedding ring, no telltale tan line where a ring had been. It wasn't definitive, but it was a clue.

Within minutes, Jason had finished his cleaning and patching. For some reason, despite the clean, fresh bandage neatly in place across Sam's brow and temple, he appeared more wounded than he had before. More vulnerable.

Jason said to him now, "You'll have a scar; you realize that. You should have had this wound stitched within an hour of it happening. The butterfly clips will probably repair some of the damage, but they can't do magic. I'll leave you a couple of extra bandages. Just leave the clips alone, they'll release when they're ready. And try to keep water away from that. Showers are okay, but don't go swimming or engage in any kind of strenuous activity."

He flicked a glance at Katherine and she blushed, not because his eyes held any kind of speculation, but due to her own unruly imaginative conjecture about possible strenuous activity. He smiled, somewhat abstractedly, she thought, and turned back to Sam. "We've got a little problem here."

Sam, apparently having forgotten his earlier anger, merely looked curious. "What?"

"All bullet wounds are supposed to be reported—"

"So?" Sam asked. His face was so innocent of calculation that Katherine realized he was totally unaware of the nature of the wound at his temple.

"That's a bullet graze you're sporting," Jason said dryly.

"It can't be," Sam said. He said it as though that settled any questions Jason might pose.

"Whether it can or can't, it *is*," Jason said. "And technically, I've got to report it to the police."

"No," Sam said quietly. So quietly that if Katherine hadn't seen his eyes narrowing and his lips pulling to a thin line, she would have assumed him unmoved.

"Do you really have to do that?" Katherine asked quickly, before the volcano she sensed in the man on the sofa could erupt.

Jason had seen it, too, and held up his hands as though warding off blows. "Whoa. I didn't say I would, I just said—" he cut a sharp look at Katherine "—bullet wounds are *supposed* to be reported."

"Thanks," Sam said wearily. He closed his eyes.

"Don't go to sleep on me yet," Jason said, and Sam's eyes flew open to eye the doctor warily and, Katherine thought, somewhat menacingly.

Again Jason held up his hands. "I don't mind bending the law, but I have a conscience. Besides, I'm incurably nosy. What you've got there is a bullet wound, and you're saying it can't be. Why?"

Sam shook his head, his expression rather forbidding.

"Is there some reason you don't want to talk about it?"

"No," Sam said distinctly, but since he didn't elaborate, he obviously meant for the discussion to end.

"No reason not to talk about it, but you're not going to, are you?"

"No."

"Why not?"

"Because I don't want Katherine involved in this."

"In what?" Jason fired back.

Sam frowned heavily and his eyes lost their sharp focus on Jason. His gaze shifted to Katherine and she read a plea in the blue depths.

"Jason..." she murmured, unable to drag her eyes from the link she felt with the impostor.

Jason ignored her, saying calmly, "You know, it's common with head wounds to encounter some trace loss. Memory loss, that is."

"What are you talking about?" Sam growled.

"Temporary patch memory loss."

Sam's face lightened as though a physical weight had been taken from him. Jason must have noticed it, Katherine thought, but he simply nodded, saying, "Feeling a little off balance? Like the world is spinning to another rhythm?"

Sam nodded, and Katherine's heart contracted as his jaw clenched and his eyes clouded.

"I want to run a couple of easy tests."

"No hospitals," Sam said distinctly.

"We don't need an X-ray lab for these," Jason answered. He held up his hand, displaying two fingers. "How many fingers?" he asked.

"Oh, for Pete's sake..." Sam began angrily, but trailed off. He slowly repeated his words, giving them a different inflection. "For *Pete's* sake..." His eyes seemed far away, then they slowly focused on Jason's hand.

Katherine was racking her brain for the sentence he'd uttered in the car when Sam announced they'd lost their pursuer, when she and Andrew were trying to persuade him to go to a hospital. Hadn't it been, *Pete has a long arm?*

"Two," he said now in a subdued, almost puzzled tone. "Two fingers." What was he thinking? Was he trying to remember what had happened to him, or was it more than that, was he trying to remember who he was?

Jason's eyes slid to meet Katherine's, then he performed the test with a different number of fingers held aloft. Sam said, "Four," then, "One," then, "Is all this really necessary? I can see just fine."

"I agree," Jason said softly. "Now, keep your head still. Follow my finger. No, don't move your head. Just your eyes. That's it." He moved his finger toward the study door and then slowly toward Katherine. Then he repeated the process up and down.

"No dilation of your eyes. Your eye-motor functions seem all right. Now let's have a look at the gray matter. Any troubles you've noticed? Odd smells? Lights?"

"Fine," Sam said.

"Let's just go over some of the standard ones, okay?"

Sam sighed as though bored. "Okay," he murmured.

"Name?"

"Sam McDonald." He shot Katherine a smile filled with wry amusement and a trace of an apology. For having accused her of playing a joke?

Jason saw the smile, but gave no indication of witnessing it. Katherine wondered if he felt any of the same feelings she'd had when this stranger called himself Sam McDonald.

"Middle name?"

"Robert."

Jason glanced at Katherine, as though in confirmation. Katherine had to shrug. She had never bothered to give Sam McDonald a middle name; somehow it had never seemed likely to crop up.

"Date of birth?"

Sam frowned, then his brow cleared. "November ninth," he said clearly and added a year. That made him forty-five, Katherine figured rapidly; he was six years older than she.

"How about work?" Jason asked. "What do you do for a living, Sam?"

Sam cocked his head at Jason as if trying to determine whether or not the doctor was joking. Apparently what he saw in Jason's eyes told him he wasn't kidding. "I'm a novelist," Sam said quietly. "I write spy novels with my wife, Katherine."

"I see," Jason said neutrally, but Katherine had known him long enough to recognize the sudden tension in his shoulders. "And how long have you and Katherine been married?"

"Ten years," Sam answered swiftly.

Jason hesitated for a moment. "And . . . where did you spend your honeymoon?"

Sam stared at Jason for several seconds, then his eyes shifted to Katherine's. The anguish she could see there rendered speech impossible. She wanted to help him, wanted to supply him with an answer no matter how unrealistic it was, no matter that it would be a lie. She had to bite her lips.

"I can't remember," he said dully. He shook his head, as if by the physical action he could clear his mind, and turned his gaze back to Jason. "I can't remember."

"That's because you didn't have one," Andrew quipped dryly, his fortitude apparently restored now that Sam's bandage was in place.

"Andrew," Katherine said warningly, her eyes on Sam. He had turned his head her way and was smiling crookedly. The expression on his face made her heart pound. It was warm, tender, somewhat apologetic, and wholly loving.

"We will," he said softly. Katherine felt a shiver send goose bumps across her shoulders, partially at the vow in his eyes, partially at the depth of sincerity in his tone, but mostly in reaction to a fleeting wish that it could be true.

She shook her head slowly, almost sadly.

His smile broadened, and some of the tension etching his face seem to lessen. He nodded, negating her denial.

"Oh, yes," he contradicted, raising his hand to forestall any objection from her. His eyes locked with hers and for a moment Katherine felt the sensation that Jason had described earlier, that the world was spinning to an odd rhythm, a beat created by her contracting heart.

The impostor said quietly, making his words a vow, his voice a caress, "I promise you, Katherine, we'll have a real honeymoon. *Soon.*"

Chapter 5

"You're suffering a concussion," Jason said into the long silence following Sam's last pronouncement. "I'm not going to kid you by saying it's mild—"

"Mild!" Andrew interjected. "The man thinks he's—"

"He's probably had enough probing for one night," Jason interrupted warningly. He looked at Sam with reassurance. "I'm quite sure these lapses in your memory will go away with a little rest. And speaking of which, I think it would be a good idea—"

"That's a relief," Sam interrupted, his crooked grin transferring to Jason.

"When you cast about, are there any other things you can't seem to remember?" Jason asked, his brow furrowing in curiosity.

Sam thought for a moment, but having apparently accepted Jason, felt free enough to tell the truth. "Yes. Some things. Little things." He looked annoyed and gave a brief snort of disgust. "Like I don't know what's in any of those drawers over there," he said, pointing to the wall unit at the far side of the living room.

"That's because you haven't—" Andrew began, only to be frowned down by both Katherine and Jason. He rolled his eyes at the ceiling and subsided.

Sam continued as if Andrew hadn't spoken, "And while I can remember watching Katherine's appearance on that talk show the other night, I can't remember either being there, or being here. It seems like I was somewhere else. But I can't remember where."

At the mention of the talk show, Katherine felt her body growing curiously weak. The interview he presumably referred to had been a particularly long one, the kind Andrew called the garden club variety. Was this how Sam knew so much about her? She'd already witnessed his remarkable memory for her novels; did it also extend to her spoken word?

As if reaching in her mind for her unspoken question, he answered, "She talked about us, I remember that. About our latest book. And about Andrew and the bookstore. And Max, she talked about Max. Even George remarked on that."

"George?" Jason asked.

Sam looked blank. "What?"

"You said, 'George talked about that.' Who's George?"

Sam shook his head. "I . . . don't . . . know." He raised a hand to his head, rubbing at the non-bandaged side of his brow, as if touch would restore his memory.

Jason reached into his yellow bag again and pulled out a packet of cellophane-sealed capsules. "Antibiotics," he said, handing them to Sam. He pulled out a pad and started writing. "Take one three times a day with meals. These'll see you through the weekend, then fill this prescription."

Jason rose and looked a question at Katherine. "Sam really should get some sleep now. Why don't we—"

"I thought concussed people shouldn't sleep," she said, ignoring the question in his eyes and the decision looming before her.

"Old wives' tale," Jason replied with a tired smile. "It probably started when a comatose patient never regained consciousness. A person with a concussion can be roused, a comatose one cannot. Sleep is usually the best remedy for a vast majority of ailments . . . concussions included."

Sam pushed to his feet, swaying slightly. Jason stepped to his side, taking hold of his arm. Again Jason's eyes begged the question of Katherine.

"The guest room," Katherine said, ignoring Andrew's wave of protest. It was Sam who verbalized resentment, but for a different reason.

"Why the guest room?" His eyes conveyed his outrage at being barred from the bedroom he obviously believed he shared with her. The notion struck her as anything but amusing.

"It's on the first floor," she said lamely.

The stranger she was about to harbor in her home looked at her for a long moment, then nodded, a rueful smile touching his lips. "You're probably smart. I'm afraid I'm not up to much tonight."

Katherine could feel the heat staining her cheeks and wished that she'd listened to Andrew's unspoken protest in the car. This wasn't a good idea.

"I can take him with me," Jason said quietly, correctly interpreting Sam's comments.

Katherine threw him a grateful smile, but before she could answer, Sam interjected his opinion of such a plan. "I'm not going anyplace." His eyes met Katherine's with a combination of daring her to object and that odd, unspoken plea she'd seen there earlier that night.

Slowly Katherine shook her head, turning to Jason. "He'll be all right here."

"What about you?" Jason asked softly.

"I can take care of her," Sam said, a ghost of a laugh in his voice. "I've managed for ten years now."

"And I'll be here," Andrew interposed, eyeing Katherine wickedly.

Sam gave him a funny look, then grinned. "Give me a hand with this, will you?" he asked, already unbuttoning his shirt.

"I'll get Max out of there," Katherine said, all but fleeing the room. She hustled Max out of the guest bedroom and down the hall to the kitchen, having to wrestle with him to keep him from trampling over her to get to his latest favorite. His sad brown eyes conveyed his displeasure at being excluded from the late-night activities.

By the time Katherine returned to the guest room, Andrew and Jason had assisted Sam in stripping down. Katherine stopped in the doorway, frozen by what met her eyes. Her newfound and fictional husband stood in the center of the room, his back to the door, his shirt, pants, shoes and socks already discarded. It wasn't his seminudity that held her in thrall, however, it was the sheer maleness of him. Wide, broad shoulders, squared with muscles, and corded with his pain and his weariness, tapered to a narrow waist and from solid buttocks flared again to long, muscled thighs. He turned then, his face still in profile to her as he said something over his shoulder to Jason.

As before, Katherine was struck by the contrasts this man presented, at one and the same time he was confused, lost by his own admission, and shockingly tough-looking.

Katherine felt her mouth go dry, yet she felt strangely liquid elsewhere. Everywhere. This self-styled Sam McDonald was all a man should be and more. A light dusting of dark hair winged from his broad shoulders to a sharp point at his navel, an arrow pointing toward other secrets soon to be revealed. As Sam tucked his thumbs in the elastic band of his briefs, he turned toward her and paused, a half grin crossing his face. His eyes lit in mischievous enjoyment. "Help me?" he mouthed, his grin expanding.

Katherine hastily averted her head, her mouth no longer dry, her thoughts as scattered as her senses.

She felt like she had the day she'd discovered that males and females were different. But this man was different than any other man on earth, she knew this with an almost grim certainty; no man had ever made her feel this way before. He left her wanting, gasping, fearful of her own reactions, wishing he'd both simply disappear and that he would stay forever.

She'd told herself that it was his words, his delusion that snared her, caught her imagination, tugged at her heart, but in the heat of reaction to seeing him, she realized she'd again played herself false; she had also reacted to the overwhelming masculinity of him.

And his damnable sense of humor. How could anyone who was obviously going through such a rough time come up with quick lines, sharp, pointed, wholly wicked remarks? Comments that made her want to laugh, made her want to share that laughter with him.

A touch at her shoulder made her jump and utter a sharp release of the tension that had been building in her almost since first sight of the stranger that afternoon in the bookstore.

"Katherine?" Sam asked. It struck Katherine suddenly, and irrelevantly, that she knew what his slightly rasped voice reminded her of now. While his touch was like velvet, his voice was like corduroy, rough and soft at the same time, warm and somehow reminiscent of a crackling fire in the deepest quiet of winter.

She dragged her eyes upward, away from his shoulders, away from his bare chest, not daring to look any lower. "W-what?"

He didn't answer; he merely leaned closer, and gently lowered his lips to hers. The heat pulsating from him threatened to envelop her, and served to hold her captive in his loose embrace. Dimly she understood that she could have pulled away easily. Even more indistinctly she knew that Andrew and Jason were standing mere steps away, watching, one or both of them either frowning or raising a hand to object.

Yet despite this knowledge, Katherine was also aware that had the room been crowded with all of her friends and relatives, had the hands so lightly touching her shoulders slid away, she still would have stayed where she was, drinking in his scent, lost in his gentle care of her lips, his tender regard of her cheeks, her bared throat.

Even as her legs weakened, as the heat in him sparked an answering fire in her, she wondered why she was doing this, why she allowed such incaution to overset her mind, her life. Humor or none, striking body or no, tender kiss or not, he was still a stranger. A complete stranger. *A stranger that knows every line of every book you've ever written,* that invidious voice inside her whispered.

He stood back and softly stroked her cheek, the love he supposedly felt for her all too evident in his blue eyes, and she knew why she had let him kiss her, touch her: it might be a fantasy, it might be a delusion, but for this single moment, for this one night, she could dream along with him. And not just because she wanted the dream, but because he needed it. To her it was a beautiful, bittersweet fantasy, to him it was salvation.

As he pulled away from her and crossed the room to slide beneath the covers of the bed, Katherine remained still, her mind working over her questions, her answers. And as she watched him close his eyes, her name on his lips, she knew she'd been lying to herself. She'd let him kiss her, had kissed him back, because she wanted him to. It wasn't a matter of dreaming along with his fantasy, it was a matter of really wanting his fantasy to be true. And like a child, she'd mentally crossed her fingers, and kissed him back, hoping that if she believed hard enough, the magic would be real. And like that child, she found herself saying over and over, like an incantation, *I do believe, I do believe.*

If she believed strongly enough would it—could it?—come true?

Ruefully, watching him shift to find a more comfortable position for his injured forehead, she knew it couldn't. She wasn't six, or ten, or even twelve years old anymore. The days of magic were long gone, locked in boxes in the attic with yellowed paper dolls, books with drawings of elves and fairies, a single, much-scratched glass slipper, and a plastic wand with crinkled, glitter-stained fronds dusting the contents of the box with the drossy red-and-silver sparkle of childhood.

Was it this sort of magic that had made him believe he was her husband, spy novelist Sam McDonald, and that he loved her, and that made him certain she loved him in return? Was he, like her, saying to himself that he did believe, he did believe?

With a sympathetic nod in her direction, Jason pulled Andrew from the room to wait for her in the hall. She crossed to the bedside and after a last glance at her stranger, clicked out the light.

"Katherine?" he mumbled, making her breath catch in her throat, making her hand still a scant two inches from the lamp.

"I'm here," she said softly and wondered if he'd heard her over the rough beat of her heart.

She heard him pushing against the covers and reached her hand out to reassure him. "Don't move. It's okay," she said. Was she reassuring him, or herself?

A warm, broad hand curled around hers, and lifted it to his lips. His lips seemed both too warm and just right against her suddenly cold fingers. His unshaven beard wasn't scratchy or abrasive as she might have imagined, but an erotic contrasting rough-soft against her sensitive skin. Like the man himself.

"Don't worry, Katherine," he said. His corduroy voice was warm with comfort, slack with weariness. "I'll be all right in the morning."

"Get some sleep," Katherine said quietly, soothingly. A wave of empathy shook her. What must he be going through? His mind must be at war with his delusion. How long could he maintain the fiction? Did he realize he was lost in a maze of some kind? She returned the pressure of his fingers with a deep, unspoken promise to stand by him while he found himself.

"Everything's okay," she lied, underscoring the message of her fingers. "You'll be fine." But she couldn't help but realize that if he stayed there much longer, she wouldn't be. She was already too caught up in his delusion as it was.

"Stay," he asked. "Sit here awhile." As if he sensed her hesitation, he added, "Please." It was so soft, so quiet, she was certain it was a word he didn't use often, and the thought made her pause anew; he'd used it several times with her already. Was it because his mind told him she was his wife, therefore use polite language, or was it something more, something that lay between the two of them, a chemistry, a certain electrical combination of two people?

Slowly, sitting on the edge of the bed, scarcely allowing her weight to rock the mattress, she complied.

"Have you been worried?" he asked.

"Worried?"

"About me."

"Yes," Katherine answered honestly and felt vaguely guilty when he sighed.

"I'm sorry. You know I'd rather do anything than worry you."

"You need some sleep now," she said rather desperately.

"Promise me, Katherine," he said.

"Promise you what?"

"Promise me you'll love me forever."

Unprepared, Katherine's breath snagged, her heart seemed to miss a stroke. She felt tears of sympathy gather in her eyes, well in her chest.

"Promise me, Katherine," he repeated. "I can't go to sleep without hearing you say it. I can't. Promise me, Katherine. Please." His voice was rough with fever, tight with the urgency he felt, but didn't strike Katherine as pathetic. On the contrary, his voice, the grip on her hand crashed into her like a fierce demand.

Slowly, almost sadly, unable to deny him this request, unable to consign him to uneasy, comfortless dreams, and despite her heart beating with painful thuds, she whispered, "I promise."

"I love you," he whispered back, "more than I ever thought it possible to love someone."

Katherine had to lean forward to hear his words, and his warm breath playing on her face only served to underscore his statement. Stiffly, finding it difficult to control her own breathing, she waited until his became slower, until she felt, with a sense of loss, his fingers slip from hers.

Gently, her heart strangely heavy, Katherine pulled erect, turned, and left the room.

Out in the hallway, Andrew and Jason had waited for her. Both turned curious gazes in her direction, one edged with speculation, the other in concern. Both pairs of eyes carried heavy doses of warning.

After a long look, Andrew stepped past Katherine to turn a key in the guest-room door.

"What are you doing?" Katherine asked, half seeing the turned key as a betrayal of the promise she'd given only seconds before. She'd lied then, to give him solace, but now it seemed she was compounding the deceit. "What if he needs something?"

Andrew dropped the key into her hand. "Unless you want me to sleep here tonight, his door is going to stay locked.

He's got a bathroom in there, complete with fresh towels and a new toothbrush, and he's got plenty of blankets. But let's face facts, dear, we know absolutely nothing about him.''

"Except that he's a Treasury agent," Katherine said firmly.

"Who also happens to be off his ever-loving rocker," Andrew added.

Jason headed off any argument on Katherine's part by agreeing with Andrew's decision to lock Sam in. He raised his hands at Katherine's sputter of protest. "No, I don't think he'd do anything to hurt you, Kath. For one thing, he's hardly in any condition for roughhousing. For another, I really think he believes he's your husband, Sam McDonald. And he's obviously feeling very protective of you.''

He cocked an eyebrow at her and she found she couldn't deny his last remark. She couldn't forget the searing anger he'd shot at Jason over an innocuous comment, and again later over the bedroom arrangements.

Jason sighed and gestured toward the living room and both Katherine and Andrew followed him, Katherine feeling dazed and more than a little conscious of Andrew's dubious acceptance of the stranger in the house.

Jason continued, "This confusion of his is most likely the result of the concussion and some deep-rooted traumatic shock.''

"That explains everything," Andrew said caustically, after Jason paused for several seconds with the apparent intention of stopping there. "It tells us everything we wanted to know." He turned to Katherine with his humor back in place. "We can relax now, Katie. Our Sam's just had a concussion and a shock.''

Jason chuckled and sprawled out on the sofa so recently occupied by their unexpected guest. He raised his legs to the coffee table and plunked his scuffed shoes onto the surface beside his yellow bag. "I have to say, this guy is brilliant. He must be. This delusion of his is almost perfect. As near as I can tell, he's suffering some form of amnesia." He held up a hand to forestall a biting comment from Andrew. "No, I don't have a name for it. I'm willing to bet there isn't one, but if you want a tag for what this man's got, you could call it substitution."

He continued, "The trauma—I'll use that word for want of a better one, Andrew—is both interesting and perplexing. The man seems to really believe he is Sam McDonald. He believes it so strongly that, in all likelihood, his name is something very similar, if not really 'Sam McDonald.'"

"Isn't amnesia fairly rare?" Katherine asked, remembering newspaper articles she'd read in which an amnesia victim suddenly encountered loved ones after years and years of leading other lives. The notion left her ice-cold.

"Oh, no," Jason said easily, shaking his head and smiling. "Everyone has certain moments of amnesia. Almost on a daily basis. It's called a trace loss, or if bigger, a patch loss.

"You drive home, and you can't really remember how you got there. You've had a few too many drinks and the next morning can't remember what you might have said, or you can remember your answers, but not the questions asked. You have whole days, whole months you can't recall. And, as we get older, years. It's the mind's way of dealing with the copious amounts of input we give it every day. The memory is a funny thing. All that we see or do, read or hear, goes in the old circuits, but how it gets filed away is a mystery to all of us."

He tapped his head and grinned. "Even to us mind readers."

"Cut to the chase," Andrew said, handing Jason a freshened drink.

Jason grinned good-naturedly and took the proffered glass. "In most cases, these lapses of memory are either so common, or so easily dealt with that we ignore them. In

Sam's case, he has gone another step forward. In his attempt to cope with whatever traumatic situation sparked what I suspect might be an almost complete or total amnesia, he supplied a ready-made alternate world.''

Katherine murmured some half protest.

Jason nodded, as though he understood. ''Oh, I admit I've never run across anything quite so complete as this. He's apparently got enough strong memories, associations and identification with *this* life, through both his attraction to you, Katherine, and—I suspect—his name, that he simply substituted an entire life-style for his own. We could try hypnosis, but I would hazard a guess that he might even block that. Except for the odd references, such as 'George' or his abstraction over certain phrases or items—and these indicate to me that he'll probably snap out of it pretty quickly. Overall, he strikes me as being fairly strong-willed.'' This last was said without any change in expression, but from the glint in his eyes, Katherine was aware this was a tremendous understatement.

''When you say 'snap out of it' do you mean he'll just wake up and be himself, and that's that? Or should we do something dramatic when the hero wakes up?'' Andrew asked.

Jason smiled. ''What, for example?''

''Well, if he's still in lala land, I was thinking that telling him the truth might be interesting,'' Andrew said.

Slowly, Jason shook his head, the smile fading from his lips. ''No, I'm not very comfortable with a direct confrontational situation.''

''What should we do? If he's still confused, I mean,'' Katherine asked before Andrew could state his obvious opinion of Jason's comforts.

Jason replied, ''In other circumstances, I would probably insist on taking him with me, either calling an ambulance or hauling him myself, to a hospital.'' He again raised a hand. "I know, you told me about his reaction to the notion of going to the hospital. And I saw it, remember?"

His eyes cut to Katherine for a swift, penetrating examination. His expressionless face gave nothing away, yet still Katherine felt as if she'd committed some crime.

He sighed. "No, I wouldn't force him to go to a doctor. It seems obvious to me that some very real danger exists for him and, as a result, his subconscious mind is clinging to the idea that he's Sam McDonald the novelist. This apparently represents safety to him."

"And the fact that *our* Sam supposedly is a former agent plays right into this fantasy?" Andrew asked.

"Exactly," Jason approved.

"So what do we do?" Katherine queried.

"What happens to him matters to you, doesn't it, Kath?" Jason asked. "You don't have to answer. I can see that it does." He smiled, but his eyes were sad, or perhaps merely tired. "I'm beginning to have hopes for you. Maybe you won't be spending your whole life taking in strays and hiding behind your novels."

Andrew piped up, "What would you call a mystery man with a bullet wound on his head who claims to be her husband, if not a stray?"

Jason simply grinned. Neither man seemed to notice Katherine's frowning thoughtfulness. "You think his memory will be back when he wakes up, then?" she asked.

Jason shrugged. "It's entirely possible. He was already having some difficulty in maintaining the fiction. His real memory is trying to reassert itself."

"What happens when it does?" Katherine asked. The question meant a great deal more to her than the simple words implied. What she really meant was, how much of his delusion, how much of his fantasy would remain? He thought that he loved her; what would be shining in his eyes if he knew that he didn't? "Will he remember any of this?"

Jason pursed his lips. "I don't know. We don't know all that much about how the memory works. I would say it's unlikely, but this guy's not your average Joe Blow with an average IQ. If he does remember, I wouldn't count on him being any too happy about it. Like I said, he's a bright man, he'd be able to understand immediately what he's done, and if that forceful personality of his is any indication, I'd hazard a guess he's likely to be very, very embarrassed."

"Meaning what?" Andrew asked.

"Meaning he'll probably want to get as far away from here as he possibly can."

"And never come back," Katherine said softly, knowing instinctively that would be the case, knowing what Jason said would likely prove to be true. Why did the thought bother her so?

Jason lifted his feet from the table and leaned forward. "And never come back...yes, that's a distinct possibility," he said, equally softly. His eyes were on his hands and when he lifted them, Katherine turned aside.

She didn't want to meet his eyes for fear he would read the pain she was sure was evident in hers. She tried telling herself the pain was all for the man in the guest room, but as she had done with him, with the promise to him, she knew she lied; somehow, in some strange way, his pain was already hers.

Jason cleared his throat and pushed to his feet. "If his memory doesn't reassert itself overnight, call me in the morning. I'll swing round and see if I can't persuade him to go to the hospital. If he refuses..." he trailed off, holding out both his hands in a surrendering gesture "...there won't be much I can do about it, unless you want to call in the police, of course. Besides, if he believes he would be in danger by going to the hospital, that could be his real memory trying to warn him."

"So what do I do?" Katherine asked.

"We," Andrew corrected. "What do *we* do?" He smiled at Katherine, his old mischievous grin.

Jason answered, "In my opinion it would be better for him if he were safely led, rather than forced, to confront his fantasy. If he were to stay where he sincerely believes he belongs, he could avoid the shock and severe disorientation that could result from a direct confrontation with a past he obviously wants to forget."

Jason stepped around the coffee table and took Katherine's limp hands in his own. "Now I have a question, Kath. What would someone be doing with a Treasury department badge?"

The question steadied Katherine as nothing else could have; this was the world she knew and understood, the world of facts and data, the world of research for her novels. "Treasury governs firearms, tobacco, alcohol and drug enforcement. If he's an operative for them, he'd be like the plainclothes detective in charge of smuggling."

"We'll call Treasury tomorrow," Andrew offered, "to see if they can figure out who he is. Can't you just hear us? 'Excuse me, but are you missing one of your agents? You are? Would you mind telling us his name so we can tell him?' It's too rich."

Jason chuckled and shook his head, but Katherine didn't find the quip terribly amusing. And she was afraid to wonder why.

After repacking his yellow bag, and setting down his glass without having finished it, Jason gave Katherine a quick hug and ambled out of her house as casually as he'd entered it. He waved over his shoulder without looking back.

Andrew wasn't as easy to send away.

"I think I'll sleep on the sofa, dear," he said when she yawningly suggested it was getting late.

"Good Lord, Andrew. The man's got a bullet graze on his forehead, he's concussed, and you yourself locked him in the guest room. What on earth do you think he could do?"

"I don't have the foggiest, dear, but you have to admit that for a guy who's been shot, who doesn't know who he is, and doesn't remember even getting shot, he's managed to do quite a bit tonight."

She pushed him toward the door to her study, then on to the French doors leading to the patio connecting the main house with Andrew's guest house. "You heard Jason, the guy's not up to much, anyway."

"Except you, dear."

Katherine was too tired to even blush. "I'll keep the door locked," she said.

"And you keep my buzzer next to you. Promise me that if you hear so much as a peep out of him, you'll buzz me."

If he weren't so serious, the conversation might have struck Katherine as humorous. "I promise," she said, and was immediately aware of this being the second time that night she'd made a promise. Snatches of poetry and childhood edicts sifted through her mind: *And I have promises to keep...*, *a promise made is a promise kept*, and *never break a promise*.

"I'll be over first thing," Andrew said, looking at her in concern.

"Of course," Katherine said, closing the door behind him, torn between relief that he was leaving and fear that he was gone. It wasn't, she admitted, that she was afraid of the man asleep in the guest room. She was more afraid of her reaction to him. Or rather, her reaction to his delusion.

Unable to resist the impulse to check on him one last time, she unlocked the bedroom door and stood in the spill of light from the hallway, watching the steady rise and fall of his chest. Unlike many men, he didn't look vulnerable when asleep. If anything, he looked tougher, the lines on his face shadowed, indistinct, making even the planes of his face a mystery. Was he dreaming the dreams of his alter life, his real life? Was that why he looked harder, tougher? Or was he wrestling with the gaps in his self-imposed fantasy?

"Who are you?" she whispered. Then, as he sighed and half rolled over, she wondered if she really wanted to know. Was it the fantasy that intrigued her or the man himself? Or was it some elusive melded element of both? She knew that oftentimes a mystery lost its charm if the solution were readily known. Would that be the case with this man? Or would the unraveling prove to hold a charm all its own?

She pulled the door softly closed and, with a moue of distaste, and adhering at least to one promise given that night, she turned the key in the lock until she heard the dull click of the tumblers slip into place. The sound seemed to echo in her heart. Leaving the key in the lock, she snatched her hand away as if the key were alive and could snap at her. Again that sense of betraying the man inside the room washed over her.

He was a stranger, she told herself firmly. Aside from his actions earlier that night, she owed him nothing. And her own whispered lie to him came up to haunt her: *I promise.*

She moved swiftly down the hall to the kitchen, reminding herself that Jason had said in all likelihood this Sam would be "himself" the next morning, the fantasy having evaporated with the night's mist. She pushed the kitchen door open, freeing Max, then caught the door open on the double hinge so that it lay back against the kitchen wall.

"The house is yours, Max. Guard it for me, will you?" It was a game they played each night, and Max, as always, responded with a yawning stretch and accepting whine and promptly padded into her study to flop down on the rug by the French doors.

The simple routine steadied her and allowed her to walk back down the hall, eyes anywhere but on the guest door, hand on the stair rail, with no more than a mere acceleration of her heartbeat. She swung onto the stairs and walked lightly up to the second floor, her mind jumbled with chaotic thoughts, her emotions curiously on hold. *I do believe.*

I can't believe. Which did she really feel? Which did she really want?

As they had with Max, the simple routines of nighttime preparation seemed to relax her, to steady her, and allowed her thoughts a chance to coalesce into some semblance of order.

Finally, she slipped naked between the cool sheets, and doused the bedside light. Loving the slow warming of the sheets, heated only by her own body, listening to the faint strains of Schubert's "Unfinished Symphony" emanating from Andrew's opened window, she found herself sleeplessly wondering what on earth she'd gotten into.

Then, remembering the jagged flesh wound, the pleading look in his eyes, she wondered, not for the first time, what *he'd* gotten himself into. How had he come by a bullet wound? Contrary to her novels, it wasn't all that common an occurrence for an agent to get hurt. And contrary to her novels, agents weren't usually anything faintly resembling the attractive stranger who claimed to be her husband.

But like the men in her novels, this Sam McDonald was in danger of some kind, and he wasn't able to say what it was or where it was coming from. Whoever was after him had obviously tracked him to the bookstore that evening. Would they be able to find him here? Katherine shivered. She had a gun. She had Andrew and Max, and, after his performance earlier that night, the stranger asleep downstairs would likely prove a worthy ally.

But she didn't know how to shoot the broad side of the proverbial barn, Andrew was in the guest house, Max was more bark than bite, and the cause of the potential danger was, at this moment, sleeping soundly.

Katherine sighed. This was getting her nowhere closer to sleep. She continued her line of comparisons between the impostor downstairs and the agent heroes of her novels and finally hit one that made her smile. He certainly kissed like the men in her books. And he looked like them. Andrew had been right; the impostor husband downstairs even looked like the fictional character she'd created for her "front."

Her smile faded as she thought of the sincerity in his tone as he'd told her he loved her, and made her promise to love him, too. Forever.

For the first time in years, Katherine heard the lonely echoes of an empty room in her heart. Let him in, the echoes seemed to say. Let him fill this dusty, too-long-unoccupied space. And unbidden, his voice added to the echoes...*Please.*

She turned to her side, as if she could turn her back against the persistent call within her, and while her attempt didn't stop the echoes, she at least was able to drift into an uneasy sleep only to fall into dreams filled with a dark-haired, blue-eyed stranger whose warm hands roamed the secrets of her body while his words plumbed the secret compartments of her heart. And in her dreams he really was the husband he claimed to be.

"Good morning, darling," he said, kissing her, his lips cool against hers.

As she'd done all night, she arched upward, meeting the kiss, aching for his touch, for his vows of love.

The smell of coffee and the soft tickle of something against her cheek confused her and she resented this intrusion into her dream-time fantasies. But the tickling didn't stop and the smell of the coffee drew her even as she rejected it.

She opened her eyes and squinted against the bright morning light, then, blinking rapidly, realized this was no dream. Bent over her, a coffee mug in one hand, a late-blooming rose in the other, the Sam McDonald of her dreams was very real, very awake, and very much still lost in the command of his substituted memory.

He was dressed in the same rumpled clothing from the day before, his face harsh with another day's growth of whiskers darkening his skin. The light from the windows was reflected in his eyes and, as she stared at him, trying to make sense of his presence in her room, Katherine felt impaled by the raw hunger in his gaze.

It was as if he were looking through the sheets and could see her revealed to him. And it seemed he could read her chaotic thoughts as well, for he set the coffee mug on her nightstand with a jarring thud that sloshed coffee onto the wood. The rose dropped to the floor, forgotten and unnoticed by him. To Katherine, the unfurling bloom appeared to fall in slow motion, symbolic of her spiraling rationality.

"Katherine," he said harshly, and in fluid motion settled beside her on the bed. "I feel as if I've been gone for years, as if I haven't kissed you in a lifetime of lifetimes."

Though she pulled back, as much in denial of the rush of welcome she felt as in true rejection of this extenuation of the fantasies he'd conjured in her the night before, Katherine had nowhere but the pillows to retreat to, and Sam wrapped his muscled arms around her, drawing her upward, closer, tighter, holding her firmly, yet gently, kissing her forehead, her cheeks, her lips.

His hands were cool against her bare, bed-warmed back and his lips against her temple were hot fire, leaving a trail of sensitized flesh in their wake.

"No," she murmured. But was she telling him or herself?

"Yes," he answered back, pressing her against the bed, sweeping the protective sheets from her naked body. His breath whistled in raggedly, and with a groan of need, he bent his head to her breasts.

She wanted to scream a protest, and wanted to cup her hand behind his head and draw him closer. Never had she felt so completely electric, as though every nerve ending in her body were in tune with his questing lips. And never had she felt so confused.

"Please," she moaned, pushing at him feebly, knowing this wasn't right, not understanding why, if it was wrong, it felt so perfect.

He groaned some answer and, using his broad hands to arch her back, he took the puckered, upright nipple of a breast into his mouth, cold-hot tongue flicking and inciting her body to riot.

"Please," she moaned, and couldn't have said what she was pleading for. Involuntarily one hand curled around his dark head, while the other, moved perhaps by the last glimmer of reason, pushed at his shoulder.

"It's been so long," he murmured, only to transfer his attention to her other breast. His tongue against her puckered nipple made her body melt, while his words served as a headlong plunge into cold water.

Katherine, gathering the final vestiges of the knowledge that he wasn't her Sam, that this *stranger* wasn't in his right mind, was living a delusion, used both hands to push him up and away from her.

"Katherine . . . ?" he asked, a note of hurt in his voice, a puzzled pain in his eyes.

Lying beneath him, her breath coming and going raggedly, her body still quivering for his touch, Katherine fought for sanity, a state of mind made all the more difficult because of his complete departure from it. Because he made her *want* what he so obviously believed to be true. If only it was, she thought, absurd tears smarting her eyes.

The man above her, this stranger who called himself Sam McDonald, studied her for a long, assessing moment. Katherine couldn't read his expression. Then he sighed, and smiled somewhat ruefully. His hands slid from behind her and he flicked the sheet back over her.

Katherine closed her eyes against the reluctant acceptance she read in his. She had been so close to acquiescence. So close to succumbing to his fantasy, to hers.

"I forgot," he said unsteadily. She opened her eyes, frowning a question at him. He still wore that rueful smile. "You're just not a morning person."

Katherine opened her mouth to deny this, but closed it again. This was his fantasy, his delusion; if he wanted to believe she couldn't rally in the morning, her hold on reality would last that much longer. Her body still tingled with the desire he'd stirred in her with his dreams, his insidious lie.

"Why did you lock me in?" he asked softly, somewhat coldly.

"How did you get out?" Katherine blurted, pulling back against the headboard, drawing the sheets up against her bare throat. She had asked the question sharply, as much to hide her reaction to his proximity as to dodge her lack of a plausible excuse.

To her surprise, he cocked his head to one side and grinned widely at her. "You knew what I was when you married me," he said, an eyebrow raised tauntingly. "There isn't a lock made that could keep me in—or out—for long."

He reached for the still-steaming coffee mug and pushed it into her hands. "Here, drink this. You look like you need it."

He rose and turned away from the bed. He didn't notice that she had taken the cup absently, her lips still parted in shock. Nor did he notice the rose stem he negligently crushed beneath his foot. Again Katherine found the rose symbolic. It was as if the rose were the very essence of logic and reason. He dropped it, forgetting it, then, abstracted, trod upon it, grinding the thorny stem into her carpet. Wasn't that what he was doing with her mind? Not to mention her heart.

"Not that I blame you for not trusting me last night—I was pretty woozy. Who knows what another clonk on my head might have done?" He turned and gave her a wry look. "If I had fallen, I mean."

Katherine frowned. This wasn't going as Jason had assumed it would. Far from having regained his own memory, and even further from feeling more disoriented, this "Sam" obviously felt more at home with his pseudo-life. Instead of shying away from the confrontation of his two sets of memories, he'd abandoned his own and embraced those of her fictitious husband. Hers, in essence.

"Do you *feel* all right this morning?" she asked, after first clearing her throat in order to do so.

"Right as rain," he said, crossing to the large bank of closet doors against the right wall. He glanced back at her over his shoulder, "To coin an old phrase." His grin was infectious, and Katherine found herself dazedly responding.

But her smile faded as he flung open the closet doors and stepped back a pace to get a better view. He stared into the rows and rows of clothing for perhaps a full minute, then slowly turned back to face her.

A heavy frown etched his brow. "Where are my clothes?" he asked. "What have you done with all my stuff? There's nothing anywhere in this house but your things."

He took a step toward her, his hands loose at his sides, his legs spread apart—fight-ready, the thought flashed through Katherine's mind. His eyes were puzzled and more than slightly cold. A muscle worked in his squared jaw.

"Katherine . . . what is going on around here?"

Chapter 6

Desperately, Katherine sought a logical rationale to offer this confused man. What might Jason tell her to say or do? she wondered, and halfheartedly cursed him at the same time. It was his fault this man was here, looking more than a little angry now that his alter ego was finding the going difficult. She shook her head, as much to answer Sam as to put the blame where it really belonged: not at Jason's door, but at her own. It had been *her* decision to have Sam stay the night, had been *her* decision to let him stay at her home until he felt better.

Physically, he was obviously all but well. Mentally, however... And now he was waiting for an answer to his question. *What is going on around here?* Should she simply tell him the truth—you're a total stranger who enacted a rescue last night, seemingly believing yourself to be my husband, a husband that doesn't exist—or should she try to spin some tale to explain the lack of clothing?

Much to her great relief, he took the matter out of her hands by waving his own. "Never mind. I don't think I want to know." This he said with a droll, little-boy-in-trouble expression. It was a practiced expression, one he'd obviously used many times in his life, and undoubtedly to great advantage. She had to bite her cheek from grinning back at him.

But what sparked that look? And why did it make her feel vaguely guilty for hiding the smile, for causing the look in the first place?

He straightened. "You can tell me later. We have a lot to talk about, don't we?"

He crossed to the bedroom door, tossing, as an exit line, "Hurry up, darling. I've already been writing for two hours this morning and I can't wait to read it to you."

"What!" Katherine called out to the empty space in the doorway. "You've been doing—what?" But her only answer was the soft thud of his footfalls descending the stairs.

Katherine lay still, propped against the headboard, her body and mind strangely numb for perhaps thirty seconds. Then, as his words settled into some sort of coherent pattern, she threw back the covers and all but ran across the room to her closet. Her legs were shaking, and her fingers, as she dragged on clothing, trembled. She dashed to the bathroom and quickly brushed her teeth and dragged a brush through her morning-unruly hair. She saw for the first time that she'd donned a gold-colored silk blouse and a trendy pair of baggy flannel trousers that emphasized her small waist. So much for believing her only desire was to get downstairs and into her study as quickly as possible and stop him from doing anything to her computer, to her current manuscript.

She'd dressed with understated sensuality. And there wasn't much doubt as to her subconscious mind's reasoning; she'd dressed to impress. She twitched the inset belt into place and bolted from her bedroom, with a disparaging wave at the unmade bed, and the scene that had unfolded there earlier.

As she dashed down the stairs, she knew, in some dim recess of rationality, that her shaking limbs had nothing to do with any fear of him possibly erasing a file or two. It had to do with his kiss, with his very presence in her home. It had to do with how much she had actually allowed the man's fantasy to enter her mind. Her heart. Her mind shied away from this admission, however, and she masked her confusion with simulated anger. "If that maniac has *touched* my computer..." she said, trying to forget that not five minutes earlier she'd welcomed that maniac's attention with every sign of alacrity.

She greeted Max abstractedly, giving him a halfhearted caress, still cursing the softhearted impulse that made her allow this stranger access to her house. What had seemed perfectly logical, even inevitable by night, seemed frightening and uncertain by the light of day.

"He better not have so much as..." she muttered, entering her study, and trailing off as she saw her fears realized.

Sam was sitting in *her* chair, at *her* desk, typing in a three-finger fashion on the keyboard of *her* computer.

"What do you think you're doing?" she asked coldly, as much to cover her uncertainty as to chastise.

He looked up, and instead of appearing the slightest bit chagrined or confused, he smiled easily. "Sit down, hon." He waved at the love seat tucked against the bank of bookcases. "I want you to hear this. Listen."

Katherine swallowed an acid comment as she weakly complied with his order. This morning the entire situation was so much more difficult than she'd imagined it might be. It was one thing to have him fantasize about being Sam McDonald, it was a whole different matter to have him actually writing and using her computer to do so.

She sat on the edge of the sofa, her hands clasped tightly in her lap, half in an attempt to control the sudden trembling, half to keep them from physically pulling him away from the one machine she relied upon for her career, the place where all her fantasies, stories, and alter lives lay stored in microchip files and strange programming symbology. In an odd way, the machine was the keeper of her dreams.

As she watched him flip the screen back to the beginning of the document he'd "written," she had to wonder if it was his touching the machine that bothered her or if it was that in touching it, he could also tap the very core of all of her secrets, all those untold dreams and longings. In every line of every page something of her lived and breathed, loved and cried, sometimes timidly, oftentimes boldly seeking acceptance, craving a knowing, understanding touch. This part of her was the real Katherine McDonald, and the most vulnerable.

The false Sam began to read. Fully expecting him to read one of her stories, and dreading it, Katherine was almost startled to hear new words, a new scene. She flushed as she realized the extent of her misconception of his fantasy and the depth of her relief that it wasn't her thoughts he was reading. His fantasy was so much more thorough than she could have imagined. He not only believed he was a writer, but was backing it up by actually writing. And letting her glimpse *his* words, his views, his vulnerability. The thought humbled her.

"'He was restless and thought that nothing ever looked as forsaken as a deserted pier at night. It looked haunted by the trips not taken, the dreams already spent. Here, scarcely moving, scraping against the dock with a beggar's scratch, boats were bound, drained of life, surrounded and encircled by dark wood and darker water,'" he read.

Katherine listened, mesmerized by his odd voice, ensnarled by the content of his words. It was more a scene than a story, but vivid in its detail, horrifying in its implication, and telling in its aching loneliness.

In his scene two men, two agents, waited on a dark pier for some evidence of the power behind a small-time gunrunner. And when an older man arrived, the two agents recognized him as their boss. He spied them and shot one of them and, without a weapon, the other was powerless to do anything to avenge his friend's death. Also wounded, the remaining agent's only hope was to drop to the cold water below, trusting the tide and the darkness to save him. He knew, with his boss after him and his partner dead, that his life wasn't worth a plugged nickel.

In his choice of words, in his sentences, she saw the lonely man who wove the tale. And suddenly she understood him for what he was, not needing any names or tags to give him. She felt she knew him as well as she knew herself.

He was a man who had loved intensely and had lost, and fully understood the price of that loss. He was a man who believed in causes and the single shining notion of "right" in a world half-mad with wrongs. A man who understood betrayal as a personal agony, an affront to his very soul.

When he looked over at her and saw that she had understood, that she had listened with far more than her mind, when he saw the film of tears coat her eyes, he fell silent. His lips parted, then compressed. And he sighed as though she'd reached into his body and laid a cool hand on the fevered brow of his heart.

Whatever else this impostor, this amnesiac was, Katherine recognized him: he was the man who understood dreams and longings and secret places in the heart.

"It's that good?" he asked, in a slightly altered voice.

Katherine started, her eyes flying to his. "What?"

"You were looking at me as though I was the sun and moon all wrapped up in a pretty package," he said, unknowingly stumbling across the simile she'd assigned to him only the night before.

"It's...*good*," she said faintly. Gripped by the fierce empathy she felt for him, with him, she couldn't elaborate. She felt she *knew* him now. Knew everything she could possibly need to know. She understood his need for the fantasy he'd created, fathomed the depths of horror he'd undergone to have to substitute another life for his own. She'd heard it in the terror, in the loneliness, in the aching beauty of his words.

So what could she tell him now? How could she tell him that she knew he was writing the story of what had happened to him, trying to tell himself, to tell her, what had transpired on that lonely pier he so hauntingly described? It was all there, she thought, the detail, the careful adherence to sequence of action, the potential explanation of what had happened to this man. And there was so much more. Sprinkled before her, hidden in his words, diamonds sparkled, life gleamed, and the most vulnerable part of him lay spread-eagled in trust.

How could she explain all this to Sam who was seated not more than a foot from her, guilelessly waiting for her to elaborate, totally unaware of all that he'd revealed to her?

All of her life, Katherine had waited for someone to come along and understand her writing, to understand her. And when someone came who not only understood her, but gave her that understanding in return, what should he prove to be? A person who would forget her when his errant memory returned.

She sighed, finding a certain measure of justice in the knowledge. *Nothing worth having comes easily.* Was that the saying? Or was it a case of a diamond ring purchased for a dime wasn't worth a dime? But she hadn't purchased him, he'd shown up, almost literally at her doorstep, his memory in his hand, and his heart on his sleeve.

"It's . . . good," she said again. Unconsciously, she held out her hand.

He looked at her seriously, a slight frown between his dark brows. Slowly he took her hand and wrapped his fingers around hers. She let the pressure of her hand tell him what words never could, that she understood, that in understanding she was at one with him.

He cleared his throat, as if the emotion were too intense to talk over. And when he spoke, she had the distinct feeling he'd been about to say something else. "I felt strange. Writing it, I mean. It was like I was writing about myself in some ways." His frown deepened.

Slowly, equally seriously, Katherine nodded. Her heart was pounding in an almost painfully dull rhythm. During his reading, she'd heard his voice falter once, then a second time. He'd resumed easily enough, but those missed beats had caused an echoing catch in her own breathing. She *knew.*

"I know all characters are bits and pieces of ourselves, but...I don't know, this seemed different somehow," he said, and looked away from her and out the window. "That scene is so damned close I feel like I could reach out and touch it."

Katherine swallowed heavily. She couldn't seem to release the sound, the feel of his words. Her mind revolved around them, holding them up for individual and then collective inspection. In the scene he'd read, a friend of fourteen years had been shot, literally in his arms. And thus had ended fourteen years of sharing football games, high-speed chases and cold cups of coffee. It had been this friend with no name who had seen the other one through the death of his wife, who had helped him pull it together after the long bout of his wife's fatal cancer. He'd stumbled during the telling of both these incidents, the death of his hero's friend, the death of the hero's wife.

If this was, as she suspected, as she *knew,* the story of what had happened to this man frowningly looking out at the inlet water shimmering in the early morning sunlight, then Katherine bled for him. His friend killed by another friend. His wife dead, after a long, agonizing illness. He, himself wounded, abandoned, his life in danger, his mind disoriented.

Studying him now, seeing his hard profile, watching the tension build in the broad shoulders, and knowing him from his reading, Katherine could tell he wasn't the kind of man who relied on people easily. Nor was he the type to admit to problems, to pain or to trouble.

But he had asked her for help. Had turned to her with his jaw rigid, and his shoulders erect and asked *please*. He had come, from heaven only knew where, a knight-errant of some kind whose entire life had gone missing, and asked for her help.

Why? Out of all the people he could have turned to, why her? As before, the notion humbled her, silenced her. Though she hadn't refused her help the night before, there was no way on earth she could do so now. Because no matter how or why he'd come to choose her, he had. And the simple fact that he had chosen her mattered. It mattered on an utterly basic level, a gut-wrenching level. And it mattered a great deal more than she could have admitted aloud.

She felt the questions trembling on her lips, blinked her eyes against the tears of sympathy forming in her eyes. "Sam," she murmured, calling him by his fictitious name for the first time.

For some reason this simple action held a more prominent meaning than it seemed to her that it should. It somehow officially named him as belonging in her life, clarified the distance between them. Random phrases came to her mind to haunt her, to taunt her. Snippets from the works of famous writers, contemporary society, and folklore raged in her: Shakespeare, "Deny thy father, and refuse thy name," or Thomas Moore: "Breathe not his name! Let it sleep in the shade, where cold and unhonored his relics are laid," or the title of an old television game show: "Name It and Claim It!" and, finally, a common native American belief that using someone's name was to capture that person's spirit.

Had she captured his spirit now? Sometime between his first recognition of her and the reading of his scene, he had captured hers.

Oddly defenseless, strangely attuned to him, she repeated his name, "Sam...?" Did she say it as tremulously as it felt inside her heart? Was this naming him a turning point of sorts? *"What's in a name...?"* Everything, it seemed. Everything, and nothing.

He turned, a half-bitter smile on his lips. Was the bitterness there because he, too, felt the significance of her calling him by name, or was it due to something else?

"You called me Sam," he said, and his face softened. "I'd begun to think you were never going to."

"I—"

"It's okay, Katherine. I understand. Things have been a little unusual lately. But when I think of what we have together, when I think of you, I know—I hope—everything is fine."

"It'll be all right," she said, but she couldn't be sure whether she was reassuring him or herself. Her throat felt raw from withheld emotions, sympathy with his crisis, concern for the crisis he produced in her. And simple, uncomplicated worry.

A clatter from the direction of the kitchen caused him to whirl suddenly, the sour smile quickly shifting to a hard straight line. His features changed so rapidly that Katherine found herself biting off a quick cry of dismay. This didn't even look like the same man who had been reading to her only moments before, baring his soul, and was nothing like the man who had kissed her so tenderly. This was the Sam McDonald of the alley, the tough agent who had ruthlessly shoved her and Andrew into the car and had driven all of them to safety despite head wounds and flying bullets.

"Andrew?" Katherine called out before Sam could do more than spin forward and take a single step toward the hall door.

"I'm in here, Katie!" Andrew's voice called out. "Breakfast is about to be served. You'd better wake Sleeping Beauty."

"It's Andrew," Katherine said unnecessarily. To her relief, Sam's shoulders relaxed somewhat, and that wary, shoot-first, ask-questions-later look faded from his face.

"Right," he said dully. "I forgot."

The words were almost frightening in their utter simplicity. Again Katherine wondered if she shouldn't just tell him the truth about his presence here. Wouldn't it be harder on him to try and maintain this self-imposed fiction?

She had to call Jason. He would be able to tell her what to do, advise her on the next step. She had to know what to do, how best to help Sam, because she couldn't let him down. Not now. Not after hearing his words, feeling them, taking them inside herself. He'd turned to her and her life. And in doing so, he'd given her something magical, himself. She couldn't leave it alone now, for his sake.

"Sam . . . ?"

"Katherine . . . ?" He imitated her inflection so perfectly she couldn't help but smile, though her smile felt wistful.

"Why don't you give Andrew a hand, and I'll—" I'll just what? she thought, I'll just call Jason for his prognosis? I'll sit here and think about what to do to snap you out of this when all I want is for you to stay exactly the way you are?

"Sounds good," he said, eliminating the need for elaboration by adding it himself. "If you'd look that scene over, I'd appreciate it."

"Sure," she agreed weakly. He was better at dissembling than she was, and she had often claimed she made a living crafting lies. She felt as she occasionally did when one of her book characters suddenly refused to be cast in the role she tried writing him or her into: helpless. And tremendously curious. As with her characters, she would have to wait and see what Sam came up with.

As soon as he left the room, she sat down at the desk, dialed Jason's number and waited for him to answer while she sent the computer cursor back to the beginning of the scene Sam had written.

Skipping the usual social amenities, Katherine immediately launched into a catalog of the morning's events the second Jason said, "Hello." She included everything but the kiss, and her reaction to it. She didn't wait for Jason to ponder the details before paraphrasing Sam's scene. When she came to the last line, the sentence suggesting the hero's life wasn't worth a plugged nickel, she fell silent.

"Amazing," Jason said.

"Is that all you have to say?" Katherine demanded.

"I haven't had much chance for anything else, Kath," he complained, but with his usual good humor. Before she could answer, he asked if Sam had titled the piece.

" 'Dark Water,' " she said.

Jason whistled softly. "Interesting."

"How so?"

"It fits."

"It all fits, Jason. I think what he wrote is what really happened to him."

"Oh, I fully agree, Kath. No, what I find interesting is the use of the title, 'Dark Water.' Metaphorically, his real memory is telling him he's in over his head."

"Or it just underscores his literally falling into the water, losing his wallet, ruining his clothes. That reminds me," Katherine added, "if I'm going to maintain this charade, how on earth do I explain his lack of clothing?"

"If, as you say, he is supplying most of the answers himself, I suspect he'll do the same here."

Katherine drew a deep breath, knowing that although she'd told Jason the basic details of the morning, she had yet to ask the principal questions: should she tell Sam the truth about himself, and, was his continued memory lapse hurting him? And the most important question of all: how long could she continue the role of his loving wife without succumbing to the beauty of it? She drew a deep breath and asked all but the last one.

Jason paused for a considerable time, then said, "Kath, I'm still of the opinion I was last night. The kindest way to lead him back to his real memory is to let it come to him naturally."

"But isn't staying here, being a part of this . . . this—"

"Alter memory," Jason supplied.

"—*fantasy*," Katherine stressed, continuing as if he hadn't interrupted, "going to actually make it more difficult for him? He seems to be struggling to paint in details of this life. When he said he forgot about Andrew, I had the feeling that was exactly what he meant. He had *completely* forgotten Andrew even existed."

"Do you want me to come get him, Kath?" Jason asked softly.

"No," Katherine said quickly. Too quickly. Jason's silence following her swift negation was a shade too fraught with careful consideration.

"No," she said again, softer this time, less hurried, and, she hoped, thoughtfully. She couldn't tell him that she was incapable of turning Sam away now. She pulled an excuse from the air. "He didn't want a hospital last night, and we all agreed it was probably for a good reason."

"And the police?"

"Same thing," she said.

"And it's too early to call the Treasury department to see who he might be."

"Yes," Katherine agreed. "Tell me, Jason. Tell me what to do."

"Kath, you're the writer. This is something, unless you want me to come take him to the hospital—or to the police, that you're going to have to play by ear."

Like she did with wayward characters.

Katherine started to say something but Jason interrupted her again. "Look, honey, I'm not trying to be callous. Quite the opposite. But playing it by ear is about all anyone could do. I would encourage signs that his memory is reasserting itself. Try to sound natural about it. A slow, easy approach would be the best thing for Sam."

What about for her? she thought, slowly replacing the phone receiver after Jason rang off. What was the best thing for Katherine McDonald? She was too strongly attracted to him, too vulnerable to the confusion and pain she read in his eyes, too conscious of the man she encountered in his writing. And, perhaps worst of all, she was too aware that in believing himself to be her loving husband Sam, he had unknowingly triggered a long-buried fantasy of her own.

"Katherine! You're free to come in now, darling!" her would-be husband called from the kitchen, the way her fantasy lover might have called her a thousand times in a hundred different dreams.

Sighing, Katherine rose and moved toward the voice that was as real today as the feel of his hands against her skin had been in the long restless night before. She wished it could be as simple as he'd implied: that all the outs, all the secrets, could come in free. No repercussions, no more danger to him, no surprises. But most of all, no goodbyes, that somehow, miraculously, he would wake up, his memory whole, and still believe he loved her.

"Fairy tales," she muttered, crossing the threshold into the kitchen.

"What are?" Sam asked, his solid bulk blocking her path.

"What?" she replied faintly.

He raised a hand to cup her cheek. His touch seemed to brand her, yet she didn't pull away. She couldn't.

"You said 'fairy tales.'"

"Did I?"

"You did," he said softly, his voice so low she wouldn't have heard it except that he was so close to her she could feel his warm breath upon her forehead.

She knew she should step back, call Jason and tell him she'd changed her mind, that he should come and collect this stranger, this terribly mixed-up and delusion-ridden stranger. But the memory of his soul-bared words, the warmth she read in his eyes stopped her, the heat in his hand held her fast.

"I love you," he whispered. Or had her heart whispered it for him? His lips lowered slowly and met hers. He tasted of coffee and cranberries, and his tongue was hot and strong as he tasted her in return.

It was no less powerful a kiss than the one they'd shared in her bedroom, but here she was fully awake, wholly in possession of her mind, if no longer in command of her heart. This was no dream, and yet, possibly because she was totally awake the kiss carried greater impact. He'd caught her unaware before; she was completely aware now. This kiss created the impression that the here-and-now was the reality, that all else had been the dream.

Unconsciously she pressed against him, her body pliant and arching, her arms encircling his neck to draw him even closer.

This, he thought, this was what he'd been waiting for. It felt for a moment as if he'd been waiting for her complete acknowledgment of what lay between them all of his life. With her soft arms around his neck, her breasts pressing against his chest, her moist satin lips beneath his, he felt the doubts he sensed in her disappear.

He'd seen the first glimmers of her total empathy with him, the way she should be, when he'd finished reading that scene to her. And he'd seen a shocking pity or sympathy. He hadn't wanted to see it, had hated the uncertainty in her eyes. But here, now, she was his, and here she offered total honesty, complete truth. Locked in his arms, whatever was troubling her about him slipped away unnoticed, and he knew with an almost fierce exultation that she was his and his alone.

"You always will be," he murmured into her silky hair, pulling her harshly against his chest, almost as if he would draw her inside of him. He wished he could. Then he would always have her with him. It was all-important to him, he knew, that she be with him always. He'd loved her for so long now. She was the very best part of him.

"Katherine," he whispered. As if physical contact weren't enough, he needed to name his love. But how could mere words tell her she was the single most important thing in his life? How could words tell her that with her in his arms he felt safe, he felt the terrible confusion of the past few days ebb like low tide, that his entire life felt whole again, perhaps for the first time in years, or perhaps for an eternity?

This is where they both belonged, linked, body to body, hearts and minds focused solely on the other. Nothing, he vowed silently, would ever take her away from him again. Not now.

She murmured something he couldn't hear over the pounding of his heart, but he felt her lips move against his shoulder. The sensations she stirred in him combined with the memory of her naked body earlier that morning, bathed in sunlight, warmed by sleep, roused him further. His hand unconsciously lowered to draw her hips against him.

Dimly Sam heard Andrew clear his throat. Katherine stiffened slowly, as if awakening from a dream and knowing that the day held no pleasure. He released her, half-afraid to look in her eyes and see the puzzling wariness return, fearful of seeing a stranger reflected in the soft hazel lights. But he had to know, had to see.

Katherine felt a wash of color sweep across her face as she met his gaze. She knew he could read the want in her, and the confusion, but didn't know what made him close his eyes with a look that spoke of actual physical pain.

A sorrow clamped his features and his mouth twisted as if she'd struck him.

"Sam...?" she asked softly, her hand raising to his beard-softened jawline. A muscle worked beneath her fingertips and still his eyes remained closed to her.

Ignoring Andrew, Katherine asked, "What is it?"

He opened his eyes then, and Katherine could see the extent of his pain, of his hurt. She didn't know what caused it, but knew somehow it was her fault, that he'd read something in her eyes that dealt him a severe blow. Slowly her hand dropped from his jaw. He didn't reach to retrieve her fingers, and his own hands slid down her arms to lie lax at his sides. His gaze was bleak and his mouth worked as though he'd tasted the bitterest of fruits.

When he spoke, his voice was hollow and dull. "What did I do, Katherine? What in God's name did I do that makes you look at me sometimes as if you don't even know me?"

Chapter 7

Sam's words cut at Katherine, neatly slicing across the fantasy he'd instilled in her mind, honing the edge sharper against the rough edges of her heart, freeing the knowledge that she must help him restore his own memory, not encourage herself to believe his delusion.

"You didn't do anything," she said truthfully. But she had. In responding to him, in fully giving in to his kiss, she had, for one blissful moment, truly joined him in his make-believe marriage, his dream memory. He would never know how difficult it was to resist this world of his devising.

"Breakfast is ready," Andrew said in a low voice. His tone was that of sympathy, and Sam turned to look at him. The two men's eyes met and an understanding of some kind passed between them.

The bitter lines on Sam's face eased and as he stepped away from her, Katherine could see that while he hadn't forgotten the moment, hadn't fully abandoned the question, he was willing to let it ride for the time being.

Katherine looked at Andrew also, half in supplication, half in question. He met her gaze with obvious discomfort, and hunched a thin shoulder in a prolonged shrug. "Why don't we eat?" he said. He might as well have said, It's not my problem, Katie, but give the hero a break, okay?

As though drugged, Katherine sat by rote and dipped into the cantaloupe stuffed with cranberries and lemon without tasting it. The eggs were braised and smothered with hollandaise, but could have been cardboard and paste for all she ate of them. She sat quiet, not hearing Andrew's chatter, but letting his voice form a blanket around her. She tore her thick crust of French bread into a million toasted crumbs in rhythm to the beating of her heart, in syncopation to the discordant command of her mind. Sam . . . this stranger in her house. . . was in trouble. Joining him in his fantasy world wasn't doing him any good; she had to get that firmly in her own head. . . and heart. She had to guide him back to his own set of memories. Only he knew what was after him, only he knew who was safe to call, safe to employ as rescue, and it was up to her to help him find the way to that knowledge.

She sighed heavily.

"I was thinking, Katie," Andrew said, touching her arm to gain her attention, "about that research you were doing about drug trafficking?"

"Drug trafficking?" Katherine repeated stupidly. She saw Sam's head slowly turn and knew, without looking for it, a frown creased his forehead.

"You know, dear, the story that needed all the facts and figures from the *Treasury department?*"

"Oh!" Katherine said, but she got no further for Sam suddenly slammed a hand palm-flat onto the kitchen table, making everything shift several inches and causing Andrew to jump to his feet.

"NO!" Sam snapped. His eyes were flinty and his mouth was a tight line of disapproval. The violence with which he'd smacked the table must have hurt, but he showed no sign of pain. "You can't call them," he added and there was no hint of a plea in his voice. It was simply a point-blank command.

"Why not?" Katherine asked much more casually than she felt.

Sam pushed to his feet, his hands planted on the table-top, his face grim with determination. "You know as well as I do that calling Treasury would be certain death."

"Good heavens!" Andrew burst out. "Why? What could possibly be dangerous about asking about...?" His nervous patter dwindled off at the implacable expression on Sam's face.

Katherine reached out to touch Sam's hand. Her hand was noticeably trembling. "Please, Sam," she said. Her heart was furiously pounding. Jason's words echoed in her mind. *Avoid direct confrontation.* "We won't call them."

His eyes swung to hers like an angry bull's follows the red cape.

"I promise," she said.

Some of the rigidity eased from his shoulders, and Katherine's heart went out to him as a shudder worked through him. His eyes seemed to lose their sharp focus and for a few anxious seconds it appeared as though he might faint. When he again met her gaze, he looked confused and worried. He slowly straightened, lifting her hand with his as he drew them from the table.

"I'm sorry, Katherine. Andrew." He released her hand and turned away from both of them, going to the French doors leading to the patio. He stood with his head against one of the small panes of glass, his hands out to either side of the door frame as if it were all that was holding him upright. He stared at the broad stretch of lawn sweeping to the sun-dappled inlet, but Katherine suspected his eyes weren't taking in the view.

"I don't know what got into me," he said simply, devastatingly. His voice was muffled and Katherine knew instinctively that he was having trouble getting the words out, not from any difficulty apologizing, but from sheer truth in the phrase. He really didn't know.

As if unbidden, the right words came to her. Please, God, she prayed, let them be the right words. Healing words. Vague words of truth, words that could be interpreted by his fantasy, that could be heard by his reluctant memory. "Sam. Listen to me. You're going through a bad time right now. It'll be all right. You're disoriented . . . you've been shot at. It's only natural you'd be confused, that things don't seem right."

Andrew made some movement. Whether it was of protest or approbation, Katherine didn't wait to determine. She continued, warming to her theme, feeling the rightness of the words, hearing them with her heart, tasting them as they mingled with the unshed tears that gathered behind her eyelids, and rested instead upon her tongue.

Another shudder rippled across Sam's muscled shoulders and down his spine. But, though he didn't turn around, he pushed away from the window. "Is this . . . these moments that don't seem connected . . . are they why you keep looking at me like I'm a stranger, Katherine?"

A lone tear escaped and spilled down her cheek. She didn't answer for fear of the tears that might follow, for fear of the words that might pour out with them. Afraid of telling him the truth.

He turned then, his eyes tracing the path the tear had carved. He crossed the kitchen with a single step and knelt beside her chair, using the back of a shaking hand to wipe away the tear.

"You should have told me, darling. I didn't know. I'm so very, very sorry. I would rather cut off my right arm than hurt you. You know that."

Katherine had to close her eyes against the raw entreaty in his. Slowly, she raised a hand to the base of his neck and he followed the command of her fingers until his head lay

against her breast. His arms circled around her waist and
drew her closer. Tenderly, soothingly, Katherine wrapped
her arms around his shoulders and gave him, through her
warmth, through her understanding of his need, the abso-
lution he so desperately sought.

How long they might have stayed that way Katherine
would never know, but the spell was broken when Andrew
spoke. "Personally," he said, and his voice was choked and
full, "I'd keep him, and damn the consequences."

Against her, Sam chuckled. His laughing breath expelled
directly through her silk blouse to her bare skin and tickled
her, making her smile in response. The shared laughter was
as full of portent and as potent as the few kisses they'd exchanged, and was as healthy as the concern and the few tears
all of them swallowed.

Katherine opened her eyes and met Andrew's smiling but
watery gaze. Sam pulled free and stood. His face was relaxed again, and the tension had ebbed from him as surely
as it had earlier wound in her.

"I'll be all right now," he said in such a low tone that even
Andrew, close as he was, couldn't have heard. But Katherine did and it made her both sad and perplexed at the same
time. He wasn't all right; he would be, she was certain of
that. But when he remembered who he was, he would go
away. Leaving her behind. That was the other end of the
equation. He would be all right, yes, but then she wouldn't
be.

"I know," she said, and she couldn't keep the sorrow
from her voice. He had already turned and was making his
way out of the kitchen and apparently didn't hear—or chose
to ignore—the etching of sadness in her answer.

"I'm going back to work, hon. That always chases the
demons away." He waved cheerfully enough as he departed
the kitchen, but Katherine noticed that he didn't meet her
eyes.

"Well," Andrew said.

"I don't think it is," Katherine said.

Andrew didn't hesitate a second in following her train of thought, and added a twist of his own. "It certainly has water," he answered dryly, sitting down. "And, despite the fact you've only known him a scant twenty-four hours, I'd say it looks like it might be pretty deep."

"Are we talking about wells or about Sam?"

"We're talking about you, Katie dear."

Katherine was silent for a moment, then she described the scene Sam had written that morning.

"You think this is what happened to him?" Andrew asked.

Katherine nodded.

"His boss, hmm? No wonder he didn't want me to call Treasury." Andrew paced back and forth for a few seconds, then asked, "So what do we do?"

Katherine shook her head.

"Did you call Jason?"

Katherine told him she had, and what Jason had said. Andrew nodded sagely, as if this fit with his ideas of what was going on.

"His memory is bleeding through," he said.

"I know," Katherine said bleakly.

"Katie?"

"Yes?"

"He has to have had pretty strong feelings for you in order to cling to this delusion."

"That's what Jason says," Katherine said.

"But you don't believe it."

"It's not that," Katherine answered, turning away from Andrew's pacing; it too closely resembled the gyrations her mind was trying to follow.

Andrew didn't speak for several minutes, busying himself at the sink, but when he did he totally shattered Katherine's hope that he'd ignored what had transpired between her and Sam in the doorway of the kitchen.

Setting a wet pan in the drainer, he asked, "Why did you let him out?"

"I didn't," she said wearily. "He said there wasn't a lock made that could keep him in—or out."

"How delicious for you, dear," Andrew murmured.

"Andrew."

"I'm not the one who kissed him like there was no tomorrow."

Katherine didn't answer this sally. She couldn't; it was too close to the truth.

"I meant it, Katie. If I were in your shoes, I'd keep him."

She smiled wanly. "He doesn't even know who he is," she said.

"So? Who does?"

"I do," she said. "You do."

"Do you really, Katie? And who are you?"

"I..." she began, then let the lackluster description die on her lips.

"I'll tell you who you are, Katie. You're a backseat driver." Then he unknowingly echoed Katherine's thoughts about her computer. "You're the keeper of everyone's dreams. You spin tales and stories that keep us on the edge of our seats, then you retreat to the background again, thinking of new stories, new nail-biters. But Katie, who's spinning tales for you?"

"Any other writer," Katherine answered promptly, but Andrew shook his head.

"Wrong. You read other writers like attorneys look at the opposition—with curiosity, with awe, and a lot of times with respect. But because of that, you seldom get caught by their tales. And now, someone comes along who spins such an outrageous tale, such a huge story, that you're hooked."

"I thought you wanted him out of here," Katherine said irritably.

"I did. Until I saw the way you look at him." He stopped and shook his head, holding out his hand. When she didn't put hers in it, he grabbed her hand almost angrily, holding her tightly, shaking her. "Don't you see, Katie? You're like Sleeping Beauty, and Prince Charming has finally come along and woken you up."

"This is—"

"This is what, Katie? Ridiculous? Outrageous? Or were you thinking of the word 'wonderful,' or 'marvelous'? Because no matter how it sounds to you right now, that's what it is. That's how you look, dear. You look...wonderful. You look alive. When was the last time you were thoroughly kissed? When was the last time your blood flowed through your veins like champagne?"

It never had, Katherine admitted silently. Never like this.

"Since when did you become a poet?" she murmured.

"The day I moved in here," he answered candidly, but he didn't let go of the subject that easily. "When was the last time you shivered at a touch, Katie?"

Never, she thought. Never.

Andrew sighed. "I'll tell you something, Cousin." His voice dropped and the attendant mannerisms fell away as well. "Watching you with him, I'd say that you are totally in tune with this man. I don't think you should turn your back on it. It would be a crime, Katie. A criminal offense. Listen to me, Katie. I'm speaking from experience here.

"Love, that get-you-in-the-gut thunderbolt kind of love, doesn't come around very often. When it does, you should grab it and hold on tight, because you may never have another chance. I know. I *know*."

Andrew's words made a rather macabre sense. He was right. Sam did make her feel alive, vibrantly, wholly alive for the first time in years. Her body seemed to thrum to a thready, erratic rhythm like the first signs of spring, a green blade here, a yellow blossom there, until the chaotic burstings became a symphony of growth.

And yet, her cousin was also absolutely wrong. Like the seasons' intemperate changes, what lay in wait for her, if she continued buying into this fantasy, was winter, that hard cold taskmaster who demanded gathering wood for burning, that would steal through cracks of her heart to chill and freeze.

What Andrew was advising was to seize the idea of spring and ignore winter's onerous cold. Live for the day, seize the moment, enjoy the person for now, for the present.

"I'm an ant, Andrew," Katherine said slowly. "Not a grasshopper."

He blinked once at her seeming non sequitur, then patted her hand. "Katie-me-girl, you're not the only one. We're all ants, ants who dream of being grasshoppers. But you have a chance, right now, right here, to see how the smarter few live." He let go of her hand and pushed to his feet.

Standing over her he didn't look like the philosopher he'd been for the last few minutes. He looked like Andrew, cousin and friend, confidant and supporter, cocky grin on his face, his eyes shadowed by a long-buried sorrow. He did know what he was talking about, Katherine thought.

"I don't think Aesop ever met someone who truly rattled his chain, do you?" he asked, turning for the patio door. "Except, perhaps, right before he wrote the lion and the mouse story."

"Sam's thorn is bigger than I am," Katherine said.

"So was the lion's thorn bigger than the mouse."

"Are you calling me a mouse?"

He stopped at the door and turned, a smile faintly reminiscent of Sam's curving his lips. "I won't dignify that with an answer, Katie." He opened the French doors, letting a chilly blast of autumn air sweep into the cozy kitchen. Katherine shivered.

Andrew turned back. "Oh, I almost forgot. Your thorn needs some clothes, dear. I'll pick some up. I can guess at his size." He stepped outside, drawing the doors closed.

With that he was gone, off to his bookstore, off to be his busy ant, and Katherine was left sitting alone in her kitchen, her only close relative walking away and a total stranger using her computer in her study. Andrew had given her a full plate to consider. He'd challenged her on every count, her loneliness, her desire, her life. And, if she were to listen to him, Sam held all the anodynes, the cures for what ailed her. Spring or winter? Which should she choose? Did she really have a choice?

As if in answer, Sam's voice called out to her from her study, "Katherine? Could you come in here for a minute?"

Her legs were shaking as she rose from the table and crossed the hall leading to the study, but a slow, tentative smile curved her lips involuntarily. And the smile felt curiously like a decision.

Her mind on hold, her heart pounded steadily in counterpoint time to her footsteps. Could she really damn the consequences, full steam ahead? It was unlike her, it was as unique as having insisted he stay for the night. Was that why she'd wanted him to stay, because something about him challenged all the rules, cast aside all conventions?

She drew a deep breath, thinking of Andrew's words, thinking of Sam's delusion. No, she may not have long, there might be no tomorrows, but she would take today, seize it and hold it. She would have to, for she knew instinctively it might have to last her forever.

"You called me?" she asked, closing the study door behind her.

Sam looked up from the computer with a smile. At something he read on her face, his smile slowly faded and his eyes sharpened in hot focus. As slowly as his welcoming grin had disappeared, he rose from the desk and stood perfectly still. Then a hand raised toward her, palm upward, wholly trusting, totally inviting.

"Katherine," he whispered.

"I'm here," she murmured back. If there was hesitation in her now, she chose to hide it, to bury it for the time being.

A detached sliver of her mind, the skittish, I-shouldn't-be-doing-this part of her, noted his shirt was unbuttoned to the waist and realized it must have shrunk in his plunge into the dark water he'd described in his scene. His bared chest rose and fell rapidly and the muscles across his chest seemed to ripple with tension. She couldn't seem to look away.

Seeing her framed by the closed door, taking in the acceptance in her eyes, the desire in her parted lips, Sam felt rooted to the ground. This was the look he'd waited for, craved until his mind seemed totally obsessed by it.

All morning, except when Katherine had been in his arms, he'd felt confused, disoriented. His fingers had felt at home on the computer keys, but he'd had the odd sensation of being in a trance while he wrote. And he hadn't been able to find a pen; he couldn't remember which drawer held the writing utensils. Even the office itself had felt unfamiliar. And the rest of the house seemed right and all wrong at the same time. It seemed the proper setting for Katherine, but he couldn't conjure any memories of himself in this house.

And now Katherine stood before him, her eyelids lowered to bedroom slits, her full lips soft, as though anticipating his kiss. He'd accused her of looking at him as though he were a stranger. He was the one who felt like a stranger now. He knew what she felt like, what scent would invade his nostrils, what she would taste like, yet he felt he'd never been with her before. The notion left him oddly defenseless. *Remember,* his mind insisted. *You don't have to remember,* his heart answered. *Just love her.*

He whispered her name again, almost as though confirming it, as though saying it would act as a charm to draw her closer.

It was her saying "Yes," in a soft, breathless voice that lent strength to his legs, that gave him the momentum to cross the room. He stopped in front of her, not touching her, his arms aching with the need to encircle her body, his heart slamming against his ribs at the fierce desire that raged through him. Yet still he couldn't reach for her. He'd dreamed this moment so many times, and woken only to find his hands buried in the pillows, his lips hot from wanting and missing the contact with hers.

He tried shoving the memory of these dreams and their lonely conclusion from his mind, but the torment caught him and held him. Where had he been when he dreamed of her? Why had he woken alone, mangled pillow gripped in white-knuckled hands, loins throbbing, her name upon his lips? Why couldn't he remember? Why did that memory hold more concrete reality than the dreams of holding her, the fantasies of loving her?

Katherine's breath caught. She felt she had only to touch Sam to completely fall apart. A single touch from him and the flames he'd sparked in her would leap to a conflagration. She felt it, knew it. And she felt the heat that emanated from him, this time not fever driven, unless the fever bore her name. His broad shoulders blotted the light from the patio doors, and his eyes searched her face as if unbelieving that she were actually standing before him, defenses down, the need pulsing in her veins as potent as his own.

She understood from his disbelieving expression that she would have to be the one to let him know that she was with him in thought and body. His memory, his real memory, was apparently erecting a barrier of sorts, or was it really coming to the surface, challenging his delusion, ramming home the falsity of the substitution?

With his memory so close to the surface, with the confusion and wonder warring on his face, this was the moment to tell him he was not her husband. It could turn the tide for him, she knew. A part of her raged against the idea. It was her turn, she deserved one moment with him. He was the one who incited this riot within her, he was the one who introduced the illusion. Now she should reap some reward, no matter how small.

Even as she defiantly tried to cling to these selfish wants, however, she knew it wouldn't be fair, wouldn't be right.

"We have to talk," she said. Even to herself, her voice sounded husky, as though it came from somewhere deep within her. "We . . . aren't . . . what you think we are."

The sudden fear in his eyes caused the half-formed explanation to die on her lips.

"We aren't?" he asked. Though he wasn't touching her, Katherine felt she could actually hear the pounding of his heart and had to fight the urge to lay her hand against his bare chest.

"No," she whispered. "Try to remember. . . ."

He turned then, away from her, almost making her cry out for him to stay close to her. But she remained silent, and he walked to the patio doors, his eyes locked on the blinding water of the inlet. As if scorched by his gaze, a white heron took wing, its ungainly body suddenly graceful in the broad dip of its flight.

As it had been in the kitchen, his voice was muffled, the rough-soft corduroy tones harsh with his struggle to deny the truth. "You're Katherine. I'm your husband. That's all there is to remember." One hand, resting against the doorjamb, bunched into a tight fist. "That's all that counts, Katherine. That's all that matters."

Katherine didn't reply, closing her eyes against his rigid control, leaning limply against the study door.

"I know things . . . shift . . . in a marriage, Katherine. Things can change. People can grow apart. People can die and you think you'll die, too."

Katherine opened her eyes, a poignant fear stabbing at her. He was remembering. He might not know it, might not recognize it, but in his words, in the painful tenor of his voice, she heard the memory of the time his wife had died. Just as she had known it was the truth in his writing, she could hear it in his harsh voice now.

"But you put the pieces together again. You learn that hope doesn't die, too. And I know this, Katherine. I love you more than anything on this earth. Without you ... I'm lost."

Nothing could have stopped her from crossing the room to his side. His words pierced every last defense she might have mustered. The emotion in his voice, the confusion raging within him, drove straight into her heart with the unerring accuracy of a heat-seeking missile and lodged there, tearing at her, urging her to respond to him.

"Sam ... ?" she asked, laying her hand upon his arm, applying no pressure, but willing him to face her.

He turned slowly. Sorrow etched every line, every shadowed plane of his face. Sorrow, and something else: a pained resignation. He had the look of someone who has been told that all hope was gone, that daylight would be darkness from this day forward.

Katherine couldn't lie to him, but neither could she bear the cold despair settling on his already burdened shoulders. "I'm here," she said tremulously. "I'll ... I'll help you through this."

"Oh, Katherine," he said. He closed his eyes and turned his face upward as if he'd been drowning and only now reached the surface for a pull at fresh air. He pulled her roughly to his chest, one hand cradling her head, the other pressing against the small of her back.

He rocked gently from side to side, lulling her, soothing himself. His arms around her trembled and Katherine's body shuddered in reaction. She murmured something, some acknowledgment of his warmth, of his strength, and he groaned in response and slowly released her.

She pulled back, dazedly, her eyes locking with his. Unconsciously she lifted her hand to his cheek, as if in question, or perhaps in answer. Sam raised her other hand to his chest, pressing it flat against the crisp cushion of hair, letting her absorb his heartbeat, letting her feel his ragged breathing.

"I need you, Katherine," he said steadily, and if she hadn't felt his irregular heartbeat, didn't see his jaw clenched tightly, she might have thought he said it easily, offhandedly.

"Yes," she answered, and this time it was total affirmation, no questions, no doubts.

His mouth twisted and his eyes closed again, but his head lowered slowly, gently, until his lips brushed hers. A butterfly touch, the softest of caresses, the light kiss shouldn't have inflamed her body, but it did. Her lips quivered, as though possessing independent life of their own.

Feeling the tremor, Sam pressed harder, his tongue flicking against her lips, parting them, tasting her, seeking greater access. "Yes," he rasped, pulling her closer, tightening his grip around her.

He felt as though he had died and was, by dint of her warm breath, her sweet mouth, coming back to life. Confusion was gone as were the conflicting memories. Thoughts of the past completely disappeared in the need of the present.

Katherine felt his heart thundering against her hand and her palm slid upward, curling around his neck, drawing him closer, pulling him deeper. The cranberries she had tasted on him earlier but had missed at breakfast were once again sweet and tart and seemed to embody the essence of spring. Needing more, wanting everything now, she clung to him as her knees weakened and her body turned to molten liquid.

His hands roamed freely, firmly sweeping down her back, across the curved planes of her trousers, over the indentation of her waist, sliding inside the opening of her blouse to wrap warm fingers around her breast. He lowered his mouth to a vein wildly beating in her throat and flicked his tongue in syncopated time to her heartbeat.

The maddening tongue, the hand so steadfastly massaging her breast served to render her dizzy. She felt as though the ground held no solidity, as though the only concrete thing on earth was Sam McDonald.

He withdrew his hand from her breast, and when she cried out, he raised his lips to capture the cry while his hand deftly loosed the buttons of her blouse.

Without releasing his hold around her, nor his lips' pressure upon hers, he swept the blouse from her shoulders. He stroked the suddenly bare skin first with his broad palms, then his tongue. Finally, as though unable to resist the urge to see her any longer, he drew back from her with a ragged breath. His eyes, scorching in their intensity, slowly memorized her every line. His hands lifted to the straps of her brassiere and, tantalizingly slowly, he inched the lacy material from her shoulders. When the lace cups were the only thing between their bare chests, he raised a finger to the center stays and jerked downward in a swift, impatient tug.

Her breasts, full with desire, nipples rigid with anticipation, fell free, jiggling with the sudden release, aching with the need for his touch. He didn't torment her by making her wait any longer. With a groan borne of his own need, his head bent to one breast while his hand cupped the turgid fullness of the other.

His tongue laved and his mouth suckled and his fingers imitated the excitement his lips created. Unable to think, unable to resist his demand, Katherine arched against him, conscious of nothing but the moment, the rightness of this day, the totality of his need, her need, his want, hers, this man, his mouth, his scent, his touch.

His free hand gripped her behind and drew her firmly between his spread thighs, continuing to suckle her even as he slowly rotated his hips, making her fully aware of his own desire for her.

Her hands roamed the broad expanse of his shoulders, fighting to free him from his shirt, returning to massage his cheek as he lavished attention on her bared breasts. Never had she felt so vital, never had she experienced this sense of total abandon.

With an oath, Sam released her, straightening, but before she could do more than utter a confused objection, he bent and picked her up as though she were of no more weight than a child, and strode out the door to the living room.

Katherine didn't say anything as he lightly, seemingly effortlessly, swept up the stairs. There was nothing to say. Any protests she might have once issued were long drowned in the liquid fire he ignited in her, any objections had dissipated with the first moist contact his mouth had made against her bare skin. She clung to him, trusting him as she had never trusted anyone before, wanting him as deeply as she knew he wanted her.

He entered her bedroom and deposited her on the unmade bed. A groan escaped him as he took in the sight of her hair spread around her like a golden aura, and then, as his eyes lowered, taking in the darker aureoles surrounding her hard nipples, his groan deepened until it seemed an extenuation of the ache in his loins.

Without speaking he swiftly unfastened the attached buckles on her trousers and rendered a silent prayer of thanksgiving for the fad of baggy pants. He swept them for her, and disposed of her panties with equal ease. Her blouse, still fastened at the wrists, and her brassiere, loosely encircling her slim waist, seemed to taunt him, and for an unsteady moment, he considered leaving them where they were.

But a touch of uncertainty was back in Katherine's hazel eyes, and he knew, instinctively, that though her body was languorous with desire, her mind could easily be frightened by impatience, by thoughtlessness.

A wave of doubt shook him. She was so much more beautiful than his dreams, than his memories, had let him know. And so much more vulnerable. She was real. She was here, and she was waiting for him. And him alone. Dimly, a stray memory reached out to touch him, to warm him. *I've loved Sam McDonald every day for the past ten years*.

"I love you, Katherine," he said slowly, his eyes linked with hers, his heart reaching for her.

Sternly holding his own needs at bay, he stretched out beside her and slowly, teasingly unfastened the bindings at her wrists. Using teeth and fingers together he pried the complex fastening on her brassiere free and swept both articles from the bed. They landed, he saw, on the rose he'd brought her that morning. He'd forgotten the rose.

And so much more. How could he have forgotten Katherine was so soft? How could he have forgotten that her lips were like satin, that she tasted like fine wine? His hand trembled and hers covered it with gentle question.

"I'll never forget this, Katherine," he said earnestly and then wished he hadn't said it, for her eyes closed as though she were in pain. He leaned over her to kiss away the hurt he'd unwittingly caused. *Please,* he said with his touch, with his kiss, *forgive me.*

As her lips parted, and her hands reached for his shoulders, a delicate, unsure touch, he knew he was forgiven, and in her instinctive undulation beside him, he understood that the past was only that, felt her wish that the present be all that mattered.

But a part of him insisted that he lock this firmly in his mind. He pulled up from her and, resting upon one elbow, he gazed down at her, his eyes tracing every curve of her glorious body.

Lying fully naked beneath his regard, her heart pounding as rapidly as a boat's engine at full throttle, Katherine raised shaking fingers to either side of his lips. Lightly she traced them, and gasped when he drew her finger inside his moist mouth, his teeth gently holding her, his tongue flicking against her sensitive fingertip.

"I love you, Katherine," he said again, around his hold on her. The harsh note of sincerity in his voice brought tears to her eyes.

"Oh, Sam," she murmured in reply, unable to voice her own emotions.

He released her finger. "This feels like the first time for us," he said unevenly.

"It is," she said, the truth searing her, the ache in her heart threatening to overwhelm her, the ache in her body a riot of urgency.

"It'll be the best time," he whispered, bending to her breasts and taking one hard nipple in a gentle mouth.

"Yes," she agreed, running her fingers through his hair.

"One you won't forget." He paused as he transferred his attention to her other breast. "I won't let you." He said it fiercely, she thought, as though it were her memory that lay hidden in the recesses of her mind, and not his.

Raising his head, and watching her, his hands began to roam the peaks and valleys of her willing body. In one sweep his hands would firmly rub from her throat to her knees and back again. He stroked her as though he were an artist and she were the canvas, lovingly, fully, and with infinite attention to detail. Rising to straddle her legs, his fingers danced along her skin, painting her with emotion, covering her with all the love he claimed to feel for her.

When she began to squirm beneath him, he exchanged his lips for the paths his hands had discovered, nipping here, suckling there, trailing feather-soft kisses along her thighs, or the underside of her breasts.

Her mind lost to the moment, lost to this caring man, her heart fully engrossed with his touch, with his ministrations, Katherine reached for him, her hand fumbling with the catch at his pants, but he eased away from her, off the bed to kneel on the floor still half-dressed. Wrapping his hands around her, he drew her naked body closer, parting her trembling legs, gazing at her with raw hunger.

"Sam...?" she queried, reaching for him.

He dodged her hand, his teeth taking his lower lip in hold. "Sh-h-h," he offered, raising his hands to her moist core. At her gasp, he stilled, then lowered his head to her thigh to kiss her while his fingers resumed their gentle, liquid exploration.

Whispering words of love, urging her to fly with him, to let herself open fully to him, Sam stroked and quested, finding places that made her cry out with pleasure, made her quake with the need for him.

"Please, Sam," she begged. "Oh, please..."

Her soft voice asking for him, asking for him to enter her nearly undid him, and he had to fight the urge to bury himself in her, to lose himself in her moist embrace.

"Not yet," he rasped, his voice scarcely above a whisper. He'd seen in her eyes that she'd been afraid he would forget this time together; he would ensure that she couldn't. Resisting the honeyed assault her scent made upon his already reeling senses, he continued to work his fingers while lowering his lips to taste her. She bucked against him and her breath snagged and harshly exhaled.

His touch was as poignant and as revealing as his writing, and captivated her as surely. Her body became the instrument and he the master musician as he called note after aching, desperate note to command. With each stroke of his fingers, of his tongue, she lost a bit more of herself to the overpowering symphony he created. Higher and higher she rose, and with each ascending crescendo of pleasure, came nearer and nearer to losing herself completely to the greatest music she'd ever encountered.

"Come with me...." she called out, no longer able to see, no longer able to hear anything but the notes he commanded.

When her legs began to quiver and her muscles tightened around his fingers spasmodically, and she clutched his shoulders as though she were drowning, his control shattered. Keeping his lips upon her, his fingers swiftly removed the last barriers between them.

Slowly he raised his head and, as though from miles away, Katherine saw his face, his eyes glassy with supplication, his jaw rigid with need. And the hunger and need were for her and her alone.

"Oh, yes," she murmured, opening her arms and welcoming him to her. With a cry of his own he entered her, filling her, hard and strong, hot and driven. He stopped, poised above her, his eyes closed, his mouth open as though in exquisite pain. Then he slowly pressed forward, deeper, slowly, then faster, then faster still.

Circling his legs with her own, arching to meet him, pressing against him, Katherine urged his completion, urged him to experience what he had given her, gave him her body with all the trust and love she'd never given anyone so completely before.

Cradling her to him, holding her fiercely, his buttocks rigid beneath her hands, he whispered his love for her, his aching need of her. He kissed her, and rocked her, and pleaded for words from her, words of love, words of promise.

And without lying, without thought of tomorrow or a thousand tomorrows, Katherine gave him the strength he needed, the music he wanted to hear.

"I'm with you, Sam," she murmured. "I'll be here for you as long as you want me." And it was the truth. At that moment, at this time, he had pulled all stops from her, had reduced all life's little immediacies to the mundane realities they were. Only this, only Sam, held any real meaning. "I love you," she whispered, tears of wonder forming in her eyes.

As if these three words were the trigger, Sam convulsed, calling her name, driving ever deeper into her until his body went rigid. He shook her, inside and out, with the fury of his release and it sparked an answering release in her. And, suddenly, without warning, Katherine joined him, not in a symphony, but in a raw, wild thunderstorm that could only be nature's creation. Together they spun on the hot winds of the desert, rode the raging lightning of a savage cloud, clung to each other through the tumultuous aftermath.

And together they returned, bodies locked, minds strangely in tune, hearts, for once, at peace. It was only later, when her thunderous heartbeat had slowed, when Sam sighed and pulled her tightly beneath him, cushioning her with his hands, his weight displaced to his elbows, his breath playing against her temple, that Katherine felt the stirrings of the reality of what she'd done. She may have forgotten that tomorrow existed, may have ignored the truth of it, but it would come whether she acknowledged it or not.

"I love you," Sam said softly. "I'll always love you. I always have. I always will."

It was tomorrow now.

Chapter 8

Katherine let the water from the shower wash the day's illusions away. Naked, clean, water sluicing over the body Sam had so lovingly tended earlier, Katherine felt totally stripped of all fantasies. Something about the familiar rhythm of the water droplets slapping the shower curtain, the lathered soap in her hands, the herbal scent of the shampoo, these all combined to spell normality in her mind.

The man sleeping in her bed, his face once again the hard features of a stranger, was in some kind of trouble. In some kind of danger. That she'd allowed herself to be lured into believing his fantasy, his delusion, wasn't his fault. It was hers. They'd loved, laughed, talked as lovers talk, stopping to eat once, pausing to sleep twice. They'd showered and fallen back into bed again. It was a day out of context, a day out of rhyme. There were no days to compare it to; it was simply as if time itself had stopped and given them this one day together, a gift of magic, a single loving frame for a wonderful fantasy. Sam had said he needed her, and Katherine believed that he did.

He quoted poetry to her, and told her a joke or two, had told her a story of a man he once knew who could accurately describe the exact heritage of a person just by hearing that person's voice, and this man could tell what town, what part of any of the fifty states that person came from. His memory bled through and gave her glimpses of the man Sam had been for the past forty years.

And his eyes had been warm with humor, hot with passion, and tender with loving as he carefully, skillfully searched her body, her mind, for clues to her inner identity. He'd tickled her, he'd laughed with her. And once, challenging a meaning of a word, he'd run downstairs to grab a dictionary, returning with a smug grin to plop the book on her bed and point to the definition in triumph.

''Think you're the only one with any brains in this family?'' he'd said and frowned when she didn't join in his laughter. He had pushed the dictionary from the bed then and stretched out beside her, drawing her into his arms, asking her what was wrong. And when she hadn't answered, he'd kissed her, and rocking her in his arms, he'd talked, low and soft, his raspy voice casting a spell on her.

The day waned as he'd waxed promises and futures, places they would go, things they would do, books they would write together, children they might someday have or adopt. He'd described a ranch in Montana where they might spend their summers, surrounded by horses and mountains, and friends who would come to stay in the bunkhouse and join them in the evenings while someone played a guitar and everyone sang songs from the sixties and drank wine from pewter mugs. His words had fallen upon her ears like newly discovered Byron lyrics, and she'd responded with the music he created in her soul.

Yes, the day had been magical, and their time together an especial enchantment, as sweet and tender as his touch, and as beautiful as the illusion he was living in, was giving her.

But now, with the water beating upon her, with the clock once again in motion, she had to face the truth. All the pretty dreams and promises were nothing more than just that: dreams and promises. Wishes borne of love, of desire, as elusive and incorporeal as the wind, as the soul. He wouldn't even remember them, nor ever remember having proffered them to her, promises empty of all but the one most precious of gifts, love.

He'd said he needed her, and it was true. But he needed her as a cool hand on a fevered brow, as a soothing ointment on an open wound. He needed her to guide him back to himself, not as a willing party to his fantasy.

She'd been the one who needed that. Who wanted it, wanted him. She still did. A quiet, implacable voice in her heart said that she always would. This was the voice she had to ignore, because the *stranger* lying on her bed, who was a stranger no longer, needed his own memories, his own life, to combat whatever it was that was out there. For himself, for his sanity, and perhaps most important but feeling only secondary, to save his life from this mysterious gunrunning boss.

As if the water splashing against her shoulders and pooling at her feet had somehow magically stripped away the rationales and the half-formed dreams, Katherine saw clearly that the time for fantasies was over. Sam's memories had to be brought to the surface. He had to be able to assimilate them so that he could be safe, mentally and physically.

Perhaps, she wished, their time together would make this blending of memories easier for him. Perhaps knowing that his delusion had been shared, that it had captured her as well, would make him accept the inevitability of having to face his own world, his own life. But she knew that no amount of wishing would make this a certainty.

As if her thoughts had called to him, woken him from his dreams of his other life, Sam pulled back the shower cur-

tain, a solemn expression on his face. As if he were aware of
her thoughts, he shook his head. His eyes were so filled with
a bleak despair, Katherine felt a stab of fear. Had his memory returned?

Despite her awareness that his memory had to return, and
contrary to her earlier resolution that she must encourage it
to come back, she couldn't help the piercing dismay that
swept through her.

So soon? she thought, and on the ragged edge of that inner cry, she again fought against the sense of unfairness
about their lack of time together. She wanted more time.

Forever. That's what she really wanted from Sam Mc-
Donald. Forever.

"We've got to talk," he said. His face was closed, his
voice dull.

The pain in her heart grew and gripped her with great fe-
rocity. No, she wanted to whimper. It's too terribly soon.

He stepped into the shower, into the water, into her arms.
She clung to him as though she could hold him there against
her for a lifetime, keep him from his memories of another
life, one without her. And he held her tightly against him,
as though this time he was following the lead of *her* fantasy, *her* delusion.

And it seemed to Katherine that the warm water caressed
them like a midsummer rain, like sorrow-laden tears, like
yesterday's promise.

"Katherine...?" he said, stepping back a pace, and
running his wet hands down her arms to take her fingers in
his. It was a simple gesture, a gentle one, and it should have
made it easier for her to bear his returning memory, but it
didn't. If anything it clarified the desire she felt for him, the
desire she knew wouldn't fade. And it was both desire for his
touch, and desire for his company. *Forever.*

"Please," she said, and had to turn her head from the
question in his eyes.

He lifted a finger to her chin to make her face him. "What is it, Katherine?"

What could she possibly say to him to make him understand her ambivalent wants and needs? She wanted him to stay with her, as the Sam McDonald who believed himself to be her husband, the man who loved her absolutely without trying to know the inconsequential details of her life, who loved her simply and honestly because he wanted to, and she knew he needed to be the Sam McDonald who was a stranger to her.

"Y-you said we needed to talk," she said, finally, hopelessly.

Awareness lit his eyes and a soft, rueful smile curved his lips. "Oh, Katherine. Did you really think it would be something awful?" His arms wrapped around her and pulled her close, and slowly he turned her around so that the water beat against her shoulder blades.

"Never, darling. Never. I could never say anything to hurt you. Don't you know that by now?"

Joy leapt in Katherine, buoying her, lifting her, giving her hands, her body new life. And knowing that the joy was selfish, was wrong, didn't make it subside one iota. Around and around in her heart the joy danced, singing, spinning on one refrain: *His memory hadn't returned.* Tomorrow wasn't here yet, she still had today...tonight. She still had Sam. For now, if not forever.

She hadn't had to utter the plea in her heart, the cry that asked for more time, for one more night. He was giving it to her.

As he rocked her, turning her this way and that beneath the hot jets, passion flared in her, and involuntarily her hands tightened their grip around his waist. His body was familiar to her now, as if they'd been together all of their lives. His hands were like old friends, knowing everything about her, his scent seemed to have always been in her nostrils, in her heart, and his salty taste would remain on her tongue forever.

Against her she felt his body responding to the gentle exhortation of the water, to the arousal growing in her, in him. She saw desire in his eyes, felt it in his hands, felt him against her.

Raising her, lifting her in his arms, he pressed a thigh between hers, parting her legs. Water ran between them, sliding over both of them, rousing her, rousing him. She wrapped her legs around his waist and leaned back from him, holding onto his shoulders. His hands cupped her breasts to the water, to his mouth, as he entered her again.

"This," he said, hands roaming from her breasts to firmly grip her behind and hold her tightly against his rocking loins, "this is what I wanted to talk about." A rumbling laugh shook him, a laugh of triumph, a laugh of communion, an open acknowledgment of satisfaction.

"I can't get enough of you," he said and his upward thrusting intensified, and increased her own rotation. "I'll never get enough." His voice was muffled as he again took a hard nipple between his teeth.

Katherine felt lost in sensation, the hot water, the cold tile, his hot mouth, his driving need for her, his burning want, his rough hands, his soft wet beard, her want, her need, her all-consuming ache. And suddenly she was spinning, more lost than ever, in a wet world of his creation, an infinitely broad galaxy of imploding convulsions. And somehow he found her there, wrapped warm arms around her and soothed her back, talked her through the shattering fragmentation of her mind and heart, of her very soul. Words of love, of respite, of repletion mingled with the water against her ears and took permanent root in her heart.

"Don't ever leave," she murmured against his shoulder, willing him to understand, knowing he wouldn't, but needing to say the words anyway.

"No," he said. "I couldn't."

But his words sounded hollow, as if even he knew he was lying to her. He kissed her fiercely then, swallowing any words she might have uttered.

It was dark when Katherine came back downstairs. Her brow was furrowed, but a smile lingered on her lips. Sam was still sleeping, his body fully relaxed, the harsh lines completely gone from his face. From the shower, where they had lingered to wash, to talk of the things all lovers talk about, the little things each cherished in the other, they had moved to the bedroom and again found a solace of sorts in each other's arms.

It was the memory of this that made Katherine smile, the knowledge that they had communicated so thoroughly and so intimately on all levels... all but one. And it was this one, the awareness that Sam had participated fully and completely while not of his own mind, that brought the furrows to her forehead.

She was hungry and confused. Food would answer the first need, but nothing short of Sam's memory staying locked inside him could answer the second.

She was halfway through a microwaved ham and cheese sandwich, a psychology book she had pulled from her storehouse of reference books opened to a section dealing with the memory, when Max's excited barking and a clatter at the front door sent her hurrying down the darkened hall to the entry. She was conscious of her damp hair and total nudity beneath her thick, terry housecoat. To her mixed relief, it was Andrew, yelling for her to let him in and for Max to stop it. She opened the door, letting in a blast of chill autumn air and a swirl of gold and red leaves. He brushed past her, a slender, cold reality carrying a mountain of crackling plastic and paper bags.

He went straight to the living room, Max happily padding behind him, cold tail pounding against Katherine's bare legs.

"What's all this?" Katherine asked, clicking on an end-table lamp. The golden glow lit the room and chased shadows to the corners.

"Clothes, Katie. Clothes. I charged them to you. He's claiming to be your husband, after all." Andrew dumped the contents of several bags onto the sofa—the sofa where Sam had lain the night before, she thought and then wondered if everything would seem colored by Sam's presence.

Andrew stood back to wave a hand at them. "Aren't they marvelous?" He turned to see what she thought and his wide grin slipped. His eyes dropped from her flushed cheeks to her bare feet and came back up again.

"Please don't say anything," Katherine warned.

He rubbed his reddened hands together. "I wouldn't dream of it, Katie-girl. I wouldn't dream of it," but his eyes said it all anyway.

"I suppose I shouldn't ask how much all this cost," she said dryly.

"No. I'll let it be my little secret. Until the bill arrives, of course. I just hope it all fits." He swung a final bag from his shoulder. "And here's some man-type toiletries. Razor, shaving cream, fresh bandages, his filled prescription, stuff like that. I suppose I should have brought them home earlier."

"I'll carry them upstairs," Katherine murmured, taking the proffered bag before sweeping up an armload of the assorted clothing, and pointedly ignoring Andrew's speculative expression upon the disclosure of Sam's new sleeping quarters. She whisked past him and out of the room, hating herself for the telltale blush that stained her cheeks.

Once in the semidark bedroom, she deposited the clothes on an armchair and considered waking Sam. But he looked peaceful for the first time since she'd met him. And a smile played on the corner of his mouth. Whatever he was dreaming, she had no desire to tear him from it. And while he was asleep, she could maintain the fantasy that much longer. When he woke, he could well be a stranger.

She dressed quietly, in a loose sweater and her baggy trousers, and slipped downstairs to find Andrew.

He was sitting at the bar in the kitchen, blandly consuming the remainder of her sandwich, reading the segment on the memory. "Do they fit?" he asked around a mouthful of melted cheese and ham, not looking up.

"He's still asleep," Katherine said diffidently, going to the bread box for some French bread and then to the refrigerator for other sandwich fixings.

"And is his memory still at large?"

Spreading ham, cheese and an assortment of fresh cut vegetables onto the tiled counter, Katherine sighed. "Yes. As far as I know."

"This is interesting," he mumbled. "Listen to this. 'There is evidence that forgetting can be initiated within an individual by his hopes, feelings, desires, anxieties, and frustrations. This type of forgetting, therefore, is referred to as *motivated* memory trace loss, or more specifically *repressive forgetting.*' And here's a story about Herr Y who consistently forgets Herr X's name, because Herr Y used to love Herr X's wife. Well, that's interesting, but not very conclusive. Oh. Wait, this next part is."

Katherine stacked another sandwich and slid the plate into the microwave. The hum of the machine made Andrew read all the louder.

"Here it is. 'The unconscious process of excluding unpleasant or unwanted thoughts is *repression.*' Get this, Katie. 'When part of one's personality, or *memory,* has been subjected to electromagnetic shock or extreme anxiety, it can become dissociated or separated from the rest of the personality.' Bingo. And, blah-blah-blah . . . 'Extensive memory loss—called *amnesia*—creates a *fugue* state.'"

Andrew continued to read, silently, ignoring the ding of the microwave. Then he shook his head. "Uh-oh. Bad news,

Katie. 'The individual in a fugue state does what many of us would like to do upon occasion—forget everything and get away for a while. Upon recovery, the earlier events are well remembered, but those occurring during the fugue state are usually forgotten....'" Andrew's voice trailed off as the implication of the words sank in. He turned apologetic eyes in her direction.

"I'd already read it, Andrew," Katherine said dully. "And Jason implied as much last night." Had it only been last night? It seemed lifetimes ago. And last night she hadn't known it would hurt so much. Last night she had been kissed by Sam, but hadn't yet traveled universes and galaxies with him. She hadn't fallen in love with him then.

"Katie...?"

"Yes?"

"I've had a lot of time to think this morning. I'm not so sure what I said at breakfast was good advice."

"It's a little late, Andrew," she said, pulling the plate from the microwave and setting it at the far end of the bar so it could cool. She pulled a slender bottle of wine from the rack beside the pantry and held it up for Andrew's inspection.

He nodded absently and went back to his supposition while she opened it. "No, I mean, what about this boss of his? If that scene he wrote is really what happened, and like you, I think it did, then this guy has already had two potshots at Sam. What's to stop him from coming around here?"

"He doesn't know where Sam is," Katherine said.

"No? He found him in the alley behind the bookstore."

"He may have followed him there."

"What's to stop him from coming here?" Andrew repeated.

"We lost him. Besides, he doesn't know us. He doesn't know where Sam is."

"Come on, Katie. That was a fairly public book-signing event. All he has to do is put two and two together, and I'd say that judging by Sam, Treasury doesn't hire any fools. Crazies, maybe . . . sorry." He held up his hand as though warding off a blow, but accepted the glass of white Rhine wine she was holding out for him. "Or for that matter, all he has to do is track down the license plate number from my car. Which, by the way, is in some serious need of repair."

Katherine waved away the last part of his statement, but addressed the former. "What are you recommending?" She sipped at her own wine.

"For starters, I think we should call the police."

Sam's voice exploded from the kitchen doorway. "No!"

Both of them whirled to face him. He'd entered so silently, neither one of them had heard him. He was wearing a shirt, a sweater and a pair of slacks that Andrew had purchased, and had shaved. The blue in the patterned sweater enhanced his deep blue eyes, and the clean planes of his face accentuated the tough image the growing beard had thinly disguised.

He had changed the damp bandage and a new dry one was plastered raffishly across his left eyebrow. He looked good, certainly, but his appearance disturbed Katherine, for despite the handsome features, he looked hard, uncompromising. Her overall impression of him was one of total determination, a face obdurate in decision, rigid in anger. He was a complete departure from the man who had shared her bed, who had lovingly explored her every dream. A stranger.

"Sam?" she asked, as though he were indeed someone else.

"No police," he snapped, stepping through the swinging door into the kitchen, letting it go with a fierce shove, sending it sweeping back and forth as if it too were unable to contain anger without physical motion. Max barked from the darkened hallway.

"I told you," Sam raged. His words were an accusation, his eyes blazed with cold fury.

Andrew's gaze darted to Katherine's, filled with questions, offering too many answers.

Had his memory returned? Katherine wondered, not knowing how to ask, not able to formulate a cohesive string of words.

Sam walked to the refrigerator, yanked it open and closed his eyes when all the condiments on the door threatened to spill out. He drew a deep breath, let the door swing shut again, then said evenly enough, "All I need is some time to work things out."

"What?" Katherine asked. "What things?" Where was he in this fugue state Andrew had described? On the side that believed himself to be her husband, or the other?

He turned to her then, his eyes cloudy, his mouth a tight line. "It's something left over from the old days, something that was unresolved when I left the Agency."

Katherine was afraid to maintain contact with him, so intense was the relief and fear that swept through her. He was still *her* Sam, but his memory was trying desperately to provide realistic answers for his confusion. She drew a shaky breath and glanced at Andrew. He was looking at her pointedly.

He was right, she thought, correctly interpreting his message. Now was the time to probe at the wounded memory. It was close enough to bleed through his current delusion, and Sam needed the abilities and skills this memory possessed if he were to deal with this murdering chief of his.

But it was so hard to probe, to push him to remember, because, in all likelihood, he would then forget her, forget their time together. Katherine looked down at her clenched hands and asked quietly, "What...was it you left... unresolved?"

"It's nothing I can't handle." He began opening and closing cabinets, muttering to himself when he didn't find what he was looking for.

"What was it?" she persisted.

"Where the hell are the damned wineglasses?"

Katherine pointed at the inverted glass rack, not five inches from Sam's head, crystal bowls pointed toward the floor. He stared at the contraption for a full three seconds before slipping a glass free.

"That's not what I meant," Katherine said slowly, watching as he poured a generous splash of wine into the glass. "I wanted to know what it was you say you can handle."

"I don't want to drag you into it," he said.

She looked at him in shock, but it was Andrew who voiced her thoughts. "Not drag her into it? For heaven's sake, she's already *in* it, up to her neck! And you can have a look at my car sometime, if you want to see how involved I am."

Sam smiled at that, adding fuel to Katherine's ire. "Granted. But only because we're married." He raised his glass at Andrew. "And we happened to have been in your car. The less you both know about it, the safer you are."

"The hell with my safety," Katherine stormed, drowning Andrew's protest. "What about yours? What exactly are we talking about here?"

Sam's expression altered as he stepped over to her. "Your safety is the only thing that matters, Katherine."

"No, it isn't," she said even as she wondered how he managed to steer the conversation away from the main point every time. If she really were his wife, wouldn't she demand to know what was going on? Wouldn't she insist that he tell her everything?

She leaned away from his outstretched hand and said much more coldly than she felt, "I have a right to know what's going on. Tell me now, Sam."

He sighed and his hand dropped back to his side. "I can't, Katherine. I'd tell you if I possibly could, but I just can't. It has nothing to do with not trusting you, or wanting to keep you in the dark, but this is too risky. If you knew anything, *anything* about it, your life could be in danger."

"Why?"

He looked surprised, then frowned. "Let it go, Katherine. Please. I promise you that nothing could ever take me away from you. Not some leftover assignment, not Pete, not even George."

"What?" she asked, the fear once again gripping her. Was it now? Was his memory going to return right now?

He shook his head again. "Nothing. Forget it."

"Are you going to forget it?" she asked pointedly.

He gave her an odd look and frowned. "Of course not," he said. He uttered a half laugh, but it sounded false at best.

"What are you planning to do about it?"

He was silent for a long moment, then he smiled. "Nothing right now," he said, reaching for the second sandwich Katherine had made. "Except eat." He raised the plate in partial salute and with the wineglass in his other hand used his shoulder to push his way out of the kitchen.

"Get back, Max," he said on the other side.

Andrew and Katherine were both absolutely quiet as the door to the study opened then closed again.

Andrew was the first to break the silence. "If we were to call the police, dear, what would we say anyway? Hello? Police? We have this amnesiac stranger in Katherine McDonald's house. Yes, the writer. This guy's name is Sam McDonald...no, not the writer...and he's sporting a bullet wound from some unknown source. Oh, and by the way, this same unknown source—who we *think* is actually Sam's boss, because of a little scene Sam wrote earlier today—may or may not have killed someone else. No, no. This isn't *the* Sam McDonald the novelist, because *the* Sam McDonald doesn't exist. Why was he writing, then? Because he *thinks* he's Sam McDonald the novelist. Can't you just picture what the sergeant would tell us?''

''I'm going to call Jason,'' Katherine said.

''Why?''

''To find out what to do next?''

Andrew pushed the psychology book her way. ''It's all in here, Katie. Read it and weep.''

Katherine considered sweeping the book into the trash bag, thought about various tortures she could arrange for Andrew, and ended by putting her chin on her hand and staring out at a random stream of light shimmering on the night-drenched inlet, ignoring her cousin, trying to ignore the knowledge that the confrontation with Sam McDonald was inevitable. Trying, but not succeeding.

''I'm off, dear. Leave Max at large tonight. At the very best he's a good alarm.''

''I always do,'' she said without looking away from that one patch of bright water. Her mind kept contrasting Sam, the lover, with Sam, the tough, confused agent. Both had their rightful place, but only one could survive. And in order for Sam to be safe, to be whole, he had to allow the agent to surface fully.

But would that make him truly happy?

And where would that leave her?

She sighed heavily and reached for the psychology book.

Sam's fingers shook as they struck the keys. Six questions appeared on the screen, questions he couldn't answer, questions that spiraled around and around in his mind like a vulture circling a dying animal.

He drew his hands to his lap, idly scratching at the unfamiliar and stiff pants, and read the screen, viewing the questions as though they were typed in a foreign language. He read them aloud, slowly, frowningly.

''Who is Pete? Why does he seem so familiar to me? Who is George? Why do I feel as if I know everything about him, but can't conjure even his face? Why does the name Devra pull such a wave of sorrow? And, why can't I remember anything about Katherine except some interview-type scenes and the fact that I love her?''

Who was Pete? Why did saying his name aloud trigger thoughts of danger, fear and an overwhelming hatred. The name tasted of betrayal and loneliness. Why?

And George. He said the name aloud and instantly a flood of memories came washing through him, scalding him, searing his heart, his mind. But he couldn't place them in his life. George had no place in his life. Sam knew that absolutely; he had been a covert operative for the CIA, and had operated alone. So, why this torrent of memories of a man named George who had been a partner and friend? Trying to answer the question filled him with frustration and a keen sense of loss. It made him feel as though his best friend had died.

Devra. He knew the name, could see her pixie face. She had possessed that rich red color of hair that glinted fire in sunlight and deep burgundy by moonlight. He could hear her voice, a throaty burr that made her sound as if she were always on the verge of laughter, accusing him of not teasing her anymore now that she was ill. He knew her birthday and the day that she remodeled the kitchen after having been so angry that she'd kicked a cabinet door in, and then tried to hide it by tearing the rest of the cabinet doors off their hinges and repainting everything a bright turquoise-blue. She had a mole just above her belly-button, a beauty mark that she'd once been embarrassed about. During her illness, the mole had disappeared as the chemotherapy had changed her features. And her fine auburn hair had fallen out. And she had died, her throaty laughter gone, her hot temper forever lost.

Fear gripped him anew and shook him. He knew these people, knew them intimately, they seemed as real and as close as though he could turn around and see them, touch them now, yet they also seemed distant, belonging to some-one else. Cardboard, and yet not.

He knew Katherine. And he knew the books they had written together. His head swiveled to the bookcases and saw the many copies of the various titles running along the middle shelves. So why couldn't he remember writing them? He remembered every line, every nuance, but couldn't re-call a single day when he'd worked alongside Katherine, typing in the words, plotting out the next book. He could remember reading them, enjoying them, but couldn't seem to conjure a single instant of involvement with them be-yond that.

Was he really suffering a concussion, or was he going in-sane?

He ran a hand through his hair and hesitated over the bandage. He winced as his fingers probed the sensitive wound. That psychiatrist, Jason something-or-other, the guy with the yellow bag, he'd said it was a bullet wound. Sam couldn't remember being shot. How could someone forget something like that? They couldn't, unless they were insane.

Or unless they had amnesia.

But he didn't have amnesia. He knew who he was, he knew he was married to Katherine. It was just that some-times Katherine looked at him as though he were a stranger. Why? Because he was acting like one. He wasn't the same Sam McDonald that he used to be with her. But how had he been before? Why couldn't he remember? Why?

None of his clothes had been in the house when he woke this morning. The clothes and toiletries he'd found this evening were all new, the tags still on them.

And Katherine had palmed him off in the guest room. Had he been gone a long time? How long would it take to totally remove all of his effects, to totally strip the house of all memories of him? Long enough so that nothing looked familiar. Nothing at all.

Why had he been gone? Why didn't anything seem familiar?

Katherine did. He clung to that. Katherine was familiar. He knew her. And she'd welcomed his embrace, had responded with glorious abandon to his touch. Yes, he knew Katherine.

And Max. He remembered Max...but it was more Max's name that he recalled, not the dog himself. He didn't remember getting Max, didn't remember ever running with him, didn't even know where the dog food was kept. But he remembered the brand of his food. Why?

What kind of special madness gripped him? Had he been drugged? Brainwashed? Or had he really gone insane?

Nagged with the unanswerable questions, restless with the sense of guilt and frustration they produced in him, he whirled from the computer and went to the bookcase. He didn't even recognize all the books, though he'd read many of them. But he had never purchased any of the classics in hardback, and the copies here were all older, cloth-bound books. Pulling one down, he saw that it was inscribed to Katherine, with a twenty-five-year-old inscription: For Katherine, may the writing bug that bit you stay with you always, John.

Sam slowly closed the book and replaced it, running his hand along the spine. He had a sudden image of himself sitting in a dorm room his first year of college reading that same book.

But he couldn't remember what college, or who his roommate had been. The boy was just an insubstantial shadow in a corner of a dim room. Had that been when he'd decided to become a writer, or had it been earlier, as Katherine's bug had been? Why didn't he know these things, when he could remember the feel of the chenille bedspread in the dorm room, could remember the smell of his roommate's cigarettes?

His eyes searched the many books for one on the mind. He found one on coping with rage, another on Irish folktales, and still another on biology. A single gap in the rows of books lay between a college chemistry text and a handbook explaining guns. Instinctively, Sam knew this would be the book he was looking for.

The fact that it was missing caused his heart to constrict. Katherine was way ahead of him. She knew something was wrong. He'd seen it in her eyes, felt it last night in her uncertain touch. Dear God, what must she be thinking? he wondered. She loved him, he knew that, he felt it, had tasted it in her kiss, discovered it anew in their lovemaking, but she had to be almost frantic with worry. He'd seen the fear in her eyes when he'd insisted she and Andrew not go to the police and hadn't been able to explain why not. He couldn't have explained; he didn't know why not himself.

That had been when the names Pete, George and Devra had slipped into his mind. They were the reasons why Andrew shouldn't call the police, but he didn't know who *they* were. If only he could explain all of this to Katherine in a way that wouldn't scare her half to death, he knew she would understand, would try to help him. But how could he tell her he didn't remember the smallest of details about their life together? How could he tell her that he remembered this unknown Devra's birthday but couldn't come up with Katherine's?

He raised unsteady hands to his head and clasped it, as though he could squeeze the answers free.

And an answer came.

What if these people he didn't know, yet knew intimately, were characters for a book? They could be. It didn't answer the questions that chased around his mind as to why he wouldn't know what and who they were, yet know everything about them, and it didn't explain why he couldn't remember any details of his life with Katherine, but it could address those three names, Pete, George and Devra.

He swiftly crossed back to the two-drawer file cabinet nestled beneath the desktop and to the left of the computer. He pulled out the top drawer and scanned the thick manila file folders lying there. The tenth folder yielded the results he sought. It was marked Character Sketches.

He pulled the file from the drawer and slowly pushed the cabinet closed. He sat for several seconds without opening the file. What if Pete, George and Devra weren't hidden in this thick folder?

And worse, what if they were?

Slowly, hating himself for the need to look, the need to explain his irrational memory, he opened the file and began reading.

He recognized most of them. Here was Michael, who had been the lead in the first McDonald thriller. And Jeannette, the counter-spy in the third novel. And David James, the tough cop who had seen one too many murderers get off on a technicality and took the law into his own hands. And Sandra, the eager young executive who discovered a drug ring by tracing a twenty-five-cent discrepancy in a phone bill. But there was no George, no Pete and no Devra.

Setting his jaw, he pulled one of the sketches from the folder and using it as a model, lost himself in typing into the computer what he knew about the three elusive characters. He typed for hours, never hesitating, his fingers flying over the keyboard, his mind spilling forth copious amounts of information.

Anger drove Sam's fingers as he typed in the words describing Pete. He was a bastard disguised as a chief, a murderer in a statesman's suit. The .38 police special he always carried seemed like a one-eyed terrorist. His white, immaculately groomed hair that had once seemed so much a part of the kindly, classic appearance, sounded part and parcel of his overall invidiousness by the time Sam was finished writing about him.

Exhausted, drained, feeling as if he were a conduit for someone else's memories, someone else's emotions, he nonetheless continued.

George was harder to describe. He had no last name, and Sam couldn't seem to think of the color of his eyes. But George loved candy bars and football games. Washington Redskins, in particular. He drove an ancient and battered Oldsmobile that at one time had been a shiny green, but was now a faded gray. His birthday was in June, making him a Gemini, which was logical, George often said, because he constantly ate for two. He was divorced—and Sam could even come up with his ex-wife's name: Dolores—and had two kids, George Junior and Jennifer. George Junior was ten and Jennifer was eight. The last time George had visited them in their home in Miami, he'd taken them to an amusement park. He'd brought back a cartoon character watch and had worn it ever since. Jennifer had given it to him.

Sam's fingers faltered, writing about George, and his breathing grew ragged. Tears blurred his eyes once, as he wrote something George said of his two kids, something about having never once regretted having children. "The day they are born, you discover some other place in your heart, a new place, a special room. And it's filled with nothing but pure love."

He knew so much about this George, yet knew nothing at all. And in writing about him, he found he missed him, missed him like hell. And didn't know why.

Finally, he forced himself to write about Devra. Even the mere whispering of her name caused him pain. *Devra.* Lovely, sweet Devra, the laughing girl that lit her parents' life, the gamin pixie that married young and died young. She brought life a special meaning and when the cancer had claimed her, it seemed the sun had gone with her. Everyone who knew her had loved her. Everyone who came in contact with her had smiled. She'd had that gift of making people seem better than they had been only moments before meeting her, and left them permanently altered by knowing her. And when she had been dying, her beauty stripped by the cancer that ate at her, she had held her husband's hand and told him not to cry for her, that she'd had her time and loved every minute of it. She couldn't bear it, she'd said, if he ever looked back in regret.

"Oh, Devra," Sam murmured, seeing not the computer screen, but a hospital room that smelled of ammonia and disease, a pale, thin ghost who looked old with pain. And he saw himself lying across her fragile, expiring body, his shoulders shaking with the sobs he fought to contain. Tears for Devra, tears for the children her diseased womb would never bear, for the Sam who couldn't save his young wife. And reading about her now, tears of sympathy for this other Sam, and tears for his own present confusion and pain, coursed down his cheeks unheeded, unchecked.

"Oh, dear Lord," he whispered, "please don't let me be crazy. Please let me remember. But don't make me remember this. Not this. Don't make this my life. I can't bear it."

He drew back from the keyboard and pushed away from the desk, burying his face in his hands, tears falling through the gaps in his fingers.

"Give me Katherine, give me anything. But not this," he cried. "No, I . . . can't . . . bear it."

Chapter 9

When her eyes grew bleary from reading and the neighbor's light across the archipelagoes had abruptly ceased, causing the inlet to suddenly become black oil instead of sparkling water, Katherine pushed away from the kitchen bar. She looked at the unfinished glass of wine and shook her head. Her shoulders ached and her body was stiff, as much from the length of time she'd spent perched upon the bar stool as from the unaccustomed activity that consumed her day. The fantasy that had consumed it.

The book, if it was to be believed, had left her little doubt where she stood. She was the bridge between Sam's fugue states. Nothing more. And she had no right to ask for more. He needed his own memories back, for his safety's sake, for his own wholeness, his health.

All evening she'd wrestled with the uncertainties in her heart, in her mind. But the passages in the psychology text were clear, and so was the urgency to rouse his errant, disassociated self.

She dusted her empty lap, readying herself for battle, squaring her tired shoulders. It was now or never, she told herself firmly. She shoved the sorrow below the surface, and consigned the butterflies in her stomach to the netherworld. She was going to go against Jason's orders and simply tell Sam he wasn't her husband. She would tell him he wasn't Sam McDonald the novelist because there was no such man. And she would tell him who she thought he might be.

And she prayed she was doing it for the best.

And hoped further that something good would come from it.

She pushed the swinging door open and crossed the shadowed hallway to the study. She opened the door without knocking and stopped in the threshold, her hand going to her mouth, her heart jerking in painful sympathy.

The sight of Sam with his face buried in his trembling hands, his shoulders shaking, the tears evident, wholly undid her.

"Oh, Sam," she said, involuntarily freeing herself from her frozen stance in the doorway. She crossed the room and wrapped an arm around his shuddering shoulders.

He tried pulling away from her, but she drew him even tighter against her.

"It's okay," she lied, tears of sympathy springing to her eyes as well. "It's . . . okay, Sam."

"No," he mumbled. "It's not *okay,* Katherine. I feel like I'm going . . . crazy."

"Oh, no, Sam. You're just confused."

He was silent for several seconds, but his shoulders stopped shaking, and he swiped angrily at his face. He stopped trying to free himself from her embrace.

"I can't remember things, Katherine," he said slowly.

"I know," she said softly.

"Lots of things. Little things. Big things, Katherine. I can't remember big things. I can't remember writing a sin-

gle book. Not one. I can't remember what you looked like
the day we married. I can't even remember getting married.
Today, last night...God, it all seems like the first time. Like
I'd only dreamed about you before and suddenly it was
real.''

"Oh, Sam.''

"I thought maybe I'd been drugged or something. I tried
blaming it on this bullet wound on my head. But I can't. I
just can't do that anymore.''

"Sam...'' Katherine said his name like a promise, and
drew a deep breath. He had to be told the truth. It wasn't
fair to him. He thought he was going insane. She couldn't
let him continue to believe that, it would only create greater
confusion.

But he continued before she could voice the words that
would tear his delusion to shreds, that would rip her own
fantasy apart.

"You asked me who Pete...George and Devra were. I
don't know, Katherine. *I don't know.* I can see their faces,
I can even hear their voices. I seem to know so much about
them, yet I can't place them. I looked in the character sketch
files and they aren't there. But they don't belong in my mind
either.'' He broke off on a half sob and thrust his head
sharply against her as he strove to drive away another onslaught of tears by looking at the ceiling. His eyes blinked
rapidly.

"I wrote some of what I know about them. And it scares
me, Katherine. It scares the living hell out of me. Because I
know more about them, the little details, the day-to-day
details, than I know about us. Than I know about you, or
Andrew, or this damned house. I don't know *anything*
about this place.''

Katherine brushed at her eyes and said before he could
interrupt her again, "You have amnesia.''

He continued as if she hadn't spoken. "I wrote and wrote,
and every word I typed seemed to bring them closer. I could

see myself in the scenes that came to mind, but it was a me I couldn't recognize. I mean, it was my face, my hands, but not my mind.''

He pushed free of her, of the chair and walked to the dark patio doors. "Have you ever woken up and not known where you were? Woken and the dream you were having lingers so strongly that your room, your bed, everything around you seems less substantial than the dream?"

"Yes," Katherine whispered.

"That's how everything feels now. Like one or the other, those people on the screen, or this life with you, one is real, the other isn't. But I'm here. I have to believe this. I have to. It's all the evidence I've got. It's all the reality I can hang on to. Like a little kid, I've pinched myself, and I'm not waking up."

He turned around. His face was ravaged and his eyes were dull with the demons chasing him, trying to make him face a life he obviously wanted to forget.

"Help me, Katherine," he said, his voice graveled with pain. "Help me."

His eyes as they met hers were tragic in their trust, in their defenselessness. His tone, as he'd uttered the plea for help, had been flat, but stark in command, harsh in his confidence that she could help him. That she would.

There were no words, no magical panacea that could salve the wound to Sam's psyche. There was nothing she could pull from some hat that would erase the unease in his soul, the disassociation in his mind. She could only slowly, gently draw him into her arms, encircle him with all of the love she felt for him, all of the sympathy, all of the bleeding empathy, and hold him so tight, so close that he might know he wasn't alone in this limbo he was suffering.

The only words she could give him were the raw and absolute truth: "I'm here for you, Sam. I . . . love you."

He clung to her as if she were the last tree in a windswept plain. "And I you, Katherine. Dear God, and I you."

* * *

A cold front swept through the Beach region that night, an icy wind whipping the leaves free of their branches, sending bare twigs to tap tap tap restlessly against the window panes as if seeking entry. Pelicans cried as reeds and rushes beat against them, chasing them from their midnight roosts, and along the inlet, boats scraped against wooden docks, seeking the freedom of the swollen waters.

Inside, beneath blankets, and snugly enfolded in Sam's arms, his body a pliant heater as it ran the length of hers and beyond, Katherine listened to the sounds of the approaching storm and thought it echoed the storm in her heart.

She'd encouraged him to sleep, to let his wearied soul rest, to let the morrow bring whatever it would, letting her touch, her lips and her promises see him through this madness, lull him to a fevered respite.

But there had been no sleep for her. Her heart, her imagination, her entire dreams of the future were wrapped up in this confused man. She was no Florence Nightingale, no Mother Theresa. She didn't want to give solace simply for the sake of solace: she loved this man. She felt the shuddering knowledge of how much course through her veins. And it did course, as Andrew had prophesied, like champagne, like the finest of fine wines, making her feel effervescent with the irregular rhythm of her heartbeat. But it didn't make her happy. Nothing could.

She'd finally fallen totally, irrevocably in love. And he would go from her life and she wouldn't even have the comfort of knowing he would think about her, remember the little things they'd said and done all day together. She would never jump when the telephone rang, her heart thudding in wild anticipation, because he would never call her. Because he wouldn't know that she'd be waiting, for a sign that he still cared.

She'd crept downstairs once, after Sam had fallen asleep, her name on his lips, his hand forming a fist around her pillow. She'd checked the doors and windows, locking them securely against the coming storm, against potential intruders. And she'd fed Max and watched as he raced around the back lawn, his winter-bred blood in love with the chill sweeping through the area, his ears flapping as he chased shadows scattered by swiftly flying clouds and an elusive moon. He'd come back, tongue lolling, eyes bright with adventure, to flop onto the rug in her study, his tail beating a tight pattern on the floor.

But all that had been hours ago, and still sleep eluded her.

Sam shifted slightly and murmured a name in his sleep. "Devra..." he said, and his voice was colored with the rich hues of sorrow, and his brow had furrowed deeply.

"Sh-h-h." Katherine cupped his cheek in her hand and whispered soothing, meaningless words to him.

"Don't leave me," he said, and though she promised not to, she didn't know if he was talking to her or if he was calling to his missing Devra. His wife, his love who had died.

When his memory returned, when he became himself again, would he, in his dream, call for Katherine, begging *her* to stay with him, to love him? Would that be her only connection with him then? A dream to be discovered on a storm-ridden night in the dim future? Would the smell of her perfume make him turn his head in an elevator, his eyes searching the women there, wondering why he suddenly thought of a house in the country somewhere occupied by a woman who had loved him so intensely on a gray day in autumn, but whose name he couldn't recall, whose face only appeared in sweat-drenched dreams?

Wishing she had the knowledge of how to lure his errant memory to wholly reassert itself while retaining all memories of her as well, Katherine stirred fitfully. Sam's hand clutched her shoulder, drawing her closer to him, his lips pressing against the nape of her neck.

"I love you," he murmured.

When his grip didn't lessen, Katherine turned to face him. His eyes were opened, clear.

"I love you, too," she said.

"You say that as if you're afraid I'll forget it."

"I am," she said honestly.

"Never," he said and raised his lips to hers. The kiss was warming, healing. It was a pledge, a vow.

He lowered his head and smiled sleepily up at her. "I love you too much to ever forget that. Without you, I'd have nothing." His eyes closed and soon his grip loosened and his fingers slid from her shoulders.

The gesture seemed a portend of things to come. Just as sleep had stolen him from her, so would his real memory. Just as the dream world claimed him now, so would his real life. And when it did, he'd forget her. She would be an elusive question mark in the morning when he woke, and he'd shake his head thinking he'd created a dream out of a television show, or the back cover of a book.

When Max started barking, Katherine's first thought was to shush him so that Sam could continue sleeping. But his barking wasn't the birds-on-the-patio bark, nor the mailman's-at-the-box ire. It was the frantic, high-pitched bark of a dog who has spotted or heard something that threatens the household. It was the bark of the intruder, the raucous, uncertain bark of alarm.

Before she could do more than cock her head and shift her gaze to the window, Sam sat up, his back rigid, the covers falling to his lap, his eyes on the opened bedroom door. He reached out and jerked open the drawer of the bedside table.

"Where's the gun?" he hissed.

Katherine frowned. "The s-study," she answered after the briefest of pauses.

He turned and shot her an inscrutable look. "I always keep it beside the bed," he said as though accusing her of something. Moving it, perhaps?

"It's in the study," she said again. She didn't add that she wasn't perfectly certain where the bullets were. She had been given the gun as a gratuity from the Fraternal Order of Police shortly after *Salt and Tears*. It was called a police special, and had been given to her in "special" tribute for her authenticity to police procedure in the story where a tough cop had gone sour, redeeming himself at the end only by self-sacrifice.

Sam looked at her for another long moment, his lips parted as though to ask her a string of questions. But he shook his head instead, his eyes cutting to the door, and the direction of Max's barking, as he swung his legs from the bed. He quickly dragged on his pants and, skipping his shirt, yanked his sweater on, already heading for the door.

Katherine imitated his actions, and followed in time to watch, from the top of the stairs, as he crept along the wall in the hallway and disappeared, a shadow melding with the darkness, into the living room.

She ran lightly down the stairs, her breath seeming to catch at each step. *He hadn't looked like Sam.* That became her heartbeat, her single thought as she pursued him. He'd looked like a stranger. Someone else.

He'd thought his gun should be by the bed, he'd looked at her as though she had no more corporeal substance than a cloud. But he'd reacted to Max's barking with instinctive, *highly-trained* responsiveness to danger.

Was it over? Was Max's frantic barking the impetus that ripped the veil of delusion from his mind?

She heard a clamor from the study and rushed through the door, calling his name, running painfully into the corner of her desk. Her office was dark, lit only by the fitful rays from the storm-clouded moon, yet Katherine could see that Sam had already located the gun. It rested in his hand like a poisonous snake ready to strike.

"Sam?" she asked over Max's continued barking.

"Where are the damned bullets for this thing?" he demanded, not waiting for an answer, but yanking drawers open.

Memory flooded Katherine and she rushed across the study, to the small cache of bullets she'd hid behind a book. She thrust the narrow box into Sam's hand.

He looked at them oddly, and then up at her.

"It's a .38 police special," he said. His tone was one of mixed wonder and accusation.

"Yes," Katherine said. She felt as if her word had been inhaled rather than the converse.

"Why?"

"What?"

Sam shook his head, but his eyes didn't lose that accusatory, distant look. He broke the chamber open and quickly stuffed the bullets into the cylinder.

"It could be another dog," Katherine said feebly.

"It's not," Sam said quietly, snapping the gun closed.

"You don't know that!" Katherine reached a hand out to detain him. He looked down at her with cold eyes that glinted in the dimmest of lights.

"Agent's intuition," he murmured, and his face, this stranger's cold face, broke into a wintry smile.

Katherine's hand fell from his arm as if it were the block of ice from which the chill emanated.

"Don't, Sam," she murmured, but didn't know quite what she didn't want him to do: not look like a stranger or not let go of the gentle Sam she'd grown to know... and love?

But it was Max who took the matter out of their hands by leaping at the glass, clawing the door with wild impatience, his bark almost human in his urgency to get to whatever was outside.

"Stay back," Sam commanded Katherine, slinking in a crouch toward the door and swiftly turning the knob.

When the door opened a crack, and the cold, storm-driven air whooshed inside, Max didn't wait a second. He shot through the narrow aperture, a blurred red streak flying across the patio and out into the night-shadowed yard.

His bark turned from frantic need to ferocious growl as he disappeared into the tall brush on the far right side of the house.

Katherine's heart jolted as she heard a man yell, and then stopped as the whine of a silencer scratched against the night like nails on a chalkboard. Max yelped once and then was silent.

"Max!" Katherine screamed, her mind reeling with vision, her heart convulsing with pain. She leapt forward, trying to brush past Sam.

Without turning, without so much as looking at her, he swiftly raised an arm to block her, and when she would have fought the restraint, he pushed her back, all but knocking her to the floor of her study.

"Stay down!" he barked.

"But Max—!" she cried.

"I'll get Max! And I'll get the bastard that shot him."

"Who would do such a thing?" Katherine murmured, but even as she asked it, her shocked mind supplied an answer. The answer Sam had already arrived at.

"Stay here," Sam said. "Promise me, Katherine."

"The lights," she said. "Turn on the floods."

"You do it. And stay here! Promise me."

"I promise," she whispered, scrambling away from him, reaching for the floodlight switch. Sam's hand clamped around her ankle, dragging her back down, making her cry out at the sudden, unexpected touch, the rough handling. He'd only been trying to keep her away from the window, from revealing herself.

"Please, Sam," she said now. "Please don't go out there. Let's call the police. It's too dangerous."

A grim smile cracked his face. "I do this for a living, remember?"

No, she wanted to cry. I don't remember. I don't know. "It's too dangerous out there for you."

"And for God's sake, stay away from the windows," he said, but his words were muffled, for he'd already turned his head and was slipping out the doors.

Down almost level with the ground, Sam seemed at one with the night wind as his dark sweater and pants melted into the darkness. He turned, his face drawn and his eyes black with tension.

"Be careful," Katherine said. "Please."

"I will," he said, tersely. "And you stay down. You're all I've got."

His breath expelled white and his words seemed to hang on the air for a moment, giving them greater meaning as they took concrete substance. *You're all I've got.*

It wasn't true. But, except for Andrew, he *was* all *she* had.

Her thoughts flew to her cousin. Had he heard Max? Had he heard the man's yell? The whine of the silencer? She turned and crept along the edge of her desk until the wall stood between her and the outside. She rose unsteadily and depressed the floodlight switch.

Almost immediately she heard a second, louder whine of the silencer. A chunk of flagstone, not three inches from Sam's bare foot, flew into the air, spinning a second, only to drop with a sharp snap to the patio. Sam flattened against the patio and rolled into the shadows to the right.

Jerking to the floor, Katherine frantically watched as Sam disappeared into the black thicket flanking the patio and far to the left of the trees that supported the floodlights.

She couldn't contain a whimper as she saw a man's shadow flicker across the lawn, a shadow too far from the house to be Sam's.

"Sam!" she cried, but the scream was louder within than without. She couldn't see him, she thought with horror, with fear. And with relief.

The upstairs lights in the guest house flicked on and Katherine saw Andrew twitch a curtain aside.

"Get back," she screamed at him, but even as she did so, she knew he couldn't hear her.

A shot rang out, drowning the echo of her voice, making her jump and cover her ears. The sound ricocheted on the water, and a screech of an angry egret punctuated it. A man yelled, then she heard Sam's voice, breathless and marked by fury.

Shadows, elongated and elastic, leapt in a macabre dance across her lawn, arms flailing, feet seemingly rooted to a dark thicket running away from the house. One of the shadows broke free of the thicket and it seemed, despite the silhouette's distortion, that one leg dragged heavily.

Another shot rang out, and Katherine moaned, as if the bullet had lodged between her breasts. *Sam!* she cried, and heard his voice telling her, *You're all I've got.*

Dragging herself from her position of safety behind the wall, she whirled around to the telephone. Whatever Sam had said earlier about not calling the police was off. Whatever else was involved, this was a simple matter of an intruder shooting at her house, at *Sam,* at her dog. Dear Lord, let Max be okay. Let Sam be all right.

As if her fingers moved in slow motion, she depressed the emergency number, 911, and before they even finished the identification tag, she barked her name and address.

"There's a man outside, he's already shot my dog. And now Sam's out there, and he's shooting at Sam."

The man on the other end of the phone quickly confirmed her address and said he'd have a unit at her home immediately.

Katherine hung up, her stomach in knots, her hands trembling so badly that the phone rattled beneath her hand.

"I'm sorry," she whispered. "I had to call them." As if he were there, and she were trying to explain, she thought out the reasons why she'd called. Sam shouldn't have to battle this alone. This was right in her backyard. Now the police could help. If nothing else, they could chase the in-

truder away. Perhaps catch him. And if he did prove to be
Sam's murdering boss, surely that would solve Sam's trouble, make it easier to accept his situation, make it easier to
embrace his own life.

Racing to the patio doors, crouching down, Katherine's
eyes raked the empty lawn. She could see Andrew doing the
same thing from his bedroom window. Where was Sam?
Where was the intruder? No shadows danced now, and no
shots sundered the stormy night.

Was Sam hurt, lying somewhere beyond the floodlights,
bleeding to death? Was he dead? And if he was alive, would
he come back to the house as Sam McDonald, the novelist,
or would he have regained his memory and be someone else?

The roar of a car's engine in front of her house sent her
whirling to face the door to the living room. Katherine
pushed to her feet and, at a crouch, ran through the living
room and down the hall to the front door. Wrenching it
open, she was in time to see taillights blurring as the car
fishtailed in her circle drive and then careened into the narrow country lane leading away from her house.

A loud shout to her right made her draw violently back
inside the doorway until she recognized the voice as Sam's.

He ran to the front door stoop and, hesitating only long
enough to shove the gun into her hands, dashed past her and
down the hall. Slowly following him, Katherine watched as
Sam once again disappeared through the patio doors.

Though he stayed close to the shadows, he didn't crouch
as he had done earlier. And presently, apparently reaching
what he was after, he bent down and with a groan audible
even at that distance, lifted something heavy.

Max, her heart told her. He was lifting *Max*.

The tears that had threatened earlier spilled over now,
making it difficult to see the image of the broad-shouldered
man and the too-still bundle he carried in his arms. A thousand images of Max flashed through her mind, seared her
heart. Max, when she'd first found him, sores on his pads,

dirt crusted around his battered muzzle, brown eyes seemingly eyeing her beseechingly to save him; lying beside the sofa, protective of the stranger in the house, as if he had recognized that the man on the couch had been through a suffering as great as the dog had once been through; waiting for her to finish a chapter, a wild run down the inlet banks already in his eyes, his tail already swishing in anticipation.

And suddenly, watching the man she loved beyond thought carrying the still form of the dog she had rescued, the dog who had lived for nothing more than a casual caress from her, a loving pat now and then, who had given his all trying to protect her, Katherine understood something of what Sam had encountered. She wanted to turn back the clock, to a time when she and Sam had not let Max out, when she would have called the police earlier, when she might have done a thousand different things that would still allow Max to be barking at the door trying to get out. Back to a time when Max had been alive, well. She wanted to change the sequence of time and arrange it to suit the way things should be.

And just for a moment, a split second of shock and horror, she wished she were somebody else. The wish chilled her and made her shudder. Is that what had happened to Sam? Had he wished so hard that it had come true?

If Sam were not walking toward her now, arms wrapped around the red-gold setter cradled against his broad chest, Katherine might have turned away and told herself to go back to bed, that this nightmare would be gone with the morning. But he was there, his breath trailing the air like the smoke from an old-fashioned train's engine.

Watching him, knowing him for the man who had felt such pain over his wife's death that he'd tried shedding the memory, for the lover who had seemingly read her every desire, for the man who had gone with a grim smile to challenge a possible murderer, Katherine understood the greatest horror of all: he was there for her now. She couldn't deny the night's events, because he was there for her.

No one had been there for Sam. No one had been there to wrap loving arms around him and tell him that life would go on. His best friend had been killed in front of him; his wife was dead. His other friend had tried to kill Sam.

These realizations gave Katherine the ability to step forward, to swing the patio doors wide to allow Sam to carry his burden inside, to meet his eyes without the desperate grief showing in her own.

"He's alive," Sam said, and in his arms, Max whined.

Katherine shut the French doors behind them, almost sick with a dizzying relief. Max was alive. Somehow she'd been granted a wish. Would she, could she possibly be granted the greatest of her wishes? She leaned her head against the cold door, grateful beyond words, fearful beyond hope.

She turned slowly to see Sam carrying Max into the kitchen. She followed, ashamed of her weak response, ashamed because she had remained inside, protected by both lover and dog, while both of them had braved everything for her safety.

She flicked on the lights of the kitchen and Sam brushed aside the psychology book to deposit Max on the bar.

"He took it in the shoulder," Sam said, gently brushing back the dog's silky hair to display a wound that bore a startling resemblance to the score at Sam's temple.

A rap on the patio door made both of them jump, Sam whirling with a ferocious growl, Katherine with a bitten cry of fear. It was Andrew, his housecoat flapping in the wind, his hair wild, his hands clasping his arms in a tight hug.

Katherine sighed audibly in relief and swiftly admitted him.

"What the hell is going on? God! Max! Is he all right? I came over as soon as I thought it was safe enough. I saw Sam carrying something...Max? Good. I thought it was you, Katie. What happened? Has somebody called the police?''

Sam cut through the stream of questions. "Do you have any hydrogen peroxide, Katherine? And get me a couple of those bandages from the bathroom upstairs, okay?"

"I'll get them," Andrew said, pushing Katherine back to the bar and rushing from the kitchen.

Blood oozed slowly from the exposed wound on Max's shoulder. The big dog whimpered as Sam gently probed the area.

"It's just a graze. He'll be fine."

Max's head, which had swiveled around to lick at Sam's arm, laid down on the bar, underscoring Sam's prognosis.

The swinging door banged open and Andrew burst in, out of breath, hands laden with medicants. "I brought everything I could find," he panted. "Is he going to be all right? Should I call the vet?" Max's tail lifted and beat the bar in silent answer.

"Get me a couple of warm, wet cloths," Sam said quietly.

Katherine quickly did as he requested.

So swiftly that Katherine scarcely had time to think about what he was doing, let alone have time to worry about any pain Max might be feeling, Sam cleansed the wound, had her hold Max while he poured the hydrogen peroxide over the gash, then squeezed almost an entire tube of antibiotic ointment onto one of the large bandages Andrew had purchased only that afternoon. Before the blood had a chance to ooze up again, he gently flipped the ointment-covered pad over the wound and ran a strip of gauze around the wound, circling it from beneath Max's legs and then around his chest as Katherine lifted the dog.

"I'm impressed," Andrew said. "Were you a vet in a previous life?"

Sam lifted Max from the bar and carried him to a blanket Katherine was laying out in a corner of the room, near

Max's food and water. He laid the big dog down and, after petting his head, straightened.

"A vet? Hardly. Too much schooling for me. But this kind of thing isn't too tough. I'm used to it. Drug dogs always take it first."

"Drug dogs?" Andrew asked, looking not at Sam but at Katherine.

Sam didn't seem to hear the question as he went to the sink to wash his hands.

Katherine pressed a hand against her forehead. She felt hot and cold at the same time. Sam's memory was crashing through, but he seemed unaware of it.

"Sam...?" she asked, aware of Andrew's sympathetic eyes on her, aware that her hands were clenched tightly against her chest, as if she could subdue her heart's furious pounding by such a ruse.

He turned, a weary smile lighting his face.

"Yes?" he asked. Something in her face made his gaze sharpen. "What? What is it, Katherine?"

The doorbell rang in answer.

Sam whipped from the sink, his face a study in concentration.

"Who—?" Andrew began.

"Stay here," Sam barked, leaping for the kitchen door.

"Sam!" Katherine called. "It's okay!"

He stopped, turning to frown heavily in her direction.

"It's just the police," she said.

The doorbell rang again.

"What?" Sam asked.

"The police. I called them."

At first she thought he would protest her action, that his earlier objections would surface. But instead, he straightened, squaring his shoulders.

"It hardly matters now, does it? He's already found us. And he got away."

Andrew elbowed Katherine, a sharp jab at her ribs. It was no less sharp than the pain in her own heart. Knowing that Sam's fugue state was at a critical turning point, that his past and present were colliding, that whatever she said could be crucial to his well-being, Katherine drew a ragged breath and forced herself to utter, "Maybe the police will be able to stop him. All you have to do is tell them who he is."

The doorbell rang a third time while Sam steadily regarded Katherine, his expression inscrutable. Then he frowned heavily.

"Tell them who he is? Katherine, you know I can't do that."

"Why not?" she persisted.

"Because if I tell them that, I lose everything."

"What?" she asked, although she was afraid of the answer. "What do you lose?"

"Everything, Katherine. Sweet heaven, I would lose you!"

"No, you wouldn't," she said evenly, though she felt her heart was breaking.

Sadly he shook his head. "Oh yes. I have the distinct feeling that if I remember who that man was, I'll wake up and you won't be here anymore."

Chapter 10

The house reverberated with heavy thudding, then over the buffeting wind rose a tenor voice: "Police! Open up!"

Sam turned—had it been reluctantly, or with relief?—and despite his bare feet, walked with heavy, measured steps down the hall. Katherine followed equally slowly, her mind reeling at his last words. *I have the distinct feeling that if I remember who that man was, I'll wake up and you won't be here anymore.*

Her hands were cold, and her heart was hot with pain for him. *For her.* What he was suffering was so much worse than she had imagined. She had thought she understood, had stood stock-still seeing Max cradled in his arms, imagining then that she comprehended Sam's desire to simply sink into another life, another self.

His memory was trying to come fully back to awareness, and it wasn't that the individual traces were too much to be handled, it was that now, knowing her, he didn't want them back.

He should have gone to the hospital. She, Jason, and Andrew should have insisted upon it. This confusion of his would probably have resolved itself by now but for her. According to the book she had read that evening, Jason had been right, but he hadn't fully comprehended the extent of Sam's desire to be Sam McDonald, husband of Katherine.

Neither had she. But she knew now.

The realization should have gladdened her but it didn't. Seeking guilt as a substitute for the pain she felt for him, she again turned her mind to the fact that they should have taken him to a hospital and sighed when she had to accept the knowledge that had they done so, his mind might have snapped back to order more quickly, but he, in all likelihood, would be dead. The man shooting at them was already a murderer. He hadn't been playing games tonight. In a hospital, Sam would have been helpless to protect himself. At least here he'd had a gun.

But what of his feelings? What of the memories he was striving to repress? What would Sam be without George, the friend of fourteen years, the man who—according to the notes in the computer—cheered the Redskins to victory and swore for thirty minutes when they didn't win and was the first man downtown when they did? And would Sam still be Sam without Devra, the woman with fine-spun red-gold hair and a dying wish to have him not cry for her?

What would anyone be without the myriad of small, seemingly inconsequential memories that made them a whole, vital being? But when he had all of these memories, Katherine thought, as he was soon to have, he wouldn't remember her.

And what would she be then?

As though watching a movie, she saw Sam open the door, again chilling the house as the storm gained entry. The police officers outside pulled back at the sudden access, the barrels of their .357 magnums pointing at the lintel, their wide eyes an indication of their blood pressure, of their adrenaline levels. Their fingers were poised on the triggers.

Sam drew back, his eyes dark, his face unreadable, his gaze locked on the weapons ready for a battle.

"Mr. McDonald?" one asked.

"Yes?"

"This could get tricky," Andrew breathed in Katherine's ear. She waved him away absently, as she would an annoying mosquito.

"We had a call regarding someone trying to break into your house by force," the policeman said, his eyes darting from the obviously calm Sam to Katherine. The still-raised gun begged the question.

"There was a man outside," Sam said. Somehow his statement sounded lifeless, like the words of an automaton. "He shot Max, our dog, and shot at me as well."

"Were you injured, sir?"

"No."

"Where was this intruder?" the policeman barked, urgently.

"In the back," Sam said, stepping out of the way. "But he's gone."

The policemen swept into the house, eyes taking in everything at a glance, Sam and Katherine's bare feet, Andrew's fuzzy house-robe and middle-of-the-night hairstyle, the blood on Sam's sweater.

As they moved rapidly down the hall, one asked over his shoulder, "How do you know he's gone, sir?"

"I chased him around to the front, but he was already in his car and he got away."

The policemen slowed and both turned back to face Sam, two sets of eyes trained on him, identical frowns creasing their brows. One of them lowered his gun to his holster and drew a narrow pad from his jacket pocket. "Did you see the license plate, sir?"

"No."

"I did," Katherine said. "It had D.C. plates."

Sam turned his eyes to her. In the deep blue depths she read a plea of some kind, and a warning.

"Did you see the number on the plate, ma'am?" the other officer asked.

Not looking at Sam, Katherine shook her head.

"And the make of the car?"

"A Chevrolet, I think. Four-door."

"Color?"

"White or maybe silver."

"Have you ever seen this car before?"

Katherine started to say no, but Andrew said, "Yes! Last night. In the alley behind the bookstore. It was the same car," he said in an aside to Katherine. Like her, he didn't look at Sam.

"What alley is this, sir?" the policeman making the notes asked Andrew.

"The alley behind my bookstore. That's The Reader's Nook downtown. Off Rudy Inlet."

"And you are?"

"Andrew Deering. I live here. Or rather, in the guest house."

"And you were there when the burglar shot at the house?"

"Yes. I heard something—Max barking, I think—and got up. I didn't see anything until Katie turned on the floods. And after that it was all kind of confusing. Shadows and gunshots and Sam chasing somebody around to the front."

The policeman nodded. "You didn't get a good look at the intruder, then?"

"No," Andrew said. "I wouldn't be able to pick him out of a line-up of two."

The police officers didn't smile. "But you believe the person to be male."

"Well, yes. I think so." He looked at Sam for the first time.

"He was male, yes," Sam said heavily.

"Are you injured, Mr. McDonald?" the other police-man asked for the second time that night.

"No," Sam said.

"You're wearing a bandage, sir. And there's blood on your sweater. I thought perhaps . . . ?"

Sam lifted a hand to his brow and smiled wearily. "No, this happened several days ago." His hand dropped. "And the blood is from the dog."

The first policeman turned back to Andrew. "You said you thought this car was the same as one that had been be-hind your bookstore. Can you tell me about that?"

Andrew again looked at Sam who nodded slowly, his face unreadable.

"It was right after Katherine's book signing . . ." He hes-itated as the officers nodded sagely, clearly knowing Kath-erine's occupation. "Anyway, we were getting in my car when *he*—" Andrew cocked his head toward Sam "—stepped out of the shadows and suddenly this other car was in the alley and somebody was shooting at us—"

"Did you report this incident?"

"No-o," Andrew said.

"Why not, sir?"

Andrew looked from Katherine to Sam and back at the police officers, his mouth opening and closing again. If she hadn't had such sympathy with their predicament, she might have smiled at her cousin's discomfiture. How could they explain to these officers why they hadn't called the police?

"It didn't seem like much when it was over," Andrew said lamely, and Katherine could see by the doubtful, suspi-cious glances the officers exchanged that his explanation sounded more like a question than a statement.

"We thought it was just some nut," Sam interposed smoothly.

"And you weren't worried when he shot at you?" the first officer asked skeptically.

"We lost him easily enough," Sam offered in what Katherine viewed as colossal understatement.

"It seems this nut may have found you tonight," the second officer said dryly.

The other officer holstered his gun and then asked, "Is there any reason you can think of that someone would be after you?"

All three of them were silent. Katherine suspected it was because they all knew the reason, but for Andrew and her the knowledge was solely based upon a single scene written by an amnesiac, whereas Sam's was for his own safety.

Apparently the drive for self-preservation was still vitally active in him, for he deflected that line of questioning by going off in an entirely new direction. "I think I hit him. He was limping before he got to the car."

The officers brightened visibly. The first one pushed open the door of Katherine's study. "Is there access to the back from here?" he asked.

"Past the desk," Katherine said and added, "through the French doors."

The second officer pocketed his notepad and followed the first, pausing only to flick on the overhead lights. The two went through her office slowly, with the same all-encompassing gazes they'd first leveled on the three household members. They took in the computer, the sofa, the bookcases, the red-and-gold leaves upon the carpet, the many drawers open and spilling contents.

As the officers paused before opening the back doors to ask additional questions of Sam, who obviously had every intention of joining them outside, Katherine whipped from the hall and dashed to the guest room and, after a moment's search, located Sam's shoes. She carried them to the study and shoved them at Sam before he had a chance to go back outside in the cold for a second time that night without benefit of covering for his bare feet.

He took them from her, and stared at them for several seconds, a befuddled expression on his face, before leaning over to draw them on. When he straightened, he lifted a chill hand to her cheek and softly traced the curve.

"I'm sorry about all this," he said, too quietly for the policemen to hear.

"I know," Katherine said.

"When this is all over, we'll get away," he murmured and leaned down to kiss her temple. "We'll go far away where no one can find us."

"Sam," she said, raising her hands to his shoulders to draw him closer. His arms wrapped around, but he didn't pull her forward, he merely patted her back. She clung to him fiercely, believing, knowing, that soon, inevitably, he would be someone else, someone who didn't know how much she loved him. "I love you," she whispered, her fingers sore from pulling him toward her.

Remember me, she wanted to say, but couldn't. Emotions choked her, threatened to spill over.

He gave her a final pat, almost a farewell touch, and drew back. His jaw was rigid and the planes of his face were harsh as though the cold outside was so much more intense within.

"I love you, too, Katherine." But he said it sadly and his eyes were haunted with regret and colored with unspoken goodbyes.

Sam turned and went out the door before she could stop him, before she could hold him there with her luminous eyes, with her frantic grasp. He had the distinct impression that he should stay, that each step he took away from her was a passage to another world, a darker, menacing world. A world without Katherine.

The cold air snatched at his breath and drove chill spikes through the knit of his sweater, and instead of clearing his head, it only seemed to exacerbate the fog that seemed to have permanently formed there.

He paused with the policemen to point out the large hole gouged in the flagstone, and waited as one of them examined the displaced chunk of stone, but his mind continued to spin furiously.

For a second, a terrifying second, while he'd been holding Katherine, while his lips had touched her soft temple, he'd had the dizzying feeling that she was a total stranger. Her fingers digging at his shoulders hadn't felt familiar, her scent had seemed different, the feel of her hair against his face had seemed soft, yes, and silky, but had been a stranger's tousled mass.

She'd said she loved him. And for that single, terrifying moment, he hadn't known who she was, hadn't known who said the words.

"Where did you first see the guy?"

"What?" he asked, his mind still heaving. His chest was tight with the effort to hold in the scream that seemed to be growing stronger with the need for release.

Her fingers had dug into his shoulders. Had she sensed his mind slipping away from her? Then her name had come to him, and with it a hundred different memories, nothing so insubstantial as dreams, but actual memories, her laughter, her taste, the way she clung to him with her body gone dewy and her eyes unfocused as she cried his name aloud and her hips bucked beneath his. I love you, too, Katherine, he'd said then, meaning it, knowing it, *feeling* it.

"Sir?"

"Over there," he said, pointing to the thicket flanking the right side of the house. "That's where he shot Max."

"Max?"

"The dog."

"Oh, yeah. Right." The policeman shuffled uncomfortably.

The second officer went forward to peer into the bushes. "Can't see much in here," he said.

"I'm sorry about your dog," said the first.

Sam frowned, not at the officer, but at the storm swirling around them. Rain, mingled with ice, began to sting his face, but it was nothing to the storm that raged inside him. Max wasn't his. Max was Katherine's dog. He'd heard her talking about Max on television. That's why he knew what brand of dog food she fed him. It had been a prelude to a commercial. But if he was Katherine's dog, Max was also his, wasn't he?

Wasn't he?

"Sir?"

Sam answered automatically. "He's okay. It was just a graze. Luckily, he was using a .38."

"How do you figure that, Mr. McDonald?"

"That's what he always uses."

Sam felt, rather than heard, the pause that followed. "Uh, Mr. McDonald, how do you know that? Sir."

He looked over at the frowning policeman. "What?"

"I asked how you know that the guy always uses a .38?"

Had he been speaking aloud? What was going on inside him? What was going on outside?

"I'm Sam McDonald," he said and shuddered as he saw not the comfortable home behind him but a largely empty apartment in D.C., and knew it was his home. And knew he'd sold the house in Reston when Devra died because he hadn't been able to bear the sight and touch of all the things she'd put together to weave a home for them, couldn't bear them because she wasn't there to give them life.

"Yes, sir," the officer said nervously.

He heard the officer, felt the bite of sleet on his face, on his neck, knew the house was not ten feet behind him, but he also felt the crisp new shirt he'd purchased so he would look good when he met Katherine McDonald for the first time. When had that been? Yesterday. A lifetime ago. When? When George had still been alive. But when was that? Why was this officer standing there staring at him as though waiting for him to say something? What had he asked?

He heard the voice of a man who carried a yellow bag. "What do you do for a living, Sam?"

"I'm . . . a novelist," he said aloud now. It echoed in his mind. He'd said it before. But was he? Why couldn't he remember writing the books? Why did he only remember reading them?

And why, when he thought of that scene he'd written yesterday—this morning?—didn't the things he'd put on paper feel as though they belonged in a book? Why did they feel as if he'd actually been there? Why could he smell the salt water, why could he taste it?

He shuddered as the scream in him fought for freedom. *Help me, Katherine.* She was the only link between past and present, between reality and this nightmare of conflicting images. But he couldn't subject her to this horror.

The police officer in front of him swam into focus. The young man stepped back warily. "Sir?"

Sam felt hot, his skin felt pricked by flame instead of sleet, and his breathing was ragged.

"Are you all right, sir?"

"I . . . yes. No."

"Why don't you go inside . . ."

The officer's voice faded, and so did his figure. Instead of seeing the lawn changing to white as the sleet covered the grass, instead of the dark strip of water in the inlet, Sam could see a lonely wooden pier stretching before him. The night was cool, and tomorrow he would meet Katherine.

"Katherine," he said.

"Yes, sir. Why don't you—?"

"Don't tell her," Sam said.

The young officer's voice sharpened on his question. "Don't tell her what, sir?"

"That I couldn't . . . remember . . . her name."

"Are you all right, Mr. McDonald?"

"I...don't feel...well," Sam heard a voice say. The world was spinning crazily around him so that he couldn't see who it was that was speaking, though the voice sounded vaguely familiar, and the thought troubled him for the person speaking sounded in pain.

Katherine, he cried, but even as he reeled to the cold, ice-covered lawn, he knew that he hadn't called aloud. His face bounced against the stiff grass and it felt like something that had already happened before, only then the ground had been wood, and the frost had been spray from the tide below a pier.

Katherine, watching the strange tableau on her back lawn, a two-in-the-morning conversation between police and this stranger that she loved without benefit of rhyme and reason, felt cold despite the blanket Andrew had wrapped around her shoulders, and the slippers he'd brought for her feet.

The three men on the floodlit lawn looked determined and businesslike, the storm to come stirring their hair, flattening their coats—in the case of the policemen—and Sam's sweater. Their breath expelled and mingled, forming a single cloud between them, a cloud that had no substance and was warmer than the night, but looked colder, looked ominous. The wind jerked it away, like a prankster intent on a malicious joke.

The fantasy was over, she told herself. She'd had a day and two bizarre nights. Was that all that she was allotted? A single scrap of time with the one man she could truly love?

She could maintain the delusion. She knew that. All she had to do was push him to believe in the fantasy, encourage him to bury the memories that troubled him so. It would be easy. She could tell him over and over, minute after minute, how much she loved him, how she'd always known he loved her. She could, with her writer's mind, painstakingly fill in the gaps for him, color every page of his empty memory with pictures, with moments, with days and nights, with meals eaten together, and the thousand things that would make the lies come to life.

She knew how to scheme, she knew how to make him dream, she knew what to say, what to do, what to touch, how to make him cry her name as though it were the final answer to every question ever asked, knew how to entice him, incite him, prod him, rouse him to be what she wanted him to be, what *he* wanted to be. She could provide the drum he needed to strike, the canvas he needed to paint. She could be the musician for the symphony he could spark in her.

Yes. She could do all of that and more. She knew everything she could say or do that would make him stay with her. But if she did, it would all be a lie. Everything between them would be a lie. Just as it was now.

She would be cheating him of everything that made him what he was. She would be creator, not enactor. Every moment, every day, she would be lying to him.

The temptation called to her, lured her to comply with the desperate need inside her. But the deeper part of her heart, the part that said that love, *real* love, meant giving, not taking, meant wanting the best for the other person, not for the self…that part said she had to let him go. She had to tell him the truth so that he could be whole. She had to free his mind so that he could choose for himself.

And knowing that when his mind accepted the memories he didn't want and supplanted the fantasy he'd lived for the past thirty-six hours, that she would be a stranger to him, she still knew she had to tell him the truth.

But she couldn't ever tell him that it was killing her to do this. She couldn't tell him that somehow, in his touch, in his belief, he'd drawn her into a web that she couldn't shake free. That would have to be her own secret, her own wound.

She reached for the French doors, his name upon her lips. But before her voice could stretch beyond her thought, she

saw him falter, then spin. Like an expended top he leaned
left and then right and slowly, gracefully, slid forward.

She ran toward him, her legs pistons, her feet skidding on
the ice that had gathered on the grass. It seemed to take
hours to reach his side, yet his face had only grazed the white
lawn a single stroke.

"Sam!" she called, and it seemed her voice echoed and
echoed across the lawn and the inlet.

As if in slow motion she saw the police officer to her left
pulling back, but bending down, reaching for Sam. To her
right, she caught movement, but her attention was fully focused on Sam. She saw, still as if in slow motion, his head
raise a second time, a white cloud escaping his parted lips,
before striking the ground again.

"I'm here!" she screamed, her arms stretching to embrace his shoulders.

His eyes seemed to meet hers, but in the glazed stare she
could see no trace of recognition.

"Harry!" the young officer yelled. "Help me over here!"

Katherine, her body the only protection from the storm
outside and in him, pressed her face to Sam's. "I'm here,
Sam," she sobbed. "There's someone here for you this
time."

The wood creaked as his head met the plank. He felt
George's weight pressing against him, driving him to the
pier.

But his cheek was cold, frost biting at his face. And the
weight upon him wasn't George. He flinched at the harsh
imposition of voices yelling, calling, exhorting. But the
world was spinning and all he could think of was Katherine.

And he heard her voice, felt her touch.

"I'm here for you," she said. Katherine said. He relaxed
against the cold ground. She was here. She was real. He'd
heard her voice, felt her touch, smelled her scent.

Katherine. He knew her. He believed in her. He *loved* her. She loved him. This was true. This wasn't a dream.

And, as though hearing it from the hidden stars beyond the storm threatening the innocent earth, he heard her voice telling him not to worry.

"There's someone here for you this time."

Why couldn't he believe it?

Chapter 11

Sam's eyes were open and he allowed Katherine to help him to his feet. The two officers supported him on either side, guiding him to the patio doors that Andrew was holding wide.

"What happened?" Andrew asked.

"I slipped," Sam said tersely at the same time one of the officers said, "He passed out."

Sam raised a hand to his forehead, staring at Andrew as if he'd never seen him before. Fear clutched at Katherine's already cold heart.

The officer said quietly to Andrew, "He was talking pretty weird, then he just keeled over." He said it as if disclaiming culpability.

Ignoring them, her attention focused on Sam, Katherine led him into the room and pushed him into the desk chair. He leaned back and closed his eyes.

"I'm so tired," he mumbled. "Everything's spinning."

Remembering Jason's statement that sleep was nature's best remedy and that concussed people should be allowed the respite, she offered to escort him to bed.

"No," he said, but his eyes were closed. "He'll be back."

"Then we'll leave," Katherine said simply. "If we're not here, he won't be able to find us."

Out of the corner of her eye she saw the two policemen exchange thoughtful glances.

"Devra is dead, isn't she?" Sam asked, his eyes open again and demanding the truth from her.

Katherine didn't know how to answer him. He wanted the truth, but that wasn't something she could in all honesty give him. She had only the pages and pages of writing to go by. If what he wrote was the truth, then yes, Devra was dead.

She compromised finally. "That's what you told me."

"When?"

"When did she die?" she asked.

"When did I tell you this? I can't remember."

"Yesterday," Katherine said.

"Yesterday. Everything seems like yesterday...time is all twisted in my head. Out of sequence...there's no cohesion."

Katherine laid a hand on his shoulder. "You need some sleep," she said. And he nodded, finally.

She rose and met Andrew's questioning gaze. "Call Jason," she said. "Ask him if he can come over again." She knew her voice was calm, even her hands were steady, but she felt she was holding everything together by a thread.

As Andrew nodded and reached for the phone, the younger of the two officers said they still wanted to look around a bit. She nodded at them absently and left the room to prepare the guest room; she wasn't sure she could catch him if he slipped on the stairs and didn't want to think what hitting his head a third time might do to him. She pulled back the covers on the bed before even turning on a light.

He was waiting for her at the door to the study. She lifted his arm to her shoulders and wrapped hers around his waist, wondering as she did so if it would be the last time she touched him so intimately.

Sam walked steadily enough down the hall, but he was bothered by the blood on his sweater. "I'm not hurt. Whose blood is this?"

"Max's," Katherine said, easing him through the doorway and toward the bed.

"Who's Max?"

Katherine knew what he meant when he'd said the world was spinning. It was spinning around her now, fantasy and reality fusing and blending, encircling her heart with bands of garrote wire that tightened and tightened, cutting ever deeper with each erratic, painful beat of her heart.

He'd forgotten who Max was. This was it, that bleak tomorrow was here. She'd known it would hurt, she'd known it would be difficult to watch, difficult to hear, but knowing it empirically and experiencing it were entirely different matters. This was agonizing death, slow, painful and torturous.

"Max is my dog," she answered finally and with regret.

"Oh," he said. Then, as if he were merely being polite, he asked, "Was he hurt badly?"

"No, you patched him up." She found it was possible to move automatically, to speak and hear, to even sound natural while every part of her was silently screaming in writhing despair.

"Here, sit down. Let me help you with that sweater. It's soaked."

Sam sat down obediently, his hands crisscrossing to pull the sweater over his head. But Katherine had no illusions left; he wasn't thinking of her, worrying about her.

Her throat constricted at seeing his bare chest, broad back, knowing that he was even now going through the process of forgetting that her hands had roamed the muscles and clung to his arms. She would never again be able to trail her fingers across his small, puckered nipples, never again follow the arrow of dark hair that pointed to other, richer treasures.

"Why don't you lie down?" she asked evenly, despite the trembling of her lips, the shaking in her soul.

He slowly complied with her request, his eyes shifting to lock on her, devouring her, seeking her hair, her shoulders, her unsteady hands, her unshed tears. Questions had often lurked in the blue depths, but always before there had been answers as well. Love had been there whether bred by fantasy or by desire, and a thousand unspoken assurances and promises had softened the shadows, the doubts. Now there were only questions and her own reflection.

"Where am I?" he asked then, giving the bands that had tightened around her heart another strangling tug, a hard yank that finally and irrevocably severed the remnants of all her dreams, her wishes.

"In my home," she said dully.

"Why?" he asked.

"I don't know," she said then, too honestly, too filled with hopelessness to soften the harsh truth.

He stared at her for several long seconds, then a ghost of a smile played on his lips as he closed his eyes. "I hope you'll be able to use it in a book someday," he said drowsily.

Katherine realized her heart had only been damaged before. Now it was broken. His casual, offhand dismissal of the last few days, the best moments of her life, the only real love she had ever unreservedly offered, shattered her.

And the tears that shock and fear had held inside spilled free, scalding her with their heat. She couldn't see him anymore, but listened to his easy, untroubled breathing.

He was asleep and she was dying inside.

"Katie?" Andrew's voice came from behind her.

"Yes?" she asked, turning around almost gratefully, but unable to stem the flow of burning tears.

"Jason's here, honey."

Who was Jason? Sam wondered. And what the hell was going on? What was he doing in a bed in Katherine Mc-Donald's house, feeling weak as a damned alley cat that got caught in a rain? And why did Katherine McDonald look at him as though he'd stolen her last best hope?

He'd had blood on the sweater he was wearing—a sweater he'd never seen before—and she'd said it was Max's and that he'd patched Max up. Even unable to account for a stretch of time, he knew he hadn't been the one who hurt the dog. He couldn't have, it was that simple. But what had happened to make her look at him with betrayal and despair etched on every beautiful plane of her face?

And where was her husband? The guy in the doorway who'd called her Katie couldn't be Sam McDonald, spy and novelist.

A stranger stepped through the door and, after a murmured comment to someone just out of sight, he proceeded to the bed. Snow dusted the guy's silver hair and stained his opened trench coat with moisture. His face was ruddy with the cold, and his lips were almost white, as if he'd been biting them. And he was carrying what looked like a doctor's leather bag, except that it was bright yellow.

The notion that he was having a crazy nightmare swept over Sam. But the guy shrugged off his coat, and the chill that he'd brought with him reached out to touch Sam. This was no dream.

The guy's hair was mussed, as if he'd been asleep. And when his coat dropped to an armchair in the corner, Sam's impression was confirmed, for this bizarre doctor was wearing a rag wool sweater over a flannel pajama top.

What time was it? Sam wondered, and then he was shocked to realize he didn't even know what day of the week it was. The last thing he could remember was getting to George's car and wrapping a sodden handkerchief around his head.

He clenched his jaw against the pain the memory roused and he saw the man standing over him hesitate.

"It's okay," he said, dragging a smile to his lips. He might not know what was going on around here, but he wasn't about to take it out on somebody that was obviously here to try and help. Yellow bag, daffodils, sunshine and all.

The doctor smiled and sat down on the side of the bed. "I'm Jason Woodard."

Sam couldn't help but notice that the introduction was more like a question. Or like a prompt. And the strangely familiar gray eyes seemed to bore into Sam's.

"Sam McDonald," he answered, fighting with the covers over him to shake the man's hand. Was it his imagination or did the man hesitate just a second before taking his hand?

"Are you a doctor?" he asked, releasing the surprisingly reassuring grip.

Jason nodded and smiled slightly. The smile was tired, and somehow deprecating. Sam found himself unexpectedly warming to this guy. How many doctors made house calls anymore? Especially during a snowstorm in the middle of the night.

Was it the middle of the night? That seemed right.

"How are you feeling?" Jason asked.

"Fine," Sam said cautiously. "But a little out of it."

"How so?" the doctor asked.

Sam hesitated, but couldn't think of a reason not to admit what was going on in his head. "I don't know how I came to be here. In fact, I don't remember a damned thing after my partner got shot."

"When was that, do you know?"

Sam shook his head ruefully. "Not unless you can tell me what day it is now."

"It's Sunday morning."

Sam calculated quickly. "It happened Thursday."

"And you don't remember anything that transpired since then?"

Sam frowned trying to remember. Random images popped and flickered in his mind like a hundred different flashbulbs going off at once: tossing a dictionary on a bed and pointing to the word *interstice,* feeling triumphant because he'd known it meant a crack or chink and Katherine hadn't . . . Katherine McDonald, wrapped in no more than a towel, long silky legs exposed, her lips full and swollen from kisses...a voice saying, 'Personally, I'd keep him'...his own voice murmuring words of love.

"Things, random images that don't make any sense," Sam said finally, shoving these odd scraps of fantasy to the dark corners of his too-shadowed mind.

"But you remember everything else?"

Sam cracked a grin. "Except for a couple of nights in Mexico when I was twenty, I'd say it's all here."

"Just not the past few days," Jason said.

"Not a scrap," Sam said and turned his head toward the door at a rough sob from someone outside the door. Katherine McDonald?

"Mind if I give a quick check to satisfy my own curiosity?"

"Check away," Sam said, fighting an urge to get out of bed and see if it really was Katherine he'd heard crying, and feeling a sharp pain in his chest at the thought.

"Okay, now follow my finger, if you will."

Sam did as the doctor asked, and within a few minutes, the doctor pronounced his motor functions to be all right and moved on to the wound at his temple.

"Healing well. Any problems? Headaches? Flashing lights? Ringing in your ears? Any bad smells?" To each question, Sam gave a negative. Jason covered the gash with a fresh bandage he pulled from the yellow bag, and sat back. "I'd have to say you're healthy."

"What about the loss of the past few days?" Sam asked, sitting up.

Jason sighed and shrugged. "What we don't know about the mind could fill the Grand Canyon. You could never regain the memory of that time, or it could snap back tomorrow."

Sam considered this, wishing he'd paid more attention to those psychology classes back in college. His roommate had been the psych major, devouring the abnormal behavior books like Sam had drunk up every popular novel that came his way. If only Johnson were here now.

"Sounds like I need a good shrink," Sam said, trying to grin.

"You're talking to one," Jason said easily and smiled.

Sam winced, more than a little embarrassed, partly at having used the popular negative word for the man's profession, but more because the person Katherine McDonald had called to doctor him in the middle of the night was a *psychiatrist.* What the hell had he been doing that the first person she'd call would be a head doctor?

For starters, he'd somehow shown up at her house with a bullet wound on his head. What had she thought? What had *he* thought?

He asked slowly, pondering the implications, "If I can't remember what happened the past few days...did I remember who I was then?" Realizing how convoluted that probably sounded, he started to rephrase it, but Jason held up a hand and chuckled softly.

"Don't try to unravel that question. It would very likely give *me* a headache. The thing that's important to know is that you didn't do anything wrong. Keep telling yourself that and, if you do have a trace return, you'll be able to deal with it a little easier."

"How did I get here?" Sam asked.

A commotion in the hall caused the doctor to turn away without answering this pressing question. Sam watched as two police officers passed the doorway and heard one of them say they hadn't been able to find anything, but that they had taken the extra precaution of calling in a report on a white or silver Chevrolet with D.C. plates.

Sam stiffened.

"It shouldn't be too hard to spot tonight...there's not too many cars out on the road in this weather," the officer's strong southern drawl reported.

But it was neither the policeman's voice nor the road conditions that had caught Sam's attention. It had been that the description of that car sounded remarkably like Pete Sorenson's sleek vehicle. Had Pete been here? Was that what all the fuss was about? Had he gotten away from Pete only to lead him to Katherine and Sam McDonald?

"What is it?"

Sam turned to see Jason's probing gaze focused on him. The doctor's face was as kindly and attentive as before, but Sam was fully aware that the man hadn't missed the fact that Sam had reacted to the policeman's words.

"What happened here tonight?" Sam asked.

Jason's expression didn't change as he quietly explained what he knew. "Somebody took a couple of shots at the house, shooting Katherine's dog, and shooting at you. You chased him off."

"I chased him off," Sam repeated slowly.

"That's what I heard."

"If he had a gun, I must have had a pretty tough time chasing after him," Sam said dryly.

Jason smiled. Sam thought he must be a hell of a psychiatrist; the smile was completely genuine. "You shot him, too. In the leg, I'm told."

Sam looked at the doctor in disbelief. His gun was safely tucked in his holster in a motel room in Virginia Beach. "I didn't have my gun," he said tersely.

"No. I understand you used Katherine's."

Before Sam could ask any of the questions that hovered on his lips, the man that had called Katherine "Katie" poked his head in the door.

"Jason?"

The doctor rose to his feet. Sam wondered if the man was always this calm, this imperturbable. "Andrew?"

So this man in the door *wasn't* Sam McDonald, wasn't Katherine's husband. Sam didn't even try to analyze the sense of relief that washed over him.

"These officers say it's getting pretty bad out there, that the roads are pretty icy. They say they'll be glad to follow you to your place...?"

"Trying to get rid of me already?"

"For all of me, you can stay here," Andrew quipped, a weary grin cracking his thin face. "But I thought we might let you have at least one night's sleep this weekend."

Jason smiled, but Sam felt cold. Had this doctor been called over here before? On his behalf? The embarrassment that threatened earlier rose again. He tried telling himself, as Jason had suggested, that he hadn't done anything wrong, but he couldn't help but wonder. And now he saw the phrase in a different light—the doctor had been telling him that, not just giving him a panacea-like mantra to chant. He had been speaking from personal knowledge.

"I'm finished here, anyway," Jason said, turning back to Sam.

Sam suddenly felt very vulnerable, too conscious of his being an uninvited intruder in Katherine McDonald's home, afraid of the missing three days, torn by the desire to ask this doctor to take him with him, not to leave him here, and by a fierce pride that wouldn't let him admit he was scared silly.

"Now I want you to get some sleep." As if he could read Sam's thoughts, and Sam dimly suspected that he could, Jason came back to the bed and held out his hand. "You'll be all right, you know. And don't worry about being here. Katherine insisted that you stay."

Katherine McDonald had insisted that he stay in her home? The thought conjured a thousand different possibilities, most too fraught with fantasy and those bizarre flickering images to consider them anything but adolescent wishes.

"You'll probably be able to put it all together in the morning. And if you don't, I'd be glad to talk to you about it if you like."

Jason gave his hand a final pump, a gesture that was easy and natural and filled with simple human kindness. Sam again fought the urge to ask to be taken with him. It was borne, he knew, not from any real desire for the doctor's companionship or championship, but from a reluctance to face the people in the hall, the people whose home he'd violated, whose hospitality was being stretched to bizarre proportions.

Most of all, he thought, watching the doctor don his coat and with a jaunty wave snatch his ridiculous yellow bag from the bed, he was reluctant to have to look in Katherine McDonald's hazel eyes and read what she thought of him. All he'd wanted to do was to meet her, have her sign her book, and maybe smile when she heard he had the same name as her husband.

That was a lie, he told himself, he'd wanted a hell of a lot more than that from her. But he never, not in his wildest dreams, would have pushed his way into her house, into her bedroom.

Jason left the room only to come back seconds later and turn the lamp switch. The room seemed inky black, despite the illumination from the doorway, so abrupt was the change from light to dark.

"Sleep," he commanded, and left again.

Sam strained to hear the muted voices in the hall. He heard one of the policemen say they'd be checking back on the house periodically through the night, but that with the storm, and with the guy having been wounded, they didn't think there'd be much likelihood of him returning to give them any problems.

Sam's lips tightened. They didn't know Pete Sorenson. If he had found out Sam was here, wounded or not, chased away or not, he'd be back. He had to dispose of Sam McDonald. This Sam. And he'd have to do it now, after the police had come and gone, secure in the knowledge they'd done their job, and do it while the household thought themselves safe for the remainder of the night.

Sam sat up, and pushed the covers aside, ignoring the slight wooziness that assaulted him. Slowly, somewhat unsteadily, he crept over to the doorway, the better to hear.

"I appreciate it, fellows," Jason's voice said cheerfully. "Lead the way."

"He really doesn't remember anything of the last few days?" came Andrew's higher-pitched tone.

"There may be bits and pieces," Jason's voice said, and to Sam standing behind the wall separating them, he sounded sad, and something else...consoling?...as if he were offering a fragile balm to someone whose heart was breaking. Katherine? Why? Why would he have the idea that her heart was breaking over his loss of three days?

And why did he feel so responsible, far beyond any embarrassment, any concern for having imposed in her household? Why did his chest tighten when he thought of her being in pain? Why did his arms ache to hold her? And most of all, why did holding her seem so natural, so familiar?

What had he done in those missing days? And why did he feel such a sense of regret at their loss?

"...but I think sleep—and no more chasing around the garden during ice storms trying to catch bad guys in the dark—will be the ticket."

Sam could almost see his shrug. "There's nothing else I can recommend. Physically, he's fine. Mentally, too. And like I said the other night, he's a bright man. And, I'd hazard a guess, emotionally pretty together. He'll come to grips with this.''

I'll have to, Sam thought. Like he'd had to when Devra died. Like the grief he felt now, thinking about the way George had been killed, thinking about never seeing George again. Like the way he felt about hearing Katherine McDonald's broken sob.

The door was opened then, and the blast of cold air that rushed in swept into the guest room and clutched at his bare chest with chill fingers.

Sam went back to the bedside, picked up the damp sweater lying on the floor and eyed it with distaste. There had to be something else he could wear. He noiselessly opened the closet door and saw his new linen jacket hanging in the otherwise empty space. He took it from the hanger, idly fingering it, remembering George's crack about shoulder pads, remembering that because of it, because he'd wanted to impress the woman in the hallway, he hadn't worn a gun that night on the pier and hadn't been able to protect George, hadn't been able to stop Pete.

And judging by the condition of the jacket, he couldn't have made much of an impression on the lovely Katherine either.

He closed the closet door silently and slid the jacket on. He turned around and froze.

Silhouetted in the doorway, her hair loose and shining gold, the only color visible, her hands flat against the rounded curves of her hips, Katherine stood. He could feel the tension emanating from her all the way across the room.

''Where...where are you going?'' she asked. Her voice was hoarse, and he knew, if he could see her, her eyes would be red from crying. The knowledge was like hot steel driving through his heart.

"I . . ." I was going to find the gun I may have shot Pete with, because he'll be back. Could he say that? It sounded crazy. It *was* crazy. But it was also true.

"Jason said you . . . needed to sleep," she said, and Sam could have sworn she had almost said something else. What?

"I don't feel. . .particularly tired," he lied. He wanted to cross the room and turn her to the light so he could see her face, so he could read her eyes. But fear held him still. What would he do if he read things he didn't want to read, or saw things he might not be able to remember?

"Please," she said raggedly. The single word, the sorrow in her throaty voice almost brought him to his knees. It reached deep inside him and wrenched painfully. He wasn't sure what exactly she was pleading for, but he would have given her anything. *Anything.*

"Katherine," he said, and even to himself, his voice sounded harsh with a longing that he couldn't even account for, a longing so powerful and so intense that it physically hurt. "I'm sorry." The words came from his soul and somehow didn't sound inadequate.

"Don't," she said swiftly, slicing at the air, as if her hand were a sword and could cut his apology neatly, stopping it before it reached her. "I can't . . ." she choked. "Just sleep, now."

She half turned and so missed his hand raised to stop her.

"We'll . . . talk . . . in the morning," she said and fled the room, not stopping to pull the door closed behind her.

Slowly, as if her presence had held him rooted to the floor and her departure freed his limbs, he crossed the room and stared out at the brightly lit hallway, and through the living-room doors.

His hands gripped the door and its opposing jamb painfully. He fought the feeling that in letting her walk away, he was losing something precious, something priceless. He wanted to call her back, he wanted to hold her in his arms and beg her to explain the elusive memories that felt like so much more than dreams.

But he didn't call her back, and couldn't explain the sorrow that settled in him like a pall and his heartache grew as he listened to Andrew ask her if she was okay, did she want some brandy? and consoling her, calling her Katie, begging her not to cry so, and finally urging her, with knowing sympathy, to cry it out.

Sam's jaw clenched against the ripping agony that shot through him at the sound of her suffering. *He'd* caused it. He knew that without knowing the reasons why. Her pain was his, and he suffered for her.

He closed his eyes, willing the voices to dissipate, to fade, to lose themselves in the churning mess of his mind. Memories rose only to slide away, tantalizing him with their freshness, with their clarity only to blur and sink into obscurity. Memories of Katherine, of touching her, of her calm voice telling him that everything would be all right, that she was with him, reached out to him, luring him, only to twist and turn and slip away again.

He opened his eyes, gasping for air. Please, he begged, though no concrete prayer formed. How could he go to her, take her in his arms and ask her if they had been lovers, if she had told him that she loved him? How could he tell her he couldn't remember that?

"It'll be okay, Katie," Andrew said in the other room.

Her name is Katherine, Sam wanted to yell. Not Katie. Not Kath. Katherine, as full and rich as her voice, as filled with mystery as her honey-colored hair. A love song that needed to be sung, a poem needing to be read aloud, tears in the poet's throat.

And it should be him out there, damn it, holding her, soothing her. It should be his shoulder that she cried upon, her warm tears soaking his bare chest, and her sensitive soul receiving the salve it so sorely needed. But he couldn't. Though he vaguely knew what to say, what to do, he didn't know what lay between them. And he had to strain harder against the sharp edge of the door to keep from going to her anyway and spilling all the confused, agonized longings for her, to keep from telling her a jumble of truth and lies, of fiction and fact, of fantasy and reality.

He must have been crazy, he thought. He must still be.

You have amnesia. He heard Katherine's voice say this as clearly as if the words were spoken aloud beside him. But he couldn't remember where he'd heard it or when.

"Amnesia?" he asked the empty hallway.

It was a scarcely more acceptable answer than insanity and made his lack of knowledge no more palatable. He raised an arm and covered his eyes with the crook of his elbow, wiping the cold sweat that threatened to engulf him.

You're not alone this time. Her voice came again from some other time, some other place. But where? When?

Whenever, wherever, she had been wrong. He was alone. He was alone with a lifetime of memories and a single cupful of dreams and a woman he wanted more than life itself crying in the next room. How alone could you get? he wondered.

This alone, he answered, and it hurt. But it hurt more because Katherine was alone, too. And hurting as much, if not more than himself.

Chapter 12

Katherine pulled free of Andrew's awkward but well-intentioned embrace.

"Tissue," she said thickly and gratefully took the handkerchief he pressed into her hand. She blew her nose and looked at the ceiling for several seconds, fighting the quiver of her lower lip.

But the tears stopped. Outwardly, at least. Inwardly, she had the feeling they would never stop. They would go on and on, a veritable flood of pain, until she drowned in them. And perhaps it was the knowledge that no other arms but Sam's could offer comfort that allowed the outward sign of her agony to fade.

"I'm so sorry, Katie," Andrew said, his fingers wrapping around hers and squeezing gently.

"So am I, Andrew." She looked around the room as if seeing it for the first time, and remembered the night Sam had come into her life, a night that seemed like aeons ago. *You changed the furniture,* he'd said. She wanted to change it now. It seemed haunted by his having touched it, talked about it.

"I keep thinking of what he said before the police came, that he was afraid if he remembered who was out there...that he'd wake up and...and I'd be gone," she said brokenly. She reached out and shifted the vase on the table, moving it unnecessarily.

"He was right," she said. "It was like he really did know." He'd known that he had loved her and hadn't wanted to let her go. And that little voice inside her tried telling her that if he'd wanted it badly enough, he would still love her. But it wasn't true, she'd wanted him so badly it felt like dying without him, but that hadn't kept his fantasy alive.

"I keep wondering what's going on in his mind now? Is he lost in some in-between set of memories? Life here, and his real life?"

"Katie, the time he spent here was real, too."

"It was the most real time in my entire life." She shook her head against a fresh onslaught of tears. "I'm sitting here wishing that it could be more than a dream to him, wishing that he'd remember." Her voice broke on a sob. "I want to go in there and beg him not to forget everything, to not let the best part of me...disappear...into some obscure and locked file in his mind, some secret compartment of his heart."

The words that spilled so raggedly seemed to be coming from a part of her that had never been allowed freedom beyond the computer keyboard. They tasted bitter, but weren't; they were only coated with the fear in her soul, and tempered with the guilt she felt over having encouraged his delusion and regret that it had finally disappeared.

Gone were the memories of how he'd kissed her, the rose he'd picked for her and later trod upon after he'd run loving hands over her responsive body. Gone was the laughter they'd shared, and the intensely personal connection she'd discovered in his writing, in his loving. Gone was Max, Andrew, and thirty-six hours of another life.

"It's all over, Andrew," she said. "It's funny...I was so deluded, I thought...I really believed, that some kind of miracle was going to happen, that he'd...that he'd still love me."

Andrew rose from the sofa and paced the room, as though wrestling with something too weighty to say without physical action. "Katie...?"

She looked at him feeling drained, resigned.

"Why don't you just tell him?"

"Tell him what?"

"Everything."

She shook her head.

"No, listen. If you tell him everything, *everything,* maybe it'll come back to him. Maybe he'll remember."

The loud peal of the doorbell cut her negative answer, startling both of them.

"The police?" Andrew asked, already starting for the door.

"No, wait," Katherine said, pushing to her feet. Her legs felt leaden, almost as nearly weighted as her chest. "I'll get it."

"Maybe they caught the guy."

"I hope so," Katherine said, not caring one way or another if they had, except that the danger to Sam would be over. But danger seemed insignificant in the wake of the last two hours.

She pulled the door open and stared stupidly at the handsome older man on the doorstep. She had so thoroughly expected the police officers or at the very least, Jason, that this white haired, well-groomed stranger with one hand negligently tucked in his pocket, the other holding a black leather card case in her direction, seemed an apparition of the storm still raging beyond him.

"Yes?" she asked.

He flipped open the card case to reveal a badge and Katherine, out of instinct, leaned forward to look at it, her eyes too swollen from crying to do more than glimpse the brass emblem with black lettering. But when she saw the U.S. Department of Treasury tag, she had to clench the doorknob tightly to keep from screaming an alarm, to keep from denouncing him as a murderer right then and there.

But this man didn't appear injured, didn't look anything other than slightly weary and very cold. His lips were a faint blue, and purple shadows smudged the hollows beneath the blue gaze that met hers so steadily.

Her mind frantically tried sorting out possible excuses for this man to be standing on her doorstep, snow gathering white upon white, the tails of his trench coat damp, the hand in his pocket somehow menacing for no other reason than that it was out of sight. And her mind fought for potential escapes, options and retributions. But her heart called for Sam . . . for the Sam he was now.

Sam would know what to do, she thought, would know if this man portended good or ill. But Sam was lying asleep, defenseless in the guest room. And Andrew was waiting in the living room, equally unsuspecting of danger.

"Yes?" she said coolly. If this was the chief who had shot George, who had shot Sam, who had shot Max, did the hand in his pocket hide a weapon? And she knew, with an instinctive grim certainty that it did. Knew that this man was the danger they'd only heard about for three days, that peril now stood on her very doorstep, a false smile on his face, cold eyes seeming to look right through her.

"I'm sorry for disturbing you so late," the man said, and his smile broadened to show even white teeth. While he undoubtedly meant to assure her of his sincerity, the smile drove her certainty home. Something feral in it made her think of wolverines, of weasels, of vultures circling a dying beast.

"It is late," she agreed, risking pushing the door inches toward the catch.

"One of our people has been in some trouble, and we're worried about him," the man said, the false smile still spanning his features.

Every instinct screamed at Katherine to simply slam the door in his face but he shifted and now she could see the distinct outline of the gun in his pocket. Would a bullet go through the door? Would it catch her before she even slammed the door? How would her dying help Sam?

"I'm not sure I understand," she said coldly, contrary to the sudden rush of panicked heat inflaming her. She inched the door another couple of lifetimes toward the catch.

His left foot raised and lodged against the door and a spasm crossed his face as his full weight shifted to his right. A tight grimace of pain rippled across his face, and the feral smile slid to a mockery of a grin.

It was him! The knowledge tore through Katherine, as gripping as the loss of Sam's memory of her still clutched at her. She shoved at the door, calling out something—who knew what?—and closed her eyes, half in preparation for the gunshot she expected, half in the desperation of pulling upon depleted strength to shut him out.

He flung his body against the door, opening it almost surprisingly easily, sending Katherine flying against the guest-room wall.

He grabbed hold of her arm and wrenched it painfully up and behind her back, making her cry out, shoving her face against the cold door. "No more games, lady. All I want is Sam."

That's all I want, too, she thought bleakly.

Sam's body felt galvanized with the adrenaline surge that shook his frame. *Pete Sorenson:* murderer...traitor... cheat.

He was *here.* Now.

And from the sound of the scuffle in the hallway, Pete was hurting Katherine. An explosion of denial rippled through him and he had to literally bite his tongue to keep from yelling his hatred of Pete for all the world to hear. But that wouldn't help Katherine. Wouldn't save her.

No, he had to wait. Pete didn't want Katherine, didn't want Andrew. He only wanted Sam. That he wouldn't leave them alive after he dealt with Sam was insignificant now... now there was still hope, there was still a chance. Because Pete didn't know he was standing here in the dark, a stealthy cat ready to pounce on a much hated rat.

If only he had that gun he supposedly shot Pete with earlier. But he didn't have it. He had his brains, though, and his training, and Pete didn't know he was in a darkened room less than ten feet away, muscles tensed, teeth clenched, breath coming in shallow gasps, heart beating rapidly, silently.

He held back, hands away from him at the ready, shoulders lightly pressed against the doorjamb, eyes on the door opening.

He didn't have to wait long. A scuffle of feet and a pained moan from Katherine that tore at Sam's resolve, and suddenly, blotting out the light from the hallway, they were framed in the doorway, her arm pulled awkwardly and painfully behind her, her full breasts straining upward, her honeyed hair spilling over Pete's hand, and the .38 barrel pressing cruelly into her temple.

And whatever plans Sam had went painfully awry.

He felt the memory of the past three days ram into his mind with the force of a linebacker intent on an eighty-yard drive and an open field before him.

Katherine!

He knew everything about her. He knew every thought she'd ever had, he'd read it all, and in reading between the lines, he'd come to know every value, every social code she held dear, every lonely place in her soul that cried. And in the past three days he'd come to know her touch, her caresses, her scent, her wants and her needs.

Seeing her pinioned in Pete's arms, her face averted, trying unsuccessfully to pull free of the bite of the barrel against her temple, her eyes red from crying, her body rigid with fear, Sam was shocked by the stunning realization of his love for her, of his insanity, of the astonishing fantasy that had gripped him—and then her—for the past three days.

And seeing her so roughly used, and knowing what had transpired on that lonely pier four days ago, he was filled with an implacable hatred of Pete.

He had to dig his fingernails into the wall to keep from springing at Pete. But if he jumped now, the gun could go off and Katherine could be killed. And despite the stunning embarrassment that seemed to infuse his veins with molasses, and despite his thousand questions that couldn't be explained by simply remembering, he knew that of all things he wouldn't be able to bear her loss.

Pete would take her room to room, looking for him. That was just fine. Because in that sudden crashing in of a thousand impressions, a hundred individual memories of the past forty hours, he'd also remembered where he'd left Katherine's gun.

"Where's Sam?" the man growled, glancing at the darkened guest room, then roughly propelling her toward the living room, his right leg dragging. He used her body as a crutch, pulling at it, nearly crushing her with his weight.

"He's gone," Katherine said, hoping the fearful quaver in her voice would be taken as the truth. Out of the corner of her eye she saw that the living room was empty. Where was Andrew?

"Don't bullshit me, lady, I'm not in the mood. Where is he?"

"He left with the police," Katherine said. If only he had, if only they all had.

"The hell he did. I was watching, sweetheart. This kind of crap may work in your novels, but it doesn't wash with me. *Where is he?*" The pressure of the gun against her temple increased, and he jerked her arm up higher, causing her to cry out in pain despite every oath she'd sworn not to make a sound.

His lips pressed coldly against her ear, his hot breath against her skin making her stomach heave at the unbridled repugnance she felt at having him touch her, at having him so near, at the helplessness he made her suffer.

"You can't get away with this," she muttered through clenched teeth, clenched as much to contain the whimpers of pain as from the extreme hatred she felt for him.

"Don't kid yourself, sweetheart. I take care of Sam and all my troubles will be over." His breathing was labored and was heavy and hot against her ear. Again her stomach protested, heaving.

Perhaps he realized he'd pressed her too far, or maybe he just felt that he had absolute control over her, for his hand cruelly twisting her arm shifted slightly, allowing her arm to lower somewhat. The surge of blood that shot through the numbed arm was painful enough to bring tears to her eyes and she blinked them away furiously, hating the weakness, knowing it would serve no purpose; the man holding her had no intention of letting her live, didn't care whether she was in pain or not, didn't care about anything.

"So where is he?"

Sam waited only until Pete's back turned for a second as he shoved Katherine into the living room, and then moved silently from the guest room down the hall. It took every scrap of resolve in him to pass the living-room entrance without leaping for Pete's exposed back. But Pete's finger was on the trigger and the barrel of the .38 was pressed against Katherine's temple.

Pete's comments rang in his ears while Katherine's sob of pain lodged in his heart.

I'll make him pay, darling, he vowed. *He'll never touch you again.* He stealthily cracked the kitchen door and slipped in the room, his eyes raking the empty bar in shock. The gun wasn't there. Where was it? He'd handed it to Katherine who set it there, hadn't he? He glanced around the kitchen to see if she might have set it somewhere else.

His eyes fell on Max, sleeping soundly on the pallet in the corner. No help there, either.

Where was Andrew?

And suddenly he knew what had happened to the gun. Andrew must have taken it and was even now trying to creep up on Pete.

Sam's heart clenched in sudden fear. Andrew would be no match for Pete. Hell, Pete would shoot Andrew just as soon as look at him. Andrew must be in the study, planning to go through the study door into the living room. And that door squeaked.

As stealthily as he'd entered the kitchen, he slipped from it, crossing the hall to push the study door ajar. He could only hope that Andrew wasn't so wired that he'd shoot him instead of Pete.

Andrew's back was to the hall entrance of the study, totally vulnerable to attack, the .38 in his hand held away from his body and pointing toward the bookcase in as inexpert a grip as Sam had ever seen. His other hand was slowly turning the knob of the living-room door.

"Andrew . . ." he breathed.

Andrew whirled around, the gun raising to point in the general direction of Katherine's computer. His eyes were wide with fright and his mouth was slack with shock.

"It's me, Andrew," Sam whispered. "Give me the gun. I'll take over from here."

A shudder of relief worked over Andrew and he crossed the room to thrust the gun at Sam. It was a wonder he didn't manage to shoot one or the other of them during the transfer, Sam thought grimly. But he took the gun with a tight smile for Andrew's attempted rescue, and quickly checked for ammunition.

Two bullets.

He might as well have had forty. All it took was one.

He snapped the carriage shut and looked up at Andrew, whose eyes met his so trustingly and so eloquently in his confidence that now everything would be okay that Sam felt a stab of conscience. He'd brought all this into their lives, had made a shambles of the past three days, and now, because of him, Andrew had been prepared to face certain death to try to save Katherine, and Katherine was even now being held in Pete's fierce grip, a gun trained at her head.

As if he read some of this in Sam's eyes, Andrew nodded, then stepped out of the way. Sam brushed past him, pointing at the hall door, raising the gun to shoulder level, aiming it, in his mind, at the narrow bridge between Pete's murderous eyes.

He sidled up to the door, facing the study, his hand reaching for the knob. He glanced at Andrew and nodded, jerking his head toward the living room. *Make noise,* he mouthed.

Andrew's eyes widened, but he stiffly drew his head down in assent.

"Katie?" Andrew called and his voice cracked. He shot Sam a sheepish grin, cleared his throat and tried again. "Katie? Honey, where are you?"

Katherine's knees sagged as she heard Andrew's call. *Run,* she wanted to scream, *help me,* she wanted to answer.

The grip on her hand tightened even as the gun at her cheek shifted. The sudden release of pressure against her temple made her feel giddy, sickeningly grateful to this des-

picable creature in her home. The barrel slid down her jawline to rest beneath her chin, digging into the sensitive flesh,
raising her head until she had to lean against her assailant.

"Answer him," he growled into her ear. His hand jerked
her arm higher, punctuating his command. "Do it!"

"Please," Katherine whispered.

He wrenched her arm, making her cry out, pushing her
toward the hallway entrance, the gun against her throat
gagging her, the pain in her shoulder making her dizzy. Her
eyes frantically ranged her living room as though she might
find hope springing from the cushions of the sofa, from the
lamp, from the book lying facedown on the end table or
from her study.

The doorknob of the study door turned silently.

"Katie! Yoo-hoo! Where are you, Katie?" Andrew's
voice rang out again. *From the hall.* In the kitchen Max
barked twice, then was silent.

"Get him in here now, or this—" he jiggled the gun sa-
distically "—will be the last thing you ever hear. Him, too."

"Andrew," Katherine croaked, unable to drag her eyes
from the study door, her voice scarcely loud enough to be
heard three feet away. The gun ground into her Adam's ap-
ple. "Andrew!" she called, louder, with greater strength.
The pressure eased.

"Do you want something from the kitchen, Katie?" Andrew called.

"Get him in here, now!" the hot voice growled. His arm
around her was trembling with the force of his command.

"In here, Andrew," Katherine called, her eyes still on the
study door that had now opened a full crack. Another inch
and it would creak. It always did. That first night he'd been
there, Sam had promised to oil it. Please remember that it
creaks, she willed. Please be careful, she pleaded silently.

She had to do something to draw the killer's attention
from the door, from the entrance Sam was making. But
what?

Deliberately she forced her body to relax, to slump against her assailant. His hand yanked on her, and she moaned at the sharp agony, but continued her drooping decline nonetheless. She shifted slightly, as if falling, hoping that since he stood behind her and couldn't see her face, he would believe she was fainting. She was close enough to it for him to sense it to be true. She abruptly went totally lax, letting her full weight droop against him, dragging him sideways, toward the hall, away from the study door.

"Get up," the man behind her snarled, knocking the gun against her cheek as he tried to keep her upright, as he tried to stay upright himself.

To Katherine the creak of the study door was as loud as the imagined crack of her assailant's pistol would be, and she was amazed when the man behind her didn't drop her to whirl and see what caused the noise. Instead he twisted her arm, swearing at her maliciously.

"Let her go, Pete."

Chapter 13

Sam's voice was as cold as the snow falling outside, and as soft.

The grip on Katherine's wrist slackened, but he didn't release his hold. He staggered slightly, shifting over her body that rested chiefly upon his wet shoes. He turned his head to face Sam but the torturous barrel of the gun once again pressed against her temple.

Sam repeated the order. "Let her go, Pete. Now."

If Katherine had needed any confirmation that Sam's memory had fully returned, his naming the man above her would have served. Her eyes sought his. He was looking directly at Pete, no shade of emotion coloring his face. He looked nothing short of dangerous dressed in his new flannel pants and a rumpled linen jacket that covered only his flanks, but hid none of the broad, silvered chest.

"I don't think so, Sam."

Sam's lips twisted to a wry smile. "Stalemate?"

"Always have a line, don't you, Sam?"

"Usually. Though I have to admit I couldn't think of anything to say after you shot George."

"Yes. I felt badly about that, Sam. I really did."

The smile didn't shift on Sam's face, nor did his features change, but Katherine, watching him, felt suddenly cold, and wondered how the man jabbing the gun into her temple could stand so calmly.

"What did you do with his body?" Sam asked. And the chill that had settled in Katherine turned to ice.

"The fish, Sam. I fed him to the hungry fish."

"I'm going to kill you," Sam said so evenly he might have been talking about taking the man for a drive in the country.

"It was a neat dodge, Sam, pretending to be Sam McDonald the novelist."

Katherine couldn't help the agonized denial that issued from her lips. Sam flicked her a cool glance, a look that told her nothing, but wholly denied the last three days.

"If I hadn't found George's car still parked in that alley, and hadn't checked with your hotel, I'd have assumed you'd left town, hotfooted it back to Washington to spill your guts. I put out an alert to the airports—you're wanted for smuggling now, you know, and for the murder of your partner—but no one had seen you. It was only by chance that I remembered your fixation with the McDonald novels."

"Your luck's run out now, Pete."

"Really? And what are you going to do, Sam? Shoot me? Fire at me now, and there won't be any way I could keep from pulling this trigger. And the pretty wife of one spy novelist dies. Or while you were ringing for her husband did you take over other duties as well?"

Katherine couldn't help the instinctive jerk that wrenched her body at the evil man's words. The gun jabbed her almost negligently.

"I can see that you did. Then I can imagine that you wouldn't be all too happy to see her die, would you?"

"What do you want, Pete?"

"Personally, I'd prefer you dead."

Sam didn't say anything, but again Katherine had the feeling that the man holding the gun on her was making a serious mistake.

"I'm afraid I can't oblige you on that," Sam said, stepping forward a single pace. The police special in his hand was trained above Katherine, presumably at the man's heart.

The gun against her jerked convulsively. "Stop right there."

"You might as well let her go, Pete. Because I'm going to kill you either way."

The hand on her wrist slackened in the man's shock.

Sam took another step. "George wasn't even armed. You shot him down in cold blood. For that alone you should die, too."

"I'll kill her," Pete said. His voice was higher pitched than it had been before. "I will."

"And I'll kill you," Sam said. "Let her go, Pete," he commanded for the third time. "She's got nothing to do with this."

"Except you won't want her killed," Pete said.

Sam took another step.

"Stop!" Pete yelled, the gun skittering across Katherine's brow.

It was her only chance to upset the stalemate, to stop this madness. She flung her body back and, grabbing with her one good arm for the man's right leg, she clawed at his blood-soaked pants with all the force she could possibly muster.

In the act of trying to catch her and watch Sam at the same time, he couldn't stop the contact her fingers made with his wounded leg. He screamed and the explosive sound of a gun report rang out, deafening her.

Instinctively she covered her head with her arm and sank to the carpet.

"Sam!" she screamed.

A second gun report sounded almost immediately, an echo of the first. And she heard one of them scream, a cry so filled with agony, a cry so harsh with pain, that she whimpered in empathy. Then she heard a heavy body crash into the coffee table, heard the Chinese vase fall and shatter. Her ears ringing, her nostrils filled with the sharp tang of sulfur, Katherine found herself unable to look up.

She lay huddled, aware of heavy breathing, the ringing of the gunshot in her ears, Andrew yelling and Max barking, but she couldn't raise her head. Which, she thought frantically. Which one had fallen?

When a hand descended to her shoulder she couldn't contain the short cry that escaped her.

"Katherine?" Sam's voice asked.

Her shoulder beneath his hand convulsed and she mumbled something. But she slowly raised her head and looked around her living room with stunned, dull eyes.

Sprawled upon the floor, alive but in agony, Pete Sorenson was gripping his shoulder, his face a rictus of pain. He was lucky to be alive, Sam thought grimly. He'd never fought anything as much as he'd had to fight the urge to send that bullet right between the bastard's eyes.

But Katherine had cried his name, a plea so strong and so powerful in her desolate voice that he'd been unable to continue his murderous thoughts. If he had killed Pete, he would be no better than him, no stronger. He had deliberately shot his chief in the shoulder, knowing it would disarm him.

He deserved every scrap of physical agony for killing a defenseless George, for throwing his hapless body to the ravenous ocean fish. And for betraying them. But most of all for daring to hold Katherine, roughly hurting her, jamming the barrel of his gun into her soft skin. For that alone, he would have killed him.

"Is it over?" Andrew asked from the doorway.

"Call the police," Sam said.

"Well, I never thought I'd hear you say that!" Andrew quipped, disappearing, but Sam had no illusions, the man was almost sick with fear, almost devastated with worry.

It was only marginally less than the fear inside Sam. But unlike Andrew's, his had nothing to do with the bleeding and defeated Pete Sorenson, guns or danger. His had only to do with what he was going to say to the lovely woman eyeing her living room with shock, her gaze landing everywhere but upon him. He couldn't force her to look at him, couldn't draw her into his arms and cradle her against his bare chest. He could only wait, his eyes still on Pete, his gun still trained on the murderer's heart.

"I'm sorry, Katherine," he said finally, and the words seemed monumentally lame.

He held out a hand to aid her rising, and though she used the leverage he proffered, she pulled her hand from his almost immediately.

Sam could feel the heat staining his cheeks, his neck. God, what could he possibly say to her to explain the last few days, the last few hours, a fantasy of the last ten years?

Embarrassment gripped him fiercely, a more violent emotion than even the desire to put a period to Pete Sorenson's life. He had acted every part a fool, picking roses, spewing poetry that he couldn't even recall whole lines of now, spinning a fantasy that was comprised of dreams and longings and wishes he'd never even put a name to before, except that Katherine McDonald had embodied them all.

And still she said nothing. No acknowledgment of his apology, no words of any kind that would let him have a single clue to her thoughts, her emotions.

He knew his cheeks were red, knew the hand holding the gun trained on Pete was unsteady, knew Katherine stood not ten inches away from him. And he began to grow angry.

"They're on their way," Andrew said coming back into the room. His presence only served to exacerbate Sam's embarrassment, the fuse on his already lit temper. *He'd known about the fantasy as well.* And knew the fool's role Sam had played.

Standing here now, flanked by the two willing partners in his unwitting delusion, Sam couldn't come up with a rational explanation for their going along with his bizarre behavior. And it was this that roused his ire, he told himself, though a part of him acknowledged that his very embarrassment caused the greatest amount.

He knew every moment of those three days, saw it through two sets of eyes, one the deluded novelist, the other his own agent's vision. He could feel, as though from a distance, all the emotions that had run through him while he thought he was Sam McDonald, husband of Katherine. And these emotions, still raw with their freshness, with their sudden freedom, clutched at his heart and gripped him with painful uncertainty.

If only he knew why she had done it. Why she hadn't just told him the truth. Why she had kissed him, let him kiss her, let him take her to bed, let him pour all the words of his aching soul into her ears. And told him she loved him in return. Why?

The sudden ring of the doorbell made them all jump, though Sam thought they should be getting used to the sound by now.

Katherine let Andrew go to the door this time. Her eyes dropped to the man on the floor clutching his shoulder, whimpering with pain. A few moments ago he'd been ready to kill her, uncaring whether he hurt her, seeming to enjoy the pain he'd inflicted on her. And he'd been prepared, eager, to kill Sam.

She heard Andrew's voice describing the recent activities in feverish detail and risked a look at Sam's hard profile. He had saved her life. She couldn't allow the words he'd spoken to Pete to weigh so heavily on her heart. *You might as well let her go, Pete, because I'm going to kill you either way.* Said with no more emotion than when he'd asked who Max was. Said casually, cruelly, deliberately.

She told herself that he'd had to say them, that he'd had no choice, but still they pressed down upon her. Because he'd said them with no memory of the emotion they'd shared. No memory of the laughter, the tears, the soul-wrenching joining.

The same officers who had come earlier entered the room with guns drawn, faces set, and snow crusted beneath their boots.

"That's all right, sir," one said, approaching Sam and leveling his gun toward Pete. "I have him now."

"You can keep him," Sam said tersely, lowering his hand, absently massaging his right arm.

Katherine knew that he'd been holding it so tensely, so rigidly that it had cramped. Like her heart was cramped, she thought bleakly, but no amount of massaging would ease that ache.

Sam stepped back, bumping into her. His eyes flew to hers in a brief, agonizing contrition, an apology far greater than the mere stumble called for. Why did his eyes look so fevered, so haunted? What was he telling her in that swift contact?

He looked away too quickly for her to know, color staining his cheeks, flushing his neck. His eyes raised to the ceiling in a rapid, furious glare, then back down at the floor. What was he thinking? Could he possibly be remembering the time they'd spent together?

A police ambulance was summoned for the still-groaning Pete Sorenson and the police began firing questions at them all. Between the explanations and the fleshing out of details of the past half hour, Katherine felt the distance between Sam and her growing wider and wider.

He met her eyes once, when she described seeing the doorknob turn and knowing he was on the other side, but his expression was unreadable. The only thing that gave her any sign that he was reacting to the conversation at all was that his hand kept clenching and unclenching in rhythmic pulses.

Sam! Her heart cried out to him, but it was to no avail, and she knew she couldn't tell him how thoroughly she'd embraced his delusion, couldn't ask him to pretend it still existed for him like it did for her. Like it always would.

When one of the officers made a reference to the night being right out of one of their books, Pete Sorenson wrenched free of the officer's hold on him long enough to denounce Sam. ''He's not any writer!'' he yelled. ''He's a killer! He works for Treasury and he killed his partner and now he's shot me! Check him out! He's not who he says he is!''

All eyes turned toward Sam, Katherine's in worry, the officers' in speculation. When Sam didn't speak, one of the officers turned to Katherine. ''Is he Sam McDonald, ma'am?''

Slowly, unable to drag her gaze from the stranger Sam had become, she nodded.

The policeman nodded and told Pete to pipe down. Then he said in aside to Katherine, ''I know your husband's an agent, or was one, and I know how much he avoids the public eye because of that.'' Pete howled a dissent, and a hard look from the policeman silenced him. ''So, we'll try to keep the press from busting down your door to get the story.''

Katherine murmured embarrassed thanks, knowing that the story would eventually spill out anyway. Pete Sorenson would keep talking, and some time, someday, someone would listen. Then the story of her false husband, the story of those missing three days in Sam's life, in her own life, would surface to the eager public's delight.

She tried to catch Sam's eyes, but he was studying the shards of the Chinese vase on the skewed coffee table. Her heart constricted as she wondered why he looked so different now. His eyes were the same blue, his jawline swept at the same firm angle, a shadow of his beard covered his cheeks, his modeled cheekbones were identical. But his full lips were drawn to a thin line and his shaded eyes gave nothing away anymore. He was tougher now, rougher. A stranger.

The police ambulance arrived then, and in the flurry of activity surrounding the loading of their prisoner, Katherine moved to Sam's side. "Thank you," she said softly.

His eyes lifted to hers in quick question, then shifted away. "For?"

"Saving my life," she said, stopping herself from adding, *for the past three days. For letting me have a glimpse of paradise, for letting me know what I've been missing, what I'll miss for the rest of my life.*

"You saved mine," he said so quietly she almost didn't hear him.

If only he would look at her, she thought. Jason had said to expect it, but surely his embarrassment wasn't so intense that he couldn't even look at her. Because if he would just meet her eyes she would be able to look into them and see what he was thinking, because no matter whether he had forgotten her or not, she *knew* him, knew what he dreamed of, knew what he loved.

But he didn't meet her gaze and she didn't know whether his words referred to the missing three days in his life or her attack on Pete Sorenson or something else, something more.

Andrew came back into the living room after having escorted the police to the door. "We have to go to the station in the morning—which, by the way, is less than twenty minutes off—and tell the whole story over again. Is this what you go through in rewriting, Katie? If it is, I'm very glad I only sell 'em. This is simply too exhausting."

"You were wonderful, Andrew," Katherine said, reaching for his hand and squeezing it.

"I was rather splendid, wasn't I? It was all thanks to the hero, here." He cocked his head toward Sam, who, although he didn't look up, smiled crookedly. "My hands were shaking so badly that if Sam hadn't taken the gun from me, I probably would have shot you, dear."

"I was terrified you were really looking for me and that man would shoot you," Katherine said.

"All a ruse. But I about wet my pants when Max barked."

A hysterical giggle built in Katherine. She glanced at Sam and her breath caught when she saw the shared amusement in his incredible blue eyes. *Sam!* It was Sam. *Her* Sam. He looked away quickly and her heart wrenched sorrowfully.

"Well. All's well that ends at five in the morning," Andrew said, his bright eyes darting from her to Sam and back again. Message was rife in his gaze and his hand underscored it as he pumped hers.

"I think I'll mosey on out to the kitchen, check on Max, and then, if you think you all can manage to hold down the fort, I'll head on home for a little snooze," he said, giving her hand a final painful, and meaningful, squeeze.

He walked out swiftly, leaving them alone.

And Katherine had never felt more alone in her life.

"Why?" Sam asked, his voice rasped and harsh.

"Why?" Katherine replied.

"Why did you do it?"

"Why did I do what?" she asked.

He looked at her then and she pulled back from the anger she saw simmering in his eyes. Why was he angry? She reached a hand toward him but he jerked sharply away from her, hurting her more than he could possibly have known.

A muscle in his jaw worked, jumping, as if he were chewing something sour, something rotten. "Where's your husband?" he asked coldly.

His question suddenly explained his reticence in meeting her gaze, his standing aloof from her, the sharp avoidance of her touch.

"I don't have one," she said, and the admission scored her. For three days, she'd had him. For three days, she'd had the husband she'd dreamed of all of her life.

"How could you?" he asked then, confusing her. She shook her head in question, raising her hand, holding her palm out. "How could you lie to me? How could you go along with a sick delusion like that?"

Everything in her cringed at the disgust in his tone, in his eyes, in the meaning of his dreadful words, but she didn't let it show on her face. "I didn't lie," she said softly, trying to draw the memory of his touch, of his love around her like a protective blanket. But the horrid connotation he'd placed on their three days together ripped at the fabric.

"The hell you didn't!" he barked at her, swinging away from her as though their close proximity disgusted him further. "All you had to do was tell me, for God's sake. You didn't have to play me along."

"I didn't play you along!" she snapped, his anger finally sparking hers.

"Then what the hell were you doing?" he all but yelled at her.

"Helping you, damn it! I was doing what I thought was right!"

"Going to bed with me? Telling me you loved me?" he scoffed, his face haggard, his voice rough with suppressed emotion. "That was helping me?"

Suddenly, awfully, Katherine realized the significance of their conversation. He remembered it all, every detail. But as the old saying went, *Be careful of what you wish, lest it come true.* She had wished and it had come true: he remembered. But he didn't love her anymore. That had died with the death of his delusion.

Her hands were shaking, and she felt as though she might never be warm again, but she summoned the strength to answer him. *He remembered and still he could say such things to her.* There was no greater hurt than this.

"I never once lied to you. Nor did I attempt to mislead you. You needed my help, I gave it to you the... best way I knew how. Whatever I said, whatever I did... I did for you. How dare you judge me for that."

"Judge you?" he asked and he looked stunned, as if she'd physically struck him. "The hell with that. All I want to know is why? You say you did it for me. Well, thanks, but no thanks. I don't need that kind of charity. If you want to find a way to come up with new plots, find somebody else to fit into your little charades."

"It was *your* charade," she said icily, as icily as her body, soul and mind felt right then.

He stopped pacing around the room, and glared at her, his eyes roaming over her for a long moment, long enough that she felt the color rise to her cheeks, then the glower faded and he looked lost. He looked like *her* Sam. "But if it wasn't for some book... why? Why did you do it?"

Not for millions could she have told him the real reason why she had "gone along with" his delusion. There was no way on earth that she could admit that his fantasy had so captured her heart that she was now committing the ultimate sacrifice... letting him go, giving the fantasy up. And she couldn't tell him that his fantasy had so thoroughly taken her that her entire life had changed because of him.

Tell him, she seemed to hear Andrew commanding her, and his voice only echoed that lonely part of her that still cried deep inside. And she wanted to, she wanted to fling herself at his feet, to beg him to stay with her, to beg him to understand the past few days through her eyes, through her heart.

But though he remembered, he didn't understand those days, what it meant to him, what it had meant to her. The terrible confusion within him was overriding his ability to read between the lines, to see the reality of what had transpired. The collision of memories overrode the emotional instinctive link between them.

"When Andrew comes back you can catch a ride with him," she said evenly, "or you can call a cab now. I don' care which you choose."

"You're not going to tell me why, are you?" he asked and he sounded puzzled, but no more than curious.

"I did tell you," she said, "and you didn't want to listen. Until you want to really know, know what *I* think, what motivated *me,* then I don't think we have much to talk about."

It was one of the hardest things she'd ever done to turn and walk away from him. Part of her wanted him to leap after her, spin her around and stop her; the other part wanted him to let her go, to give her time to think, time to sort things out, time for him to sort things out. He didn't say a word as she left.

He watched Katherine walk regally to the stairs and mount them without looking back, her spine stiff, her profile presented, her chin high.

He was a fool, he thought. He'd accused her, attacked her, not simply sat down and held her hand and asked her to tell him about the last few days. He knew them, he remembered them, but she was right, he hadn't asked how she felt about them, what had motivated her to join him in the belief that he was her loving husband. All he'd wanted to know was something that would have given him a blanket excuse for his behavior, something that would make him feel better about his part in the three-day drama.

Slowly he went into the study, the room where he'd spilled so much of his life, pouring it innocently, stupidly into her computer, the room where she'd held him while he cried, the place where he'd first begun making love to her. He stared around him, riveted by its simplicity, by its functional nature. The computer dominated her desk, though a thousand things seemed to satellite around it, dictionaries, thesaurus, a book on psychology, the scene he'd written thinking it to be the start of a new novel, the bits and pieces that contributed to the McDonald novels, the scraps and morsels that made Katherine who she was, what she was.

He almost turned and went for the stairs that led to a room that he had seen once upon a dream, but he reached for the telephone instead. He could shake her, drive her to her knees, or get down upon his own, but until he understood what she claimed she'd already told him, he knew with an utter surety that she would never spell it out for him.

This was something he loved about her books, something he understood to be intrinsically essential to her nature, the need to leave so much hidden behind the scenes, between the lines. It was something his self-imposed alter ego had loved in Katherine herself. But he wasn't that sappy guy who had quoted poetry and picked the last rose of autumn. He was a tough agent who had been through a tough time.

And he felt like he was lying to himself as he dialed information and secured the number for a taxi.

And looking at the past three days objectively, he suspected that he didn't deserve to be offered the information on a silver platter.

"Can you send a cab to Witch Duck Point, last house on the Point," he told the dispatcher. "It's a crummy night, I know, so I'll pay double."

It was only after he'd hung up that he realized he didn't have a dime on him, that the cabby would have to wait while he went inside the motel, got a new key, and got into his room to retrieve some spare cash, that he'd be going out in the cold morning dressed no more warmly than he was right at the moment.

But moreover, he had the definite feeling that by leaving Katherine McDonald's house he was probably making the single greatest mistake of his life.

Chapter 14

Max barked happily, flushing from their hiding places the juncos, cardinals and the other birds that were hardy enough to handle the damp coastal winter. Katherine watched him, his shoulder completely healed now, whatever memories he had of Sam locked away in his mind. Life had gone on for both of them, but for him, the big shaggy animal that had been cradled against a broad chest, there was no constant, nagging pain that threatened to overwhelm him at every pass.

For Katherine, the hurt was ever present. She stumbled across reminders a thousand times a day and was haunted by a hundred memories presented as dreams every night. If she reached for a wineglass, she remembered how he'd searched the cabinets, unaware they were inches from his head all along; if she curled up with a book to read, she'd remember how he'd said he loved that particular author's work; if she sat behind the computer, fingers poised over the keyboard, she could see him sitting there, head in his hands, tears in his eyes and pages and pages of his life on the screen before him.

A hundred times in the past two months she'd regretted her parting words to him. She regretted their harshness, their chill insensitivity. And a dozen times a day she would find herself staring at the telephone, her hand twitching to pick up the receiver and punch in the Washington, D.C. area code, just to hear his voice, to try, despite the distance in miles and thought between them, to answer the questions he'd posed to her that final night. To tell him *why* she'd done what she did, why she'd said she loved him.

But she'd be talking to a stranger. She'd be talking to another Sam McDonald, as different and as changed as the difference in the seasons. That part of him she'd grown to know and love was locked deeply away in his mind, remembered but despised.

She had seen him twice since that fateful morning in her living room. And both times, at the initial formal complaint at the police station, and again at Pete Sorenson's preliminary hearing, she might as well have faced someone she'd never met before. Or an enemy.

He'd met her eyes across the noisy, crowded station, and his jaw had tightened, his lips had drawn to that line she knew portended anger, displeasure or extreme discomfiture. And his eyes, those blue eyes she'd seen warm with loving, hot with desire, they had been chips of ice, the kind that freezes everything it touches, sending shivers of pain throughout the body until it buries slivers of frozen indifference deep in the heart.

Everything about his stance warned her: *You don't know me at all.* And she didn't. She didn't know him. Not anymore. And he didn't know her either. Because if he had, he couldn't look at her coldly, he couldn't imagine the things he'd accused her of doing. It was the one thing she'd never taken into account, that he would still remember, yet hate it. Hate her for loving him.

And when she'd seen him at the hearing, he'd been standing in a doorway, too cool and crisp-looking in a dark business suit, the broad planes of his face clean-shaven and too smooth, too distant. She'd had to pass directly between him and the man he'd been talking with, had to actually touch him to clear the doorway. He'd smelled of some subtle cologne, making his scent a mystery, pleasant but oh, so different, and her heart had ached unbearably at the elusive reminder that he wasn't her Sam.

Andrew, just behind her, had stopped. "You look fit, Sam," he said quietly.

"As a fiddle," came Sam's wry reply.

"Everything all straightened out at Treasury?" Andrew had asked, making Katherine want to scream. He, of all people, knew what torture it was for her to see Sam, to be so near him, and have him look right through her.

"Almost. They've brought in a new director."

"I imagine he'd be pretty nervous. All eyes on him, and all that."

Sam had chuckled and the sound played on Katherine's heart like a discordant melody. This is unfair, she had wanted to yell. What did I do that was so *wrong?* He'd asked her for her love, and she had given it to him without reservation, loving wholly and freely for the first time in her life. How could that be wrong?

"Well, don't be a stranger," Andrew had said lightly, but Katherine could feel the tension in his hand beneath her arm, and knew his parting shot had been deliberate and pointed.

Sam had uttered a grunt that could either be taken as assent or skepticism, as vague and ambiguous as the day the sky first grays with winter clouds and everyone looks up with atavistic awe, wondering what it portends.

She'd seen him on television, news accounts playing heavily on his quasi-secret identity as Sam McDonald the novelist. He'd deflected most of the questions regarding his status in the McDonald household by either answering with a no comment, or implying his presence in her house had been part of a careful plan to roust Pete Sorenson.

She wondered if he had watched her as well. And if he had, what he'd thought, what he'd remembered. It had taken about two weeks, but as she'd suspected, Pete's accusations had finally taken hold in the minds of the press and soon she'd been besieged by reporters hungry for a juicy scandal. Where had her husband been during this? Was it possible that the Treasury agent was her real husband? Why had she consented to his stay in her house? What had been in it for her... a new novel? The questions all seemed the same as Sam's *why?* and made her squirm as she lied, never once admitting she'd done it out love for a perfect stranger.

They had even tracked down Jason Woodard after a casual remark from Andrew and subjected him to pointed questions. He had remained his usual unperturbable self and answered sparingly, using client confidentiality as his excuse for not elaborating. When asked who was his client, Sam or Katherine, Jason had simply raised his hands and smiled.

But the hardest part of all came just a month ago, four weeks after the final parting in her living room. A reporter had finally investigated deeply enough to discover that Katherine had never been married, that there was no novelist Sam McDonald. She had been born Katherine Leigh McDonald, and had remained that to this day.

She had been flooded with requests for interviews, hounded with offers for talk shows, and her book sales had shot up dramatically. But she turned down all but the most essential interviews, avoided talk shows, and even canceled a book-signing event in Alexandria. The questions asked always had to do with Sam, and though time had passed, her heartache had not. Still her lips quivered when she and Andrew talked about him, and her eyes seemed permanently heavy from crying in her sleep.

Watching Max now, as he happily frolicked, his large paws kicking up the dusting of snow that had fallen the night before, she wondered anew why something that had only lasted three days, a fantasy that had served to wake her, as Andrew had said, like Sleeping Beauty, shouldn't have faded by now, slipped into that part of the mind that governed dreams and wishes, why she couldn't just carry it upstairs to the attic and bury it in the boxes holding the remnants of her girlhood fantasies and the glitterless wands. Why, after two months, was it still so alive for her? Why did her body ache for his touch, why did her lips still curve when she opened her dictionary, or her fingers tremble when they trailed the books on her shelves?

She'd tried burying herself in a new novel, spending hours each day punching in the words of a new story, a new nail-biter as Andrew called them. But what had come through wasn't a spy thriller, it was every raw, shattered emotion inside her. What appeared on the screen, and then on the neatly typed pages from her printer, was the story of Katherine McDonald falling in love for the first time in her life. It was the story of three days in paradise, and the hell that followed, the story of a woman who learns that her life had been no more substantial than the stories she told until Sam had come to show her what reality was, what truth meant.

She'd cried when she'd read the pages, when she saw her heart laid open for all to read. And she'd cried again when she reread it. Finally, knowing this was a story that couldn't hide in her computer, that shouldn't lie in her desk drawers growing dusty with time and neglect, knowing it was a story that all women, all men, should read so that they too could grab hold of life and live it as lovingly as they might a fantasy, she called her agent and told him about it. And told him the title, *White Lies*. To her horror, her voice had broken while describing the book proposal, but her agent had ignored her graveled speech, and after some hesitation, said he thought it was a good idea, and one, now that the story of the fictional Sam McDonald was finally out, that would be a good start for books under her name only. With nerveless fingers she'd packaged the proposal, several chapters and a synopsis, and sent it to him.

He'd gotten back to her in a surprisingly short time with an offer on the book and asked her to go ahead and send in the rest of the manuscript when she was ready, but that with the public eye on Katherine right now, the sooner the better.

She'd rapidly gone to work on the most difficult project she'd had to write to date. This wasn't creating, it was remembering, it wasn't drawing a story from thin air, it was airing her very soul. She let her answering device handle phone calls, and refused all invitations.

Just last night Andrew had taken her to task for burying herself away again, hiding from the world. And when she'd said she was working, he'd shaken his head.

"That's not working, Katie, that's beating yourself over the head. Besides, it doesn't have a happy ending."

"But it has a true one," she'd said.

"Only because you won't call Sam."

"I can't," she'd said. "He's not the same Sam I knew."

"Are you certain of that?" he'd asked.

Yes, she was certain. Painfully certain.

Jason had dropped by later, prompted no doubt by Andrew, his yellow bag absent, his warm smile at her disposal. "Tell me about your book, Kath," he'd said. She let him read what she'd sent her agent instead. He'd read it carefully, smiling a few times, frowning over a couple of places. He'd handed it back to her thoughtfully.

"That bad?" she asked.

"Not bad at all. Quite good. It's some of the best writing you've ever done, Kath."

"What's wrong, then?" she'd asked reluctantly, suspecting an Andrew-inspired speech would follow.

"It needs a dedication," he'd answered, surprising her.

"That's all?"

"For a book like this, it's everything."

So, she was watching Max play, her computer screen blank, the cursor blinking at her, her mind going over Jason's words, her heart fighting her mind for the words to slip before the book, the words that would lay this book at someone's feet, giving them her whole heart, her total soul.

Finally, sighing, she began to type. There was only one thing to say.

Sam stared at the house for a long time. He hadn't seen it in two months, and realized now he'd never once seen it by daylight, hadn't known that it was a combination of red brick and white clapboard and that another room jutted, dormer style, from beyond where Katherine's bedroom lay.

Two months had passed, months he'd filled with work, with George's kids, with trying to forget Katherine McDonald. But when he sat down to work, paper trails to chase, cases to unravel, all he could think about was a pair of hazel eyes filled with tears. And when he'd walked hand in hand with George Junior and his sister, Jennifer, telling them about their daddy, how much he'd meant to him, all he could hear was Katherine's rich voice softly telling him that everything would be okay, that she would see him through this. And when he sat down over a beer and a bowl of chili, a football game on television, trying to forget her, all he could think about was three confused days in late autumn when love had seemed right and loving had been easy, and giving had been as natural as breathing.

Her parting words still stung him, still cut him to the quick. *I did tell you, and you didn't want to listen. Until you want to know what I think, what motivated me, then I don't think we have much to talk about.*

He'd thought about that statement so many times that the words spun around in his mind like a rotating Mobius strip, twisting and turning, having no end or beginning. Each time he tried plugging in an answer to the *why* she had done, said, what she had, the strip shifted, tantalizing him, taunting him. And her eyes filled with tears, her voice choked with emotion haunted him.

There was only one answer, but it was an answer he was sure he'd come up with all on his own, an answer borne of his desire for her, his three-day fantasy that turned into the most real thing he'd ever done in his life. And he'd decided that he would have to put the notion from his mind, his heart, and try to let time heal the still-bleeding wound in his soul, like it was doing with the memories of George, like it had done with Devra. All he could really do was hope that he was wrong when he thought that this time, time healing the wound might be impossible.

But he would have done it, pretended that the pain of not holding her in his arms, the agony of not seeing her laughing face, her passion-dewy body, would eventually fade into a dull ache if Andrew hadn't called him late last night.

Typically, Andrew had started the conversation with a series of quips, but somewhere in the crackling phone line, he'd become deadly serious.

"Katherine's sold another book. All this hoopla over which-Sam's-which has finally given her a chance to break out under her own name."

"That's good," Sam had responded dully, unaccountably irritated that something good had come out of all this for Katherine.

"Well, it is and it isn't. Because the story she's writing doesn't have a very happy ending."

Sam couldn't think of anything to say; Andrew seemed to be trying to tell him something, but he wasn't sure he wanted to know what it was.

When the silence stretched long enough that Andrew must have realized Sam wasn't going to reply, the young man sighed heavily. "She told me what she said to you that last morning, about what motivated her to act as she did during that time, Sam."

Despite the miles separating them, despite the fact that Andrew couldn't possibly have known how deeply her words had cut him, Sam winced.

"Have you figured it out?"

"I have a few suspicions," Sam had answered guardedly.

"Well, you can call me every kind of a busybody—and you'd have lots of company—but like I told her one day about two months ago, what you two had together was real. The real McCoy. And if I were in your shoes, I'd come on down here and sit in front of the fire and talk about it. Really talk about it."

"I'll think about it, Andrew."

"You do that, Sam. And if you ever tell her I called you I'll conk you on that hard head of yours until you can't remember next summer."

Sam'd had to chuckle, but he'd thought of nothing else since he'd hung up the phone. Did he have the guts to sit down beside Katherine and talk about those three days in autumn, really talk about them? Did he have the guts to ask her if his suppositions about her motivations were correct?

Did he have the guts not to?

So he'd called Treasury and said he was heading out for a couple of days, got into his car and driven the two hundred miles to sit behind the cold steering wheel, staring at her house, at the unbroken snow on her front walk, at the trees, at the sky, at anything and everything so he wouldn't look at his shaking hands, wouldn't see his pale face reflected in the rearview mirror. .

With an oath that seemed to come directly from his very soul, he swung open the car door and slammed it behind him. No guts, no glory.

Katherine stood beneath the water of the shower, letting the hot water beat away the torment of writing the dedication for *White Lies*. Had she written the words so that Sam would read them and call her? Had she written them as a plea for him to come back, or had she typed them so that he might understand?

The water was having absolutely no effect in washing the memory away; her tears were as hot as the shower itself, and nowhere near as cleansing.

She turned the faucet off and quickly, roughly, toweled herself dry. She slid into her tatty bathrobe and padded down the stairs. What she wanted now was a hot cup of coffee generously laced with brandy. She smiled, because Andrew had obviously come in while she was showering, and anticipating her, had already brewed a fresh pot. The aroma wafted on the cool air in the hallway. A glance at the living room told her he was on the same wavelength: a fire crackled cheerfully in the fireplace, cushions already tossed on the floor.

She stepped through the kitchen only to find it empty.

"Andrew?" she called, leaving the kitchen, surprised to find her study door closed. She pushed it open cautiously, half-afraid that as jumpy as he'd been lately, she would startle him.

His name died on her lips as she saw who was sitting behind her computer busily typing. Her heart seemed to lurch once, jerking painfully, before it resumed beating, and the new rhythm was light and too rapid for comfort. Her breath seemed to catch in her throat, choking her. She felt dizzy and weak with the shock of seeing Sam McDonald sitting where she'd so often longed to see him. For a moment she wanted to close her eyes and open them again to see if the vision was real, then didn't want to because she didn't want to know.

"Sam . . . ?" she asked finally, when he didn't look up, didn't turn her way.

His fingers stilled, and Katherine had the impression that his entire body froze as well. For a heartbeat's length of time

he stayed perfectly poised, then slowly, achingly slowly, h
raised his head and met her gaze.

The fire in his blue eyes stretched across the room and
burned her, shot into her like a flaming arrow and ignited
the blaze he'd tried dousing with his icy words, with his cold
gaze.

"Katherine," he mouthed, as if he couldn't believe sh
were really there, the way he'd mouthed it the first time sh
ever saw him, the way he'd whispered her name so many
times in so many dreams.

"How did you get in here?" she croaked, unable to say
what she really wanted to say, clinging to the doorknob to
stay erect.

A slow, almost hesitant smile curved his lips as he rose
from the desk chair, terrifying her that he would move for
ward, would touch her and she would fall to her knees to beg
him to stay. "I told you once there wasn't a lock made tha
could keep me in . . . or out."

Distrusting the sudden treacherous hope that leap
through her like a violent wind, knowing all too well th
despair that follows such hope, she tried to look away, bu
found herself unable to break the contact. She knew he wa
seeing too much in her eyes, too much memory, too mucl
life, but she could only stand there and let him read her a
easily as he'd read any of her books. Loving him had taugh
her that her emotions, her dreams, were only as real as sh
allowed them to be. That believing in the dream, striving fo
it, was the only important thing on earth.

"I've thought about what you said," he murmured, and
stopped to clear his throat. His hands were shaking, sh
noticed, and his face was as pale as hers must surely be. Th
idea that he was nervous didn't steady her, but only exac
erbated her own anxiety.

"I've thought and thought about it," he said. "And I ca
only come up with one reason why you said what you

did . . . why you said you loved me, why you let me come to your bed, Katherine. Only one reason.''

Katherine blinked her eyes against the hope that threatened to kill her with its intensity, and the fear of what he might say.

"And that is, you meant what you said," he rasped harshly and dragged his searing gaze from hers. "Just that simple. That you really meant it. You really meant that you loved me, meant that you wanted me." A shudder worked through him and his breath expelled on a harsh rattle of relief.

"That's all, Katherine. That's all I had to say. But I had to come tell you that. I couldn't . . . live with myself . . . if I hadn't let you know that I understood *why* you said you loved me. Why you gave yourself to me like that."

The tears that had only been clouding her eyes now spilled, hot and damning, down her frozen face.

"And . . . if I'm wrong, Katherine . . . if that wasn't the reason, if there was some other reason you . . . loved me then, said . . . you loved me . . ." he trailed off, turning his back to her, his hands clenching and unclenching at his sides, the knuckles white, his head tilted back, eyes on the ceiling, "then I don't want to hear it. I don't . . . want to know.

"I was just going to write that in your computer, and leave it. And go. But you're here now."

Still unable to speak, all the love she had for him aching for him to turn around, aching for him to hold her, aching for him to tell her why he wouldn't want to know if he'd misunderstood.

"I've had a lot of time to think," he said roughly. "When those three days just snapped into my mind, my memory, all I could think about was not wanting it to . . . end. I was . . . embarrassed at the things I'd done, things I'd said, but most of all, I didn't want those days to be . . . over. I just wanted them to go on forever . . . I wanted to . . . stay. And I was so damned scared that it wasn't as real for you as it had been for me. That . . . that I don't know . . . that I wouldn't have you anymore.''

Katherine couldn't bear the pain in his words, the rigid line of his jaw, the tear she saw upon his rough-shaven face.

''Sam . . . ?'' she whispered tremulously.

''When I saw you that day at the police station, you looked at me as if I were . . . somebody else, someone you didn't even know. I thought I was going to die.''

''So did I,'' Katherine whispered, willing her legs to move forward, toward him, willing him to turn around so that he could see that he hadn't been wrong, see that she hadn't just loved him those three days, that she loved him still.

''Sometimes,'' he said, his voice raw, his soul vulnerable, ''only rarely, do time and circumstance combine to give a man a second chance. A second chance at life . . . a second chance to love. A second chance to be what he wants to be, *who* he wants to be.''

''A man would be a fool not to take that chance,'' Katherine said, her hand reaching for his arm. He shook as though by electric shock at her touch. The shudder worked up and through him like life pouring into an empty vessel.

''Do you mean that, Katherine? Do you really mean that?''

''I do,'' she breathed, and it was a vow that came from the most open and trusting part of her, the part that had been unable to resist the promise in a fantasy, unable to withstand the love that poured from a stranger's gaze.

He turned then and stared at her for a long moment, his blue eyes filled with want, his heart utterly defenseless. When his hands raised to wrap around her, they were shaking still, but with love, not fear, with hope, not despair.

Slowly, so achingly tenderly, he drew her into his arms, pressing his lips to her temple, one hand behind her head, completely still, the other at the small of her back. As her arms wrapped around his waist, pulling him closer, wanting to crush him to her to make up for the lost two months, the lost time, he strengthened his hold as well, his hands roaming, seeking, his lips covering hers, a torrent of pent-up longing snaring them both.

Sometimes murmuring, sometimes groaning words of love, words of apology, he freed her body from the easy confines of her bathrobe and tore at his own suit, until they stood face-to-face, bare of restrictions, devoid of deceptions.

"I love you, Katherine McDonald," he said, closing his eyes, pulling her harshly to him, enfolding her tightly against his rigid body.

He tasted the same, she thought a little hysterically, and that new cologne mingled with her own scent to create a smell unique to both of them. And he was *her* Sam, all of him, every part of him. And she took him gratefully, wildly, in joy and in harmony. And he took her the same way, and soon there were no doubts between them, no questions, only answers, and promises, and as they reached for that spinning universe that governs explosions and implosions, Katherine knew that with Sam, in loving Sam and believing in that love, all her wishes, all her dreams had come true. That loving him would be the greatest and best reality.

"Tell me about your new book," he said later, holding her loosely, playing with her hair, first tousling it, then smoothing it, taking a strand and running it along his cheeks, his throat.

"It's about you," she said simply. Happily. And maybe a little drowsily.

"So, do I get to read it?"

Katherine shook her head. "Not now. I feel too contented right now. But I'll show you this...." She rose awkwardly, using his knee to push up.

She read what he'd written on the screen, tears of joy blurring her vision for a moment, seeing his love for her in print, his terse statement of understanding her motives, understanding her reasons, and a final, unfinished question that she'd interrupted when she came into the room. *Katherine, will you please. . . ?* Would she please what? Forgive him? She already had. Love him? She already did, she always would. Smiling gently, knowing the words would be forever locked into her computer, that somehow they lent a note of total reality to his return, she carefully saved the file and named it *Reunion,* then called up the dedication to her book.

Sam's warm arms stole around her and pulled her back against his body, a gesture both casual and exciting at the same time, the touch of a lover who feels comfortable in familiarity and whose easy affection conveys an alluring knowledge.

Katherine didn't say anything as the words lit the screen and neither did Sam as he read them. When he finished, his arms tightening, his hands flexing, he sighed. ''Read them aloud, Katherine. Please.''

Tears filled her eyes so that she couldn't have read anything, but she didn't need to see these words, they were engraved on her soul.

'' 'Dedicated to Sam McDonald, who will always remain my loving husband, if only in my heart. It is he who taught me the truth. Wherever you are, Sam, know that I love you and know I always will.' ''

''Look at me, Katherine,'' he said, his voice rough with command.

She turned her head, but couldn't see him through the haze of tears. His hands cupped her face, his thumbs brushing away her tears. ''I have loved you,'' he said, ''since that first McDonald novel. And when I was hurt, you saved my life, my sanity. You took me in and gave me all of yourself. Don't think I don't know what that means.''

His hands lowered to her throat, then to her shoulders. ''You called me your 'loving husband.' Would you be will ing to try that marriage with the real Sam McDonald this time?''

Katherine's hand stole to his cheek, felt the moisture there, and pulled him down for a lingering kiss. ''Yes,'' she whispered. ''Oh, yes, Sam. You see, I couldn't live without you now.''

A triumphant chuckle escaped him, and he clasped her tightly against him, rocking her, loving her.

''What on earth are you laughing at?'' she said, but she was smiling, too; the time for pain and tears was over. The time for living was finally here, finally at hand.

''I seem to remember promising you a honeymoon.''

''So you did,'' she agreed, feeling as if her heart would burst with the exultation of having found his love.

''And I seem to remember saying we'd do it in a few years.''

She lightly slapped his firm buttocks. ''You were vague, but the word you used was 'soon.' ''

''Oh, that's right. I remember now.''

And in his kiss, in his knowing hands stealing across her body in wonderful familiarity, in sure reality, he let her know just how much he remembered and how much remembering they would both be sharing in the far-flung future.

* * * * *

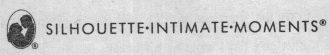

COMING
NEXT MONTH

#401 DESERT SHADOWS—Emilie Richards

Private investigator Felice Christy's latest assignment was driving her crazy! Stuck in a convent pretending to be a nun in order to protect a *real* sister, she had to deal with new handyman Josiah Gallagher, too. His drifter act didn't fool her for a moment. But did he spell trouble for her mission . . . or her heart?

#402 STEVIE'S CHASE—Justine Davis

Chase Sullivan's shadowed past made him a loner by necessity, *not* by choice. Then sweet Stevie Holt stepped into his life, and he dared to dream that things could be different. Suddenly he realized that he'd placed Stevie's life in danger, and unless he did something—quickly—they would *both* be dead.

#403 FORBIDDEN—Catherine Palmer

Federal narcotics agent Ridge Gordon's cover as a college football player didn't stop him from making a pass at sexy English professor Adair Reade. But when new evidence pointed to her involvement in the very drug ring he'd been sent to bust, he fumbled. Was he falling in love with a drug runner?

#404 SIR FLYNN AND LADY CONSTANCE—
Maura Seger

When Constance Lehane's brush with date rape ended in tragedy, she hired criminal lawyer Flynn Corbett to defend her against a possible murder charge. Instinctively she knew that his passion for the law would save her, yet the flames that burned between them hinted at a different sort of passion altogether. . . .

AVAILABLE THIS MONTH:

**#397 SUZANNA'S
SURRENDER**
Nora Roberts

#398 SILENT IMPACT
Paula Detmer Riggs

#399 TOO GOOD TO FORGET
Marilyn Tracy

**#400 A RISK WORTH
TAKING**
Judith Duncan

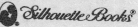

Take 4 bestselling love stories FREE

Plus get a FREE surprise gift!

SILHOUETTE® OFFICIAL SWEEPSTAKES RULES

NO PURCHASE NECESSARY

1. To enter, complete an Official Entry Form or 3" × 5" index card by hand-printing, in plain block letters, your complete name, address, phone number and age, and mailing it to: Silhouette Fashion A Whole New You Sweepstakes, P.O. Box 9056, Buffalo, NY 14269-9056.

   No responsibility is assumed for lost, late or misdirected mail. Entries must be sent separately with first class postage affixed, and be received no later than December 31, 1991 for eligibility.

2. Winners will be selected by D.L. Blair, Inc., an independent judging organization whose decisions are final, in random drawings to be held on January 30, 1992 in Blair, NE at 10:00 a.m. from among all eligible entries received.

3. The prizes to be awarded and their approximate retail values are as follows: Grand Prize — A brand-new Ford Explorer 4×4 plus a trip for two (2) to Hawaii, including round-trip air transportation, six (6) nights hotel accommodation, a $1,400 meal/spending money stipend and $2,000 cash toward a new fashion wardrobe (approximate value: $28,000) or $15,000 cash; two (2) Second Prizes — A trip to Hawaii, including round-trip air transportation, six (6) nights hotel accommodation, a $1,400 meal/spending money stipend and $2,000 cash toward a new fashion wardrobe (approximate value: $11,000) or $5,000 cash; three (3) Third Prizes — $2,000 cash toward a new fashion wardrobe. All prizes are valued in U.S. currency. Travel award air transportation is from the commercial airport nearest winner's home. Travel is subject to space and accommodation availability, and must be completed by June 30, 1993. Sweepstakes offer is open to residents of the U.S. and Canada who are 21 years of age or older as of December 31, 1991, except residents of Puerto Rico, employees and immediate family members of Torstar Corp., its affiliates, subsidiaries, and all agencies, entities and persons connected with the use, marketing, or conduct of this sweepstakes. All federal, state, provincial, municipal and local laws apply. Offer void wherever prohibited by law. Taxes and/or duties, applicable registration and licensing fees, are the sole responsibility of the winners. Any litigation within the province of Quebec respecting the conduct and awarding of a prize may be submitted to the Régie des loteries et courses du Québec. All prizes will be awarded; winners will be notified by mail. No substitution of prizes is permitted.

4. Potential winners must sign and return any required Affidavit of Eligibility/Release of Liability within 30 days of notification. In the event of noncompliance within this time period, the prize may be awarded to an alternate winner. Any prize or prize notification returned as undeliverable may result in the awarding of that prize to an alternate winner. By acceptance of their prize, winners consent to use of their names, photographs or their likenesses for purposes of advertising, trade and promotion on behalf of Torstar Corp. without further compensation. Canadian winners must correctly answer a time-limited arithmetical question in order to be awarded a prize.

5. For a list of winners (available after 3/31/92), send a separate stamped, self-addressed envelope to: Silhouette Fashion A Whole New You Sweepstakes, P.O. Box 4665, Blair, NE 68009.

PREMIUM OFFER TERMS

To receive your gift, complete the Offer Certificate according to directions. Be certain to enclose the required number of "Fashion A Whole New You" proofs of product purchase (which are found on the last page of every specially marked "Fashion A Whole New You" Silhouette or Harlequin romance novel). Requests must be received no later than December 31, 1991. Limit: four (4) gifts per name, family, group, organization or address. Items depicted are for illustrative purposes only and may not be exactly as shown. Please allow 6 to 8 weeks for receipt of order. Offer good while quantities of gifts last. In the event an ordered gift is no longer available, you will receive a free, previously unpublished Silhouette or Harlequin book for every proof of purchase you have submitted with your request, plus a refund of the postage and handling charge you have included. Offer good in the U.S. and Canada only.

SLFW - SWPR

SILHOUETTE® OFFICIAL SWEEPSTAKES ENTRY FORM

4-FWSIS-2

Complete and return this Entry Form immediately – the more entries you submit, the better your chances of winning!

- Entries must be received by **December 31, 1991.**
- A Random draw will take place on **January 30, 1992.**
- No purchase necessary.

Yes, I want to win a FASHION A WHOLE NEW YOU Sensuous and Adventurous prize from Silhouette:

Name _____ Telephone _____ Age _____

Address _____

City _____ State _____ Zip _____

Return Entries to: Silhouette **FASHION A WHOLE NEW YOU,**
P.O. Box 9056, Buffalo, NY 14269-9056   © 1991 Harlequin Enterprises Limited

PREMIUM OFFER

To receive your free gift, send us the required number of proofs-of-purchase from any specially marked FASHION A WHOLE NEW YOU Silhouette or Harlequin Book with the Offer Certificate properly completed, plus a check or money order (do not send cash) to cover postage and handling payable to Silhouette FASHION A WHOLE NEW YOU Offer. We will send you the specified gift.

OFFER CERTIFICATE

Item	A. SENSUAL DESIGNER VANITY BOX COLLECTION (set of 4) (Suggested Retail Price $60.00)	B. ADVENTUROUS TRAVEL COSMETIC CASE SET (set of 3) (Suggested Retail Price $25.00)
# of proofs-of-purchase	18	12
Postage and Handling	$3.50	$2.95
Check one	☐	☐

Name _____

Address _____

City _____ State _____ Zip _____

Mail this certificate, designated number of proofs-of-purchase and check or money order for postage and handling to: Silhouette **FASHION A WHOLE NEW YOU Gift Offer,** P.O. Box 9057, Buffalo, NY 14269-9057. Requests must be received by December 31, 1991.

ONE PROOF-OF-PURCHASE

4-FWSIP-2

To collect your fabulous free gift you must include the necessary number of proofs-of-purchase with a properly completed Offer Certificate.

© 1991 Harlequin Enterprises Limited

See previous page for details.